**Sigrit had just l(
would be losing**

In the afternoon both children sat at the kitchen table doing their homework. Through the window they saw the mailman deliver the day's mail. Ludwig rushed outside and got everything out of the Zeller box.

"Look, *Tante* Erika," he said, all excited, "letters from uncle."

She opened the letters, one after the other and stared at the dates. Looking disappointed, Erika glanced at the telegram again.

"Each letter was written before November seventh, the day he was declared missing."

"Then in a few weeks you'll get the letter he is writing at this very moment," said Ludwig.

"I hope so. I'll read these letters later. Now let's see what the youth bureau has to say. Pray for good news."

Erika opened the letter slowly. She read it in silence while the children watched anxiously. Then she lowered the letter into her lap and sighed. When Sigrit saw the stunned look on Erika's face, she started crying.

"*Tante* Erika, what does it say?" asked Ludwig.

"They feel I'm not a fit guardian for you. They have found a family in Bavaria that is able to take you in. We are to pack your things for travel."

Seven-year-old Sigrit's happy and structured life in Germany ends suddenly one afternoon in 1944. With her parents dead, she is forced to travel with a woman who hates children while being taken to live with strangers. Even her fourteen-year-old brother is yanked away from her side. When the war ends, Sigrit is once again separated from those she loves. With so much tragedy in her young life already, how will she find the courage to face what her future brings?

Sigrit is the poignant tale of war, tyranny, cruelty, love, hope, and kindness. Follow Sigrit and her family as they struggle to survive in war-torn Germany.

KUDOS for *Sigrit*

Sigrit by Ellynore Seybold-Smith is a touching story about a seven-year-old girl who lives in Germany in 1944. We see the cruelty of the Nazis, the destruction of war-torn Germany, and what people must do to survive. We are shown how really vulnerable the children were, who had no choice but to do what the adults told them to do, even if it wasn't in their best interests. I, for one, learned a lot I didn't know about the end of World War II. The story has a ring of truth that makes me wonder if the author was there in Germany at the end of the war. Either that, or she really did her homework. – *Taylor Jones, Reviewer*

Sigrit by Ellynore Seybold-Smith is an interesting look at life in Germany during World War II. It is certainly not a place where I would want to be. If you were a woman, even an ugly one, you stood a good chance of getting raped by Russian soldiers when they came through after Germany's defeat, pillaging and looting, bent on revenge. If you were a man or teenage boy, you were either drafted by the Germans or sent to prison camps by the Russians, whether you had been a combatant or not. The author's characters seem very real and her story authentic. I found evidence of authenticity in the small, everyday details of the people's lives. *Sigrit* is moving and poignant. It gives you a glimpse of the darker side of war when the attacks are to your homeland. – *Regan Murphy, Reviewer*

Out of the rubble of WWII Germany, Ellynore Smith constructs a tale of destruction, loss, love, and hope. *Sigrit* delves both into the unspeakable depths of human cruelty as well as our capacity for kindness, even amid the bleakest of circumstances. – *Richard N. Jahna, Professor, Arizona Western College*

SIGRIT

by

Ellynore Seybold-Smith

Ellynore Seybold-Smith

A BLACK OPAL BOOKS PUBLICATION

GENRE: WOMEN'S FICTION/MAINSTREAM/ROMANTIC ELEMENTS

This is a work of fiction. Names, places, characters and incidents are either the product of the author's imagination or are used fictitiously, and any resemblance to any actual persons, living or dead, businesses, organizations, events or locales is entirely coincidental. All trademarks, service marks, registered trademarks, and registered service marks are the property of their respective owners and are used herein for identification purposes only. The publisher does not have any control over or assume any responsibility for author or third-party websites or their contents.

SIGRIT
Copyright © 2013 by Ellynore Seybold-Smith
Cover Design by Jackson Cover Design
All cover art copyright © 2013
All Rights Reserved
Print ISBN: 978-1-626940-68-0

First Publication: OCTOBER 2013

All rights reserved under the International and Pan-American Copyright Conventions. No part of this book may be reproduced or transmitted in any form or by any means, electronic or mechanical, including photocopying, recording, or by any information storage and retrieval system, without permission in writing from the publisher.

WARNING: The unauthorized reproduction or distribution of this copyrighted work is illegal. Criminal copyright infringement, including infringement without monetary gain, is investigated by the FBI and is punishable by up to 5 years in federal prison and a fine of $250,000.

ABOUT THE PRINT VERSION: If you purchased a print version of this book without a cover, you should be aware that the book is stolen property. It was reported as "unsold and destroyed" to the publisher, and neither the author nor the publisher has received any payment for this "stripped book."

IF YOU FIND AN EBOOK OR PRINT VERSION OF THIS BOOK BEING SOLD OR SHARED ILLEGALLY, PLEASE REPORT IT TO: lpn@blackopalbooks.com

Published by Black Opal Books **http://www.blackopalbooks.com**

SIGRIT

CHAPTER 1

Goerlitz, Germany 1944:

A repulsive, pungent odor assaulted Sigrit's nose and gripped her throat as she rushed home from school. The hard knapsack on her back contained her books and slate. The slate's sponge and drying rag hung out of her knapsack on a string, swinging in the breeze, dancing with her long, brown braids. There was a painful lump in her stomach—not alone attributed to the almost incessant hunger. She rushed by the smoldering rubble that only yesterday was an elegant apartment house. Her neighbors' prized possessions and daily necessities had been turned into black ugliness.

Why she felt anxious she did not know. Sigrit tried to ease her fears by imagining herself entering the cozy kitchen and seeing her mother standing over a pot of potato soup. She could almost hear her mother's greeting, asking the usual question of how school was, and had she learned anything new today. Then, a realization hit her like icy rain—

her mother's face, the face she had seen and loved for seven years, remained blank. Sigrit's forehead broke out in sweat in spite of the crisp November air.

Arriving at her apartment house, she saw her father's bicycle parked near the doorway. A sight that usually brought joy, it only increased her fear. What was Papa doing home from the factory in the middle of the day on Monday? Had the factory been bombed? No, that could not be. All the workers would be busy trying to salvage the remains.

Sigrit ran up the stairs, sometimes skipping a step, a recent accomplishment she was proud of. On the third floor, she unlocked the glass paned apartment door and entered. Her ears strained for the voices of her parents. None were heard.

"Mama, Papa, where are you?"

Silence.

She ran through the apartment calling, then screaming, "Mama, Papa!"

Finally she went to her own room. There she found a note stuck to her mirror. Somehow that piece of paper represented the cortex of her fear. She did not want to know what it said. If only Ludwig was here, she would be less afraid.

"I won't read it. It's only a note telling me that Mama and Papa had to be away for a few minutes. If I don't read it, they'll be back and tell me what they wrote. I'll just go to the kitchen and see if there is anything to eat."

Try as she might, she could not pull herself away. She kept staring at the paper, straining her eyes to make out a word or two. Without being aware of it, her legs moved her toward the hypnotic object. She felt the note contained bad news and if she did not read it, the bad news would go away.

Closer and closer she moved. The note was written in a clear print, not the old Germanic script she would have to get someone else to read to her. Mama loved writing in the old script, not only for its uniqueness, but also for its beauty—letters with many sharp edges looking like rick rack.

Finally, she read:

> *Our darling daughter Sigrit,*
>
> *We are sorry that we have to leave you, but we are going to a better place. We have been working against the evil regime that is ruling our beloved country. We do not wish to fall into their talons, which we are about to do. We will always love you and your dear brother, Ludwig. Always stick together and remain good friends.*
>
> *God bless you both and keep you safe.*
> *All our love, your mother and father,*
> *Elisabeth and Erwin Lachman*
>
> *DO NOT GO UP INTO THE ATTIC!*

Alone, she went to the attic.

ඓඔඓ

The light in the room was dim and the heavy drapes were tightly drawn when Sigrit woke up. Frau Weiss from the second floor sat at her bedside stroking her hand.

"Ah, my dear, you are awake. Herr doctor came and gave you a sedative. I'll stay with you tonight. Everything will be all right, you'll see."

No, Sigrit did not see. She'd forgotten what was wrong. Then she remembered and started screaming again. Frau Weiss hugged her, spoke softly, and cried until Sigrit's screams subsided into dry heaves. She knew the sight in the attic would never leave her as long as she lived. Her body ached from being brought to the brink of exhaustion just a few hours earlier. Every cell in her small form seemed to relive the trauma of finding her beautiful Mama and tall, fun-loving Papa hanging from the rafters on two ropes—the two people most dear to her in all the world reduced to a most gruesome sight.

Sigrit had stared at the open bulging eyes for a full minute before she started screaming. She collapsed onto the wooden floor and lay still for a while, staring at the bodies. Papa dressed in his good Sunday suit and Mama in one of her favorite green dresses and green suede shoes, dressed as if going to a dance.

Sigrit whipped her arms and legs, screaming and crying until some neighbors heard her and carried her off. The women tried to comfort her with no success. Finally, someone fetched a doctor who gave her a sedative.

The next day SS men in black uniforms and Gestapo in plain clothes filled the apartment. They were searching every drawer and closet, even cutting upholstery that looked like something could be hidden in it.

Usually the neighbors were gathered in the large inside stairway, while the children would amuse themselves sliding down bannisters, but this day no one was to be seen.

Everyone stayed locked in their apartments, making the house as silent as a tomb.

Sigrit sat in the Weiss's apartment on a child's chair, clutching her old teddy bear. Her pale face had no expression and her glassy eyes stared into space.

"Don't you have an aunt in the city here?" asked Frau Weiss.

"Yes, I was expecting her to come and get me," Sigrit answered softly.

"Maybe she does not know what is going on here. As soon as Fritz comes home from school, I'll send him to get your aunt. Do you know her address?"

"Yes, Reichert Street 2."

"What is her name?"

"Erika Zeller." Once said, Sigrit hugged her bear and sucked her thumb, something she had not done for years.

As soon as Fritz, arrived his mother told him to take his bicycle and get Frau Zeller. Less than an hour later, Erika appeared on her bicycle dressed in a blue, tailored suit with a chic little hat on her brunette, curly hair. When she entered the apartment, Sigrit clung to her as if afraid that if she let Erika go, she too would be gone.

"What is going on here?" Erika asked.

Frau Weiss whispered the events of the day before, hoping Sigrit would not hear her.

"Oh that poor child," said Erika, stooping down to hug the little girl. "Where is Ludwig?"

"He is camping with the Hitler Youth," answered Sigrit, starting to cry. "He's coming home this evening." Just looking at her aunt made Sigrit sad. Erika looked so much like her dear mama.

"You are coming home with me. Now I'll go and get some of your things,"

Erika went up one flight of stairs and the first thing she encountered was an SS man guarding the door.

"No one is allowed into the apartment," he said.

"I need to get some of my niece's things. Let me speak to your superior."

"Commandant Schnellhauser," he called into the dwelling, "there is someone to see you."

Soon a tall man in his forties dressed in a well-fitting, brown suit appeared. His narrow face and prominent nose reminded her of Frederick the Great. He looked every inch like a Prussian policeman. Looking into the apartment, she saw a number of plain-clothed men and some in their black SS uniforms searching through every closet and drawer. All the things that had been gone through were laying on the floor in neat piles.

"Who are you and what do you want?"

"I am Erika Zeller. My husband is an army doctor on the Eastern Front. My sister lived here and I am taking the child home with me. I need to get a few of her things."

"I can't allow you to come in here and take anything away."

"At least would you give me her coat and some clothes?"

"I'll tell you what I'll do, I'll have my men pack up the children's things and you can come to my office to get them." He reached for a child's coat hanging on a hook near the hallway door and handed it to her. Then he took a pad of paper out of his pocket and said, "Tell me your address. The *Jugendamt* will get in touch with you concerning the children."

The word *Jugendamt* sent fear into Erika. "Why does the youth bureau have to get involved? I am the closest relative the children have, and I'm perfectly willing to care for them."

"Bureaucracy, we have to follow procedure."

"What about the bodies of my sister and her husband, where are they?"

"They are at the mortuary. I have made arrangements for internment tomorrow at ten in the morning at the *Friedhof.*"

"Could you tell me what they are accused of having done?" asked Erika.

"We can discuss that when you come to my office to get the children's things. Would tomorrow afternoon be good for you?"

"Yes."

"Then I expect to see you about three o'clock. Good-bye,"

Erika extended her right hand to him and when he shook it, she looked into his gray eyes, seeing some friendliness, something she did not expect to see in a Gestapo officer.

Leaving her bicycle in the care of Frau Weiss, Erika took Sigrit by the hand and they started walking. The little girl's eyes were glassy and blinked little. Occasionally the sun peaked through the clouds, adding a little cheer to the otherwise gray day. Even the three- and four-story apartment buildings with fancy facades and wrought iron balconies looked bleak. What was left of the bright flowers of summer was now black and brown. Some of the pots were still sitting outside like faithful sentinels, adding to the dreary atmosphere.

Passing Saints Peter and Paul Church, Sigrit asked to stop. They entered the large Gothic church that had always impressed her. Now the building seemed cold and unfriendly. The structure built to glorify man's faith in God now only appeared as a monument to architects and masons. Sigrit knelt down, folded her hands, and closed her eyes to pray. No thought of prayer came to her, only the horrible sight of her mother and father hanging from the rafters.

"Oh God, how can you let that happen? If you are good, how can you? Is your goodness an illusion? Are you only an illusion? Holy Jesus, give me a sign that you exist."

She stared at the large wooden cross hanging above the altar. "Jesus, prove you exist, make the cross swing."

The cross hung still.

"Can't think now, can't pray. Goodbye God, Jesus."

It was dusk when Ludwig who was fourteen arrived. He gave his aunt a polite handshake and bow. Erika put some precious bread and cheese on the kitchen table and the three ate supper in silence. While they lingered over some hot tea, Erika laid a hand on Ludwig's shoulder and urged him to express his feelings. He rebuffed her.

"I don't want to talk." He got up, put on his jacket, and headed for the door. "I'm going for a walk."

The door closed with a bang.

☙❧

Erika and Sigrit passed the evening in the kitchen. A heavy, dark-velvet drape kept the cold out and prevented the light from the electric lamp from being seen on the street, and possibly by airplanes. The wood fire in the dual, fuel kitchen range gave off a cozy, dry heat. The stove had four gas burners and a gas oven with a coal or wood stove attached. The top was flat, enabling one to cook on it. The radio softly played classical music.

Erika sat on the cushioned corner bench with a book on the table reading fairy tales. The girl lay on the bench with her head in her aunt's lap, being soothed by her pleasant voice, the crackling of the fire, and the heavenly notes of Mozart. Sigrit gently went into dreamland where her parents were still alive and loving her and all was well in her world.

By midnight Ludwig was still out and Erika became very anxious. Finally there was soft tapping on the apartment door. Erika rushed to the door and opened it cautiously. Her eyes opened wide and her nostrils expanded with breath. Ludwig stood at the door, one eye swollen shut and tinged with red and purple. The blood under his nose was dried and smeared on his face. With his clothes dirty and torn, he stood there, obviously trying to focus his good eye and keep his balance. He staggered forward, aimed for the nearest chair, and flopped down.

"What happened?"

Ludwig looked up, hiccupped, and spoke in an intoxicated slur. "I was with my friend, Rolf, in his father's wine cellar. You should see how much wine he has. Of course, the father was at one of his Nazi meetings. We boys got rid of some of the old stuff he has. I must say, some of that fifty year old wine was pretty good."

"Who beat you up?"

"Oh, that! On the way home we ran into some brownshirt hooligans. They were hogging the sidewalk, so we got into a fistfight. No big deal. We just stepped over them, but we did not have to step into the street."

"What happened to the gang of hooligans as you call them?"

"Oh, we beat the devil out of them, but they all got up and cussed us out."

"Do they know you and Rolf?"

"Naw, don't worry about me, I'm fine. What can happen that is worse than already has happened?"

"Don't ever think that things can't get worse—they can. There is some hot water on the stove. Wash up and I'll give you some pajamas. You can sleep in the guest room. Tomorrow is going to be a difficult day."

"Thank you, *Tante*." For a moment the boy looked small, sad, and vulnerable. Then he took a deep breath, straightened his shoulders, and assumed a defiant look in his one good eye.

CHAPTER 2

The next day Erika and the children went to the cemetery. Two black wooden coffins lay on biers in the mortuary. One lonely wreath sent by Erika and the children was the only funeral piece. The morning was cold and damp, threatening a downpour any minute. The inside of the chapel seemed even colder than the outside. The only three mourners sat near the coffins, each staring at the small bouquet of flowers on their laps. Silently they waited, each with their own thoughts, too stunned to cry. As the minutes crept by, the cold assaulted their bones. The smallest person felt it the most.

"*Tante* Erika, I'm cold," Sigrit said. "Why are we sitting here so long?"

"We are waiting for the minister to come and conduct the service," replied Erika. "Why don't you go outside and walk around a bit to warm up. Just don't go too far away."

"Yes, *Tante,* I'll do that."

Outside, Sigrit saw Commandant Schnellhauser and about half a dozen men standing nearby. Some wore uniforms and others were dressed in suits and coats. The Lutheran minister walked up, exchanged a few words with the Gestapo men, and then headed for the mortuary. Without as much as a nod or smile toward Sigrit, he walked briskly past her and entered the chapel. She quickly followed him and took her seat between her aunt and brother.

The middle-aged, tall, and thin minister stood near the coffins, opened his book, and read the service for the dead in an unemotional monotone. When the grave diggers quietly entered the chapel, the minister quickly concluded the service with a brief prayer. He motioned to the grave diggers with a nod of the head. Four old men carried each coffin, followed by the minister and the three mourners, to an open grave. After a second quick prayer, they lowered the first coffin into the cold earth.

Sigrit was the first to throw in half of her flowers and a handful of dirt. She looked at her aunt and asked, "Is that Mama or Papa in there?"

"I don't know." Erika asked the grave diggers if they knew. No one did.

"It makes no difference," one grave digger said gruffly.

"I have to know. How can I say goodbye to Mama or Papa if I don't know who is where?" A torrent of tears poured out of Sigrit's eyes. "Open the casket, I want to know. Please, *Tante*, open the casket. Open it, open it!"

Sigrit pounced on the coffin lying on the ground and tried to pry the lid open, screaming and crying.

Taken aback by the outburst of the seven year old, Erika looked around for someone to help.

Commandant Schnellhauser came over and told one of the grave diggers to open the coffin. The man said he needed a hammer and walked toward the chapel.

Then the Gestapo officer spoke to Sigrit. "Calm down, child, we shall open it and you can see."

He stooped down and stroked her hair. Sigrit composed herself, got to her feet, and extended a small hand to the man.

"Thank you, kind sir," she said, keeping her eyes down. When she raised her head and looked into his gray eyes, she noticed a trace of a friendly smile. To everyone's surprise, Sigrit flung her arms around the man's neck and kissed him on the cheek.

The man returned her affection with a quick hug then rose. "Here comes the man with the hammer," he said.

The worker quickly pried opened the lid. Reluctantly the three mourners and the officer looked at Elisabeth, the recently beautiful, vibrant woman, now stiff as a statue and starting to decay. The skin was yellow with blue tinges, the eyes were closed and beginning to sink in. She wore the same green dress she had on when they found her in the attic.

"Your mother looks peaceful," Erika told the children. "Put the flowers in with her."

They laid the flowers on her chest, then the coffin was closed again. Hurriedly the grave diggers lowered it into the grave on top of the first casket. As the mourners walked away they could hear the dirt hitting the wooden lid making a hollow drum-like sound.

"Frau Zeller!"

Erika looked back and saw Commandant Schnellhauser walking briskly to catch up with her. They stopped and waited.

When the man approached them he said, "I just want to remind you that the children's clothes and things are in my office."

"Yes, I shall be there at about three this afternoon."

"I can have one of my men help you carry the things home, so you don't need to bring anyone with you."

The statement startled Erika, but she calmly looked the man in the eyes and, with a shy smile, told him she would see him then.

In the afternoon Erika rode the streetcar toward the Neisse River. She got off in an old residential section and located a Victorian villa that was taken over by the Nazis in 'thirty-nine. When the woman saw the red flag with the white circle and, in her opinion, the ugly black symbol, fear hit her like an icy wind.

Take even breaths, just take even breaths. You are just getting some things.

Composing her face into a self-assured look, she straightened her back and walked toward the imposing house. She passed some bushes when suddenly a soldier in SS uniform stood in front of her.

"What do you want?" he asked in a surly voice.

"I have an appointment with Commandant Schnellhauser."

"Follow me, I will take you."

The young man opened the massive oak door for her and led her past another guard in the foyer, up a large stairway. All the doors to the rooms were shut, but one could hear typing and voices behind them. The soldier led Erika to a door marked with the number ten and knocked. In response to a voice, he opened the door and nodded for Erika to enter. He then closed the door behind her from the outside.

"Won't you sit down," said Commandant Schnellhauser, sitting behind a massive, carved oak desk in front of a window.

"Thank you," said Erika, taking a chair across the desk from him.

The man studied her intensely for a full minute before he spoke softly. "Did you know that your sister and her husband had been active in the White Rose Underground Movement?"

"White Rose? I never heard of it. What is that?"

"They are traitors that print up false propaganda and secretly distribute it. Your sister knew English, right? We found a shortwave radio in their home, she would listen to BBC."

"How do you know that?"

"People telling on their neighbors keeps us in business. We had been tailing them for a long time, hoping to find their contacts."

"Why are you telling me this? Do you think I am involved? I have a job—I'm a nurse in the hospital. I don't have time to work against Germany." Tears came to her eyes and her voice got louder. "My husband is a doctor on the Eastern Front. I would never do anything that could demoralize our troops." She reached into her purse, pulled out a white handkerchief, and dabbed her eyes.

"I want to ask you," he continued, "if you had known what they were doing what would you have done?"

Erika was silent for a minute then whispered, "I don't know. I really don't know."

"How do you feel about them hanging themselves?"

"I just don't understand that. How could they do that to those poor children?"

"Now, we have the problem with the children. Their guardianship has to be determined by the *Jugendamt.*"

"Why should that be problem? I am willing and able to take care of the children." Tears welled in her eyes. "After all, I am their closest relative."

"It's not that simple. The *Jugendamt* is concerned that the children's guardian be capable of giving them the proper upbringing, following the party line. Someone will come to your house and interview you. I'm just telling you what to expect."

"Thank you," she whispered, wiping her tears on her hanky.

"Now let me have a driver help you with the children's things. He can take you home in my car."

He picked up the phone, spoke quickly, then hung up. Rising, he walked around the desk and extended a hand to Erika. "Thank you for coming. Now if there is anything I can do to help, don't hesitate to ask."

Erika rose, gave him her hand, and allowed herself to be escorted to the door. "I can't thank you enough. Good day, Commandant Schnellhauser, heil Hitler."

"Heil Hitler."

CHAPTER 3

Hannelore Kempf got off the streetcar on Reichert Street. With an air of authority, she walked past three-story, gray-stone, row houses to number two. Some children were playing catch in the street. When they saw her face they immediately stopped their game and stared at her.

Damn ill-mannered children, they ought to be all sent away. Haven't you ever seen a birth mark before? Just because I have one doesn't mean I have the devil in me. Just because of it, does not give the world a right to beat on me.

She thought of the time she was in elementary school. *Classmates made my life a living hell. I was beaten and laughed at just because of my port-wine stain. Even my mother would call me ugly. I did nothing to deserve this face. Just keep staring brats—I hope you get a face full of infected pimples.*

She stopped at the corner house and found the name *Dr. Rowald Zeller* under the doorbell. She pushed the button for the apartment bell. Soon the door buzzed and she entered the building. On the first floor a door stood open and a woman in her twenties smiled at her.

What a damn pretty bitch. Every hair in place; beautiful, clear blue eyes with long dark lashes; pretty smile; even, white teeth. Wish I could call her a painted hussy, but she has no make-up on. Bet she bats her eyelashes and gets anything she wants. Well, bitch, you're not getting what you want from me.

"Frau Zeller?"

"Yes."

"I am Fraulein Kempf from the *Jugendamt*. May I speak with you?"

"Of course, please come in."

Erika led the woman into the parlor. "Thank you for coming. Just have a seat and excuse me for a few minutes, I will get us some hot tea. It'll feel good on such a cold day."

Hannelore was grateful to have a little time to observe her surroundings. The room was furnished with simple, but elegant furniture in the Biedemeyer style. She sat on the comfortable sofa and studied the pictures on the wall. Prominent was a photo of Hitler, the kind one could buy at any photography shop. What really stimulated her attention were some smaller pictures. There was a picture of Hitler with a soldier with a doctor's insignia on his uniform. Hannelore assumed that was Dr. Zeller. Her heart skipped a beat seeing her hostess in a picture, dancing with Albert Speer.

That bitch with Albert, my handsome Albert. What would I give to be embraced by Albert. Only saw him from the distance once and fell in love, and she's dancing with him. Damn. Got to be careful. She seems to know all the right people.

Erika entered, carrying a tray containing a pot of tea, two cups and plates, and a plate of cookies, a real luxury. She set it down on a low table in front of the sofa then cranked the table higher to make it comfortable to eat off of.

"Oh what a practical table. I've never seen one like that before."

"My father-in-law made it for us. He was a very clever man," Erika said while pouring tea. "Please have some cookies, I baked them myself."

"Thank you, don't mind if I do."

Sitting across the table from Miss Kempf, Erika dared to take a close look at her. She was trying to figure out how old the woman was. A purple swollen stain covered the left side of her forehead, over one eye, and half-way down the cheek. Her mousy brown hair was pulled back in an austere bun at the nape of her neck. The round, black-rimmed glasses added an unwittingly comic touch. She wore no make-up or jewelry to soften her look. Her suit was the color of her hair with narrow white stripes. Erika was among the majority of people who would never guess her age at only twenty-six.

"Frau Zeller, tell me, how are you related to the Lachmann children?" Hannelore asked while opening a notebook.

"Their mother was my sister."

"Did you know that she and her husband were involved in the White Rose anti-Nazi movement?"

"Of course not. I just can't imagine Elisabeth being involved in underground activities against our homeland." Her voice got higher. "I tell you, her husband must have murdered her. To do that to the children. I just can't imagine." She wiped tears on her napkin.

"Where are the children?"

"They're in school." Taking a deep breath to compose herself, Erika continued, "I felt it best for them to resume their normal activities as soon as possible."

"How are they doing?"

"Considering that only three days ago they had the shock of their life and then that awful funeral, they are holding up remarkable well."

"Are you their closest relative?"

"I am. I will be able to keep them, won't I? I love the children."

"We'll have to determine that."

"How can you doubt that I can give them a loving home? Especially Sigrit, she is a very affectionate child who needs a lot of love and attention."

"Love is one thing, but would you be educating them with the right political philosophy?"

"Of course, I will." Erika waved her arm at the pictures on the wall. "Some of my best friends are top Nazis."

"In that case you have nothing to worry about. People like you get everything they want," Miss Kempf said sarcastically. She looked at her watch. "It is getting late. Goodbye, Frau Zeller, you will hear from us."

"But what about some food-ration stamps? I need some extra ones for the children. Don't you take care of that?"

"See your friends about that. Heil Hitler."

Miss Kempf picked up her attaché case, slipped the notebook in, and headed for the door. Erika was stunned at the woman's quick departure.

A short time later Miss Kempf was led into Commandant Schnellhauser's office.

"Good you could come, Fraulein Kempf," he said. "Now tell me, how did your meeting with Frau Zeller go?"

"Herr Commandant, you should see the pictures she has in her parlor of Hitler and Speer. She says she is friends with them."

"That is very interesting. Now how do you feel about her being guardian of the children?"

Careful how you answer that. Who knows? That man might be smitten by her. "She seems a capable housewife and loving person."

"I want you to find a reason to have the children removed from her care. Send them to upper Bavaria or the Lake Constance area."

Schnellhauser's statement shocked and pleasantly surprised Miss Kempf. With a smile she asked, "Why that far away?"

"The farmers in that part of the Fatherland know how to raise children. They teach them to work hard."

"Your heart is in the right place. Not many people agree that children should earn their keep at a young age. I had to."

Hannelore walked on air when she left the Gestapo Office. It was the first time her opinion was backed up by that powerful office. She knew her supervisor at the youth bureau would want the children to remain with the aunt. And in her heart, she felt that would be best for the children.

She had not taken this job to do what was good for children, but to punish them. All of the bullying she had endured as a child, and she was still being pestered by children, made her hate the little creatures.

I could not have gotten a better job. I deal with miserable children and can add to their misery.

At six in the evening she was still in her office when her supervisor entered.

"Fraulein Kempf, your workday ended an hour ago. Don't you want to go home?"

"Is it that late already? I got so involved in my job I forgot to look at the time. I'll be going home as soon as I put the files away."

"Just leave them out. I want to have a meeting with you at eight in the morning in my office. We need to discuss the cases you're working on."

"Very good Frau Betz, I'll see you then, good night."

"Good night, Fraulein Kempf, heil Hitler."

"Heil Hitler," she said as she walked out the door.

The young woman entered her cold, dark apartment. Before she turned on the electric light she closed the heavy dark drapes of her kitchen and her one room. She turned on the gas to a low flame under the pot of potato soup.

After today, I need to cook another big pot of soup. It seems potato soup has become the new national dish. I'll stop at the butcher's tomorrow. Maybe I can get some meat. Sure would be nice to have a stew again.

Hannelore cooked only once or twice a week. The rest of the time she heated up leftovers. While the living room slowly got warm, she went into the bathroom, washed herself, and put on an evening gown she had hanging on the door. She unpinned her bun and let her hair fall half-way down her back. With a silver hairbrush she brushed her hair so it fell over the disfigured side of her face. Then she lined her right eye with some eyeliner and put lipstick on her full lips. She decorated her right ear with a rhinestone earring and slipped a plain gold band on the third finger of her hand. With her right hand on her hip she looked at her good side in the full length mirror.

"Good evening, beautiful lady. Now get dinner on the table before the husband gets home."

Hannelore ladled the soup into a bowl of gold-rimmed china and took it into the living room. After turning on the radio to popular music, she lit two candles and ate her modest meal, imagining herself in a beautiful house with a rich husband who passionately loved her.

Later that evening there was an air raid. Hannelore heard the sirens blaring throughout the city and listened to her neighbors scurrying down to the basement. She stayed quietly in her room, wearing the long silver gown and pretended she was sitting beside Albert Speer who ardently loved her.

Soon the all-clear sounded and the people went happily back to their apartments. It had been a false alarm.

CHAPTER 4

During the week following the funeral, Sigrit and Ludwig's lives fell into a normal routine. Every morning the children walked to school, carrying books in their knapsacks and a few pieces of firewood in their arms. All the students had to contribute to the consumption of the iron stove in each classroom. The classes were large, over seventy students, but the teachers had no discipline problems. Anyone who did not heed them had to sit in the far corner of the room where no heat reached. Students with the best grades had the privilege of sitting closest to the stove. Sigrit did her work well and enjoyed her place near the stove where her body sucked up the heat.

At one time she had felt almost guilty, sitting in the privileged spot, but not anymore. The other children in the second grade who had been her friends were no longer talking to her. On the playground she walked alone. When she came near others playing catch or jumping rope, they ignored her requests to join in the games. They all acted as if she did not exist. After she walked away she could hear them laughing at her.

The only person who still treated her the same was the teacher. The woman, who was in her sixties, entered the classroom saying, "Good morning, students."

Everyone quickly stood up and answered, "Good morning, Mrs. Teacher."

Then she would put on her crisp white lab coat and light the fire. She walked along the neat rows of desks and looked at everyone's homework. Anyone not having their homework completed got a double load of work that day. She did most of her teaching either at the black board or sitting at her desk on a platform two steps higher than the students sat.

On the way home from school, Sigrit was walking alone when she heard her name called. Ludwig was running to catch up with her.

"I figured I'll walk with you," he said.

"They're not talking to you either."

"No, all day long my classmates either ignore me or hit me."

Tears welled in her eyes. "I guess I can consider myself lucky. They just ignore me, but it hurts."

Ludwig put his arm around her shoulders and pulled her close.

"Don't cry, little sister, this too shall pass. Meanwhile try to ignore those stupid kids and think of happy times."

"When I think of happy times, I remember Mama and Papa and then I start crying. I don't even remember a time when there wasn't a war. I just pretend I'm a beautiful princess and no one speaks with me because they're all jealous."

"Hey, that is a good idea. I'll try it too. I'll be a knight who is the hero of the kingdom and an ugly princess wants to marry me."

"Are you going to marry her?"

"No, I'm in love with a beautiful tavern wench who brings me free beer while doing cartwheels."

Sigrit laughed. "Does she spill much?"

"Not a drop."

The rest of the way home the children came up with more and more outlandish scenarios. They both were laughing when they entered the apartment and found their aunt sitting in the kitchen over a cup of tea and a telegram.

"It is good to see you children laughing," she said as a greeting.

Ludwig was the first to see that her eyes were red. "Have you been crying, *Tante* Erika?"

"Yes, my dears, I got some bad news," she said waving the telegram.

"What does it say?" asked Ludwig.

Sigrit stood next to him with eyes wide and her mouth open.

"Your Uncle Rowald is missing in action on the Eastern Front."

"Missing?" Sigrit said.

"Yes, that means he is either dead and they haven't found his body or he was taken prisoner."

Ludwig hugged his aunt and said, "Don't worry, he is too big a man to be dead and they wouldn't find his body. You can be sure he's in a prison camp eating dinner and laughing over someone's jokes. When the war is over, he'll be released."

"I hope you're right. What makes you so smart at fourteen?"

"It runs in the family."

At the word family the boy became silent. His eyes went into a blank stare and his mouth drooped at the edges. The pale face was highlighted by green discoloration of the week-old bruises. His dark, straight hair looked dull, adding to his dispirited demeanor.

"I was lucky this morning and got a bone at the butcher's." Erika said as she pulled herself together. "Today the soup has eyes. Wash up for lunch, you two."

In the afternoon both children sat at the kitchen table doing their homework. Through the window they saw the mailman deliver the day's mail. Ludwig rushed outside and got everything out of the Zeller box.

"Look, *Tante* Erika," he said, all excited, "letters from uncle."

She opened the letters, one after the other and stared at the dates. Looking disappointed, Erika glanced at the telegram again.

"Each letter was written before November seventh, the day he was declared missing."

"Then in a few weeks you'll get the letter he is writing at this very moment," said Ludwig.

"I hope so. I'll read these letters later. Now let's see what the youth bureau has to say. Pray for good news."

Erika opened the letter slowly. She read it in silence while the children watched anxiously. Then she lowered the letter into her lap and sighed. When Sigrit saw the stunned look on Erika's face, she started crying.

"*Tante* Erika, what does it say?" asked Ludwig.

"They feel I'm not a fit guardian for you. They have found a family in Bavaria that is able to take you in. We are to pack your things for travel."

At the word travel Ludwig became pleasantly excited.

"We'll all go together. Maybe you can live with us in Bavaria."

"No darlings, Fraulein Kempf from the *Jugendamt* will take you. But don't worry, I have friends. I will try to get them to keep you here with me."

"I want to stay with you, *Tante*. I don't want to go to Bavaria," said Sigrit with big tears running down her face.

Erika hugged both children at once. "Don't worry, I'll see what I can do to keep you here."

Ludwig simply said, "Bavaria is supposed to be really nice. It has mountains and skiing. I've never seen real mountains."

Later that afternoon Erika was escorted into Commandant Schnellhauser's office.

"How nice of you to come and see me so soon," he said. "To what do I owe this pleasure?"

"Commandant Schnellhauser, thank you very much for seeing me. I have a problem, actually two problems. Hopefully, you can help me with one."

"What is it, Frau Zeller?"

"It's about the children. The *Jugendamt* wants to take them away from me and ship them off to Bavaria. Please, don't let that happen. Those children, especially Sigrit, really need me. To think of taking them away from a person who loves them and handing them over to who knows who. I just can't understand their logic."

The middle-aged man rose and walked to the door. He opened it and looked out into the hall. No one was in sight.

He shut the door and walked up behind Erika's chair. Gently he put one hand on her shoulder and spoke softly. "Frau Zeller, don't waste your energy fighting it. I want to tell you that your niece reminds me very much of my own daughter when she was seven. Unfortunately, she died two years ago."

"I'm terribly sorry to hear that."

"Thank you. What I will tell you now is in the strictest confidence. If you tell this to anyone and it gets back to me, I will deny this conversation."

"You can trust me. I can keep secrets."

"The war will be over soon."

"That is wonderful," she said, rubbing her cheeks with her hands.

"It won't be wonderful when the Russians come. They have suffered harshly and they will be looking for revenge."

"Why? What has been going on? My husband is missing on the Russian front."

"I'm sorry to hear about your husband. Do you have any friends or relatives in western Germany? Anyone you can visit for an extended time?"

"I have a sister-in-law in Stuttgart and some cousins in Cologne, Why?

"It might be a very good idea for you to visit one or the other for a time. Allow the children to be taken without a fuss. Then after the war is over, you'll all get back together. Believe me, it can't last much longer."

"But what if my husband comes looking for me?"

"Tell your friends and neighbors where you'll be. If—I mean when—the good doctor comes looking for you, he'll find you. Now where do you want to go, Stuttgart or Cologne?"

Erika thought about it briefly then replied, "Stuttgart."

He took a paper out of a drawer and wrote on it. Then he stamped the paper and handed it to her.

"Here is your travel permit. It's a valued document."

Erika rose and extended her hand.

The officer took it and said, "Goodbye and good luck."

"Goodbye and heil Hitler."

"Stop that Hitler crap."

That remark startled Erika and she looked at him, very surprised. Then she smiled. "Goodbye, kind Sir, God be with you."

He smiled, took her hand, and walked her to the door. Without another word they parted.

Then he returned to his desk and did something he had not done for years. He put both elbows on the desk, folded his hands against his forehead, closed his eyes, and prayed.

CHAPTER 5

A few days later Erika was sewing the seam on Sigrit's teddy bear. Ludwig and Sigrit were sitting at the table in the kitchen, silently watching every move, and intensely listening to their aunt. Two bulging knapsacks sat on the floor.

"Fraulein Kempf will be here soon," Erika said. "She might seem gruff at first, but she really is a very nice lady. You can't help noticing the large port-wine stain she has on her face right here," she said, placing her hand on the left side of her face. "But you have to ignore it. Don't stare at her, but don't avoid looking at her. When you speak with her, look into her eyes, and above all, always speak politely to everyone."

"Even if they don't speak polite to me?" asked Sigrit.

"Even then, you know how to act and speak politely. Always do it. Promise?"

"I promise," whispered the girl.

"Now each of you have all your relative's addresses in your little notebooks. Just in case you lose them, the addresses are in the teddy bear. I took leave from the hospital, and I'll be going to live with your Aunt Lydia in Stuttgart for a while. You can write to me there."

"We'll do that, won't we, Sigrit?" said Ludwig.

She nodded. "Yes."

"The war will be over soon and then I'll get you and we'll come back here. Right now we're all going on vacation. Just think, you won't be going to school for a few days. Once you get to Bavaria, you'll go to a new school and make new friends."

Ludwig's eyes lit up. Bavaria, getting away from school here, mountains, and a train trip—he was ready for the adventure.

The doorbell rang. Erika went to the house door and escorted Hannelore Kempf, carrying a small suitcase, into the apartment. She made the introductions.

"Fraulein Kempf, this is Ludwig Lachmann."

"Good day, Fraulein Kempf," said the boy, shaking her hand with a firm grip and bowing from the waist.

"Good day, Ludwig," she said, looking critically at the boy. She was expecting he would be a little boyish lad, instead of this tall handsome young man.

I know what I would like to do with him. I just wonder if I might be able to get away with it.

"And this is his sister, Sigrit."

Sigrit shyly shook the woman's hand, looked into her face, and smiled while she curtsied.

Pretty child, big blue but sad eyes, pretty rosebud lips. She reminds me of a doll I once had. Always wished I looked like that doll.

"Good day, Sigrit. Are you two ready to go on a trip with me?"

"Yes, Fraulein Kempf," answered Ludwig.

Hannelore and the children, accompanied by Erika, took the streetcar to the train station. The passenger platform was crowded with people. Most of the waiting travelers were women and children. Many carried their possessions in sheets and blankets, tied together at the corners. The train station was heavily patrolled by police. They did not give the women much of a glance, but male travelers were challenged to show identification and travel permits. Ludwig immediately attracted attention and two policemen requested to see his papers.

"How old are you?" the older policeman asked.

"Fourteen," Ludwig answered quickly.

The policeman said to the two women, "It's hard to believe he's only fourteen." He handed back the papers and walked away.

When the train slowly pulled into the station, Erika gave the children a quick hug.

"Goodbye, and don't forget, as soon as you get there to write to me at *Tante* Lydia's."

"Goodbye, I don't want to leave, but I'll be brave like Snow White," Sigrit said, fighting back tears.

Sigrit's attention was drawn to the black steam engine passing a few feet from her. She watched in awe as the large iron wheels, propelled by rods, slowly went by. Clouds of steam hissed out of the engine, not only from the smoke stack, but also out of the bottom. Momentarily she was wrapped in white vapors. She could smell the clean, sharp odor of the steam. She wished she could disappear into the steam and go to a place where there was no war, no death, no hunger, and no cruelty. Where everyone loved one another and no one caused pain.

Just before the train came to a complete halt, Ludwig grabbed Sigrit by the right hand. Miss Kempf took her left hand and the three rushed to get to an open car door. They had to keep their bodies close together and hold on tight, so as not to be wrenched apart by the crowd trying to get on the train.

Miss Kempf elbowed her way through and herded her charges into the half-filled car. They found an empty compartment and took seats. Quickly the compartment made for six was occupied by another five people. Other passengers resigned themselves to standing in the passageway. At least they were lucky enough to get *on* the train.

Ludwig opened the window and called to his aunt. She pushed her way close to the train and grabbed the boy's hand. They were able to exchange only a few words when the conductor blew the all clear whistle and the train slowly pulled out of the station. Ludwig leaned out of the window and watched as the people on the terminal got smaller. He kept his eyes on his aunt who was smiling and waving a red handkerchief. He waved back until the train rounded a curve and the terminal was out of sight. Then he pulled his head in and closed the window.

Erika's acting skills helped her hide her sadness when everyone left the house for the train station. However, seeing so many people traveling alarmed her. With the train out of sight, she turned to go home.

Turning around she almost fell over a toddler sitting on the cement platform. His mother was trying to coax him to get up and walk. The little boy wore a crudely made harness with a rope attached. The woman pleaded with the child to obey. Her face had a resigned look of suffering that looked as if it had been going on for longer than she cared to remember. The fact that the child gave her grief was only another cross in her life. At least the baby in her left arm was sleeping, and she was fortunate to have a large battered suitcase to hold all of their belongings. People walked by them with annoyance, trying not to breathe.

"Here, let me carry your suitcase or the child," offered Erika.

"Thank you, if you would carry the suitcase, I would certainly appreciate it. I'm looking for a room to spend the night. Do you know of any hotel in town?"

"Yes, there is one right across the street. I'll go with you."

"The woman picked up the very tired little boy and carried him under her arm. Her long black skirt almost swept the street. Her hair was hidden under a dirty, blue wool kerchief that had a fold, bringing the material over her forehead.

At the hotel, there was a large number of people waiting to check in. Erika went to the front of the line and inquired if there might be a room available. The clerk looked up with a sneer, but seeing a beautiful woman with an air of authority, he quickly changed his demeanor and told her rather politely that the hotel was booked solid.

When Erika told the woman that there was no room, her face fell.

"I suppose we can find a spot at the train station and get some sleep."

"You will do no such thing. You can sleep in my apartment. Come, we'll get the streetcar in the next block."

"Oh, gracious lady, how very generous of you. Bless you, I can't thank you enough."

"Think nothing of it. I'm sure you would do the same for me. Would you mind telling me where you are coming from?"

"We are from a small village near Breslau. The Russians are there and we were lucky to escape with our lives."

"I'm very sorry." Erika led the woman, carrying the two children, through a tunnel under the railroad tracks out on to the street. Soon a streetcar came. They got on and sat down. Both women sat in silence during the short ride. People did not talk where others could hear, not even to exchange names.

By late afternoon the two children were bathed, fed, and sleeping in the bed that had been used by Ludwig. Erika scrounged around the cupboard trying to find enough food for the woman and herself. Having had the children for two weeks without additional food stamps exhausted her supply. She was totally out of stamps and there were still five days left in the month. The only food in the house was a little bread, a bouillon cube, and an onion.

"Onion soup coming up," she said to herself.

The woman entered the kitchen as Erika was putting the soup on the table. She wore a long red skirt with a wide black hem and a black velvet bodice fastened with silver filigree buttons. Her crisp white linen blouse was decorated with cut work embroidery around the neck and on the full short sleeves. A long, white linen apron matched the blouse. Her blonde hair was parted in the middle and two thick braids were piled across the top of the head like a tiara. The woman's eyes were close set, giving her face a full look in spite of her general gauntness.

When she spoke, her green eyes radiated with animation. "That bath felt absolutely wonderful, I feel human again. I can't thank you enough, Erika."

"You look beautiful, Jutta. Is that the folk dress of your region?"

"Yes, and this skirt is over thirty years old. The blouse and apron are not much newer. We had to leave so quickly all I had time for was to grab some children's clothes and this. I figure there is enough good material in the skirt to make something out of it. Are the children still sleeping?"

"I just checked them and they're sleeping like babies. Now you eat this soup while I get ready for work. I'm a nurse and I have night duty."

"Aren't you going to eat?"

"I can eat at the hospital." Eating at the hospital meant eating food the patients had left on their trays, provided there had been no visitors.

While the woman ate, Erika went into the cold parlor and looked around. She picked up a silver bowl and left the apartment. On the third floor she rang a doorbell. An aristocratic looking old lady opened the door.

"Oh, Frau Zeller, what a surprise. Won't you come in?"

"Thank you." She held out the bowl. "Frau Greis, would you still like to have this bowl?"

The woman's eyes lit up. "Yes, definitely. Let me show you what I can give you for it."

༄༅༅

The train moved slowly through the flat countryside. Miss Kempf read a book. The children stared out of the window, watching the endless fields and forests slowly go by. The day was mostly cloudy and the rhythmic bump-bump of the train's wheels, hitting the spaces between the tracks, put the passengers almost into a trance.

"Fraulein Kempf," Sigrit said timidly.

"What?"

"Why is the train moving so slowly?"

"Because our evil enemies like to bomb the tracks. The engineer has to keep a sharp eye out for damage so he can stop in time." Then she put the book back in front of her face, signaling an end to the conversation.

The other passengers in the compartment, four women and one old man sat in silence. Occasionally, Sigrit caught one old woman's eyes and the woman smiled at her. Sigrit returned the smile, grateful that someone on the train, besides Ludwig, liked her.

When the train stopped at dusk, Ludwig opened the window and stuck his head out, looking for a terminal. He only saw fields. People in the passageways started disembarking the train. The friendly old woman moaned,

"Not again, at this rate we'll never get to Nuremberg."

The conductor opened the door and said, "Tracks are bombed. All out and walk ahead about a kilometer and wait for another train."

Miss Kempf finally put her book down and glanced out of the window. She suddenly became quite animated and looked out on the other side of the train to confirm their location. "Come children, put on your knapsacks, time to go."

When they got off the train, she took them away from the tracks.

"Fraulein Kempf, aren't we going to catch the train?" asked Ludwig.

"Children, we are in luck. We are only about five kilometers away from my mother's. We'll go there for the night, sleep in a bed, and take the train tomorrow. Come on, we can be there in a little over an hour."

The three travelers walked on a dirt road as the red sun quickly dropped behind trees, illuminating the gray clouds and promising good weather tomorrow. Sigrit had problems with her knapsack slipping off her shoulders, and she slowed down to adjust the straps. Finally Miss Kempf got impatient with the delays, took the knapsack, and put it on her own back.

"Thank you, Fraulein, would you like me to carry your suitcase?"

"No, child, it's not heavy."

Tante Erika was right. She really is a very nice lady, thought Sigrit while hugging her teddy bear.

CHAPTER 6

The travelers could see a square church tower with the sharply pointed steeple first. Then they saw the tiled red roofs of the houses.

"That is Eichdorf ahead," Miss Kempt said. "My mother lives there in a house almost four-hundred years old," she continued with pride in her voice. "I was born there."

"It looks like a farm village," said Ludwig. "Does your mother have animals?"

"Yes, she does."

"Good, I'd like to see them."

Frau Kempf had finished feeding the chickens and was going into the house when she looked down the road. One of the three figures walking toward her looked familiar. Not paying any more attention, she went into the house and started making potato dumplings. A knock on the door made her wipe her floured hands on her apron with annoyance before she opened the door.

"Oh, it's you. So you finally get around to visiting your old mother, and you bring more guests without letting me know ahead of time. I suppose you want to spend the night."

"Good evening, Mother. It is so good seeing you again. How about a little hug?"

"Can't you see I have my hands full of flour? Who are they?" she said, nodding toward the children.

"This is Ludwig and Sigrit Lachmann."

"Good evening, Frau Kempf," the children said together, making a bow and curtsy without shaking hands.

The woman looked at the children and smiled. "Pretty children. Why couldn't I have had children that looked like that? I suppose you're hungry. Hannelore, show them to the spare bedroom and have them wash up, then help me make supper."

While the children were getting settled, Hannelore stayed in the kitchen, helping with the cooking.

"Who are these children and where are you taking them?"

"Mother, they are orphans and I'm taking them to a family near Munich."

"I want you to leave the boy here."

"I can't do that. I have orders to deliver them to these people in Bavaria."

"Hannelore, I'm running this farm by myself and I need help. I want that boy."

"What happened to the man you had?"

"You mean the Bulgarian? They needed him in a factory. My farm isn't big enough to qualify me for getting any more labor. I'm getting old. By the way, not only didn't you come for my sixtieth birthday, I didn't even get a card."

"I'm sorry, Mother, but I was tied up at work. I did send you a card and present. I hear the mail is getting mighty slow nowadays. Maybe it will still come."

"You can give me a present now by leaving the boy. You owe it to me. I am your mother. If you would know the pain you gave me giving birth to you and—"

"Yes, I know. You have told me often enough. Then you were disappointed that I was no great beauty."

Hannelore looked at her mother critically. *She was lucky Father married her. I bet, if she wouldn't have had a sizable dowry, she'd be a bitter old maid now. Her eyes are small with eyelids drooping like valances over the corners. There are more blood vessels on her nose. It's getting bigger and more bulbous all the time. Her body is thick and shapeless, but that is to be expected at her age.*

"Besides, that boy might get snatched away from you before you get to Bavaria," her mother continued. "They are drafting fourteen and fifteen year olds for the *Volkssturm*. I have seen them, those kids are little."

"And if I leave him here, what is to prevent him from getting drafted?"

The woman thought for a minute. "I know, I'll dress him as a girl."

"You can't do that. Besides, I have the responsibility to get him to Bavaria."

The woman looked her daughter straight in the face and said, "Hannelore, let me put it this way: if you don't leave the boy here, you can leave right now and never come back."

"Maybe I could tell the people who are expecting him that he got drafted, or that he ran away. But if someone finds out I left him here, I don't know what they'll do to me.

I'll surely get fired, maybe thrown in jail. When I first saw him, I thought of leaving him with you to make your work easier. See, Mother? I do consider your welfare."

"I'm glad you think of me and my hard life here while you have a clean office job and live in grand style in the city."

Frau Kempf went to the stove and lifted the lid from a large pot. Steam and a most delicious aroma of smoked pork impacted the kitchen. Hannelore felt weak with hunger. She looked out of the window and saw the fading light and gray clouds, with the wind whipping bare branches in the trees. If she left now with the children, they might have to sleep in the fields. The thought chilled her to the bones.

"Mother, you are more important to me than my job. You will have to help convince the boy that what we are doing is best for him. We don't want a big scene in the morning."

"I knew you would understand. Now tell those children to come and eat."

ಆಾಯ

The city was pink in the early dawn light as Erika wearily made her way home from the hospital. She wished she had nothing to do but sleep for the next twelve hours. When the children were living with her, she'd had a hard time sleeping during the day. There was all the tension of events, the death of her sister and brother-in-law, the funeral, the interrogations by the Gestapo and the youth bureau. Then the children were taken away while all she could do was smile and tell them that it was for the best. She almost forgot another terrible event—receiving the telegram informing her that her husband was missing. So many bad events at one time, it was more than one could absorb.

She felt like just crawling into a hole and pulling a blanket over her head, but she had no time for that. She had a house guest. She needed to talk with the woman more and find out what was happening on the Eastern Front. The news she read in the paper or heard on the radio never mentioned that the Eastern Front was well inside Germany.

Even at the hospital, the hoped-for quiet night did not materialize. There were a number of refugees being treated for bullet wounds. Some of the wounds were several weeks old and had never been professionally treated. The people she saw came from the east and northeast. Many had no idea where they were going, only west. They were running for their lives, running away from the Russians and toward the Americans or British.

Erika had planned to go to Stuttgart shortly before Christmas, but the situation, being as it was, made her consider moving the departure date up radically.

Quietly she entered the silent apartment.

Good, maybe I can catch an hour of two before my guests get up.

Erika woke suddenly and looked at the clock. It was almost noon. She got up quickly and went into the kitchen. Jutta was there, nursing the baby, while the two year old boy sat on the floor studying a red ball.

"Hello, did you have a good sleep?" asked Jutta.

"Yes, thank you. Forgive me for not getting up and making breakfast. I did not mean to sleep that long."

"No problem, Erika, I just was so bold and helped myself. I don't expect you to wait on us. Just having a roof over our heads is a luxury, not to mention warm, feather beds. Please allow me to serve you lunch."

"If it makes you feel better, you can do that, but there is no hurry, finish with the baby."

Erika stooped down and picked up the toddler, kissing him. The boy laughed and hugged her.

"What a handsome boy you are. Now Auntie has to get dressed and then I want to talk with your mother."

The two women and small boy enjoyed a feast of frankfurters on rolls accompanied by sauerkraut.

"Erika, I know this food costs you dearly. I can't thank you enough for all you are doing for complete strangers."

"Yesterday we were complete strangers, today we are friends. We both are innocent victims of war. Both of our husbands were yanked away from us to fight in some useless conflict. I don't know if my Rowald will ever return, and you know that your husband will not come back," Erika said with tears welling in her eyes. "So much pain, so much suffering—for what?"

Jutta's eyes opened wide with surprise. "You shock me. Forgive me, but I thought you would spout the party line of glory and honor and love for Hitler."

"You must have seen the photographs in the parlor."

"Yes," Jutta said apologetically. "I went in there looking for fire wood. I did not go into the yard for wood because I don't know which is your wood pile."

"No problem. The picture of myself with Speer and my husband with Hitler are fakes. The photographer nearby is my friend and he dubbed them for me. I was hoping to impress someone."

"Did you?"

"I don't think so. If I did, it didn't work. Now we better make some plans for the near future. It's no use you traveling alone anymore. If you want, I'll be glad to travel with you."

"That would be wonderful."

"Where are you going?"

"I am hoping to get to Frankfurt. I have an aunt and uncle there, but what used to be a one day trip now can take a week or longer. I just got to the point where I would get on any train going west."

"Then we will go together and split up when we get closer to those cities. Do you have travel permits?"

"No"

"They're available at the police station. You can leave the children here while you get it"

"Erika, you are too kind."

"We can also go through my clothes and pick ourselves some good traveling clothes. I think my clothes will fit you."

"If you have them, I would like to have more urban dress. But I'm sorry. I can't give you anything but a little money for them."

"I don't want your money. Who knows if this house will survive the war and all would be lost anyway? I can't take much. The rest might as well be put to good use."

The rest of the day the two women carefully picked out clothes from the ample supply of Erika's pre-war wardrobe. Erika took some of her precious china and crystal pieces, along with some additional clothes and bartered them for groceries from her neighbors, the butcher, and the grocer.

For the journey each woman chose hiking clothes, consisting of wool pants, sturdy shoes, and down filled jackets.

The things they carried were put into canvas backpacks. Erika put some sterling silverware and her jewelry, along with one good dress in the bottom of hers.

"I wish they would invent throw away diapers," Jutta said.

"Good idea. We'll make them." Erika took many of her towels and cut them into diaper size pieces. "We'll take them in a large shoulder bag and just throw them away."

"We better do it secretly," Jutta said, "or we'll get some dirty looks from fellow passengers for being so wasteful."

Erika laughed. "If anyone gives us a dirty look, we'll offer them the soiled rag."

"You're right. I'm sure they'll want it."

"Fortunately, I'm off tonight. I'll call my supervisor and tell her that I have to take leave for a few weeks. I know she will have a fit because we are already understaffed."

"Where do you have to go to make the phone call?"

"Into the bedroom."

Jutta's eyes widened. "You have your own phone? I've never been in a house with a phone."

"Yes. You want to make a call?"

"I don't know anyone who has a phone, but could I hear someone speak on it?"

"Yes, come along."

After calling the hospital, Erika called her friend with the photography shop and told him she was going to Stuttgart. After a brief conversation, she let Jutta have her first telephone conversation.

"What a wonderful invention. To think of it, we haven't had electricity until just a few years ago," Jutta said, all excited.

"Now we'll both have a good supper, hopefully a quiet evening, and a good night's sleep," Erika told her. "We better be at the train station by five in the morning. We might get a train then."

Providence cooperated with them. It was a night without an air raid. They both enjoyed a feast of meat, potatoes, and vegetables washed down with beer. Jutta relished the luxury of drinking whole milk for the first time since she started the journey. She worried that she would lose her milk and her four-month-old son would starve to death. With a belly full of good food, a warm place to stay, and having a clean body, the world looked a lot less threatening. Suddenly her eyes brightened.

"Erika, how would it be if I don't go any farther? Suppose I stay in your apartment while you go to Stuttgart. I can keep it clean and take good care of your things while you are away. Then when you come back, I'll move out. I have some money and I could pay your rent while I'm here. I know this is asking a lot, but you would have a much easier time traveling without me and the children. Why don't you think about it?"

She is right. Traveling with those two children would be difficult. From what I hear, Frankfurt has seen a lot of bombing. Her relatives might be dead or homeless. Then what would she do?

"Well, Jutta, are you sure you would want to stay here, not knowing anyone? But it would be a lot easier than traveling. I suppose you'll be as safe here as anywhere. You know, it would be a winning situation for both of us. Yes, I trust you to stay here."

Jutta hugged her host with enthusiasm.

"Thank you. Oh, thank you so much, thank you. I will take good care of your furniture and everything. I'll even sew your towels back together."

The rest of the evening Erika told Jutta the ins and outs of life in Goerlitz. Suddenly she felt free. She had no one to look after, no one would call her nurse or depend on her to provide. Now she was only Erika Luise Zeller, a woman without responsibility and going on a trip. She felt free and ready for adventure.

Tomorrow I will leave my comfortable apartment and start a journey into the unknown. It has been a long time since I have seen the land the poets and writers praised. I have to look beyond the destruction and enjoy the mountains and fields and streams.

Her youth had been serious and disciplined. She'd lived with her parents in a spacious apartment in Goerlitz. After her nurse's training, she worked in the hospital but stayed in her parents' house, paying rent. She met Dr. Rowald Zeller at work, dated him, and fell in love. After they were married, she moved into his apartment. They had put off having children, then the war came and they were separated.

In a way she envied her older sister, Elisabeth. As soon as she was old enough she left home and got herself a job as a nanny with a family in New York City. When she returned after three years, she surprised everyone by marrying her childhood sweetheart, settling down, and having children.

Erika walked through her apartment, taking mental pictures of the expensive furniture and fine china that was left. All the things that tied her to a place she suddenly felt alien to. Things and duty had kept her prisoner. Yesterday she could hardly imagine living anywhere else, but now she felt free.

She took the picture of Hitler off the wall and tore it up. Then she tore up the fakes with the famous people. The studio portraits of family members went into her knapsack.

After pouring herself a glass of wine, Erika raised her glass and said, "Here's to you Rowald, wherever you are. I hope you are well and will return." She took a sip. "Here's to you Elisabeth, my adventuresome sister, wherever you are. I hope you are happy."

She took another sip and raised the glass again. "Here's to everyone else in my family. May you all be well and happy."

Before the last swallow she raised the glass once more. "And this is to you, Erika—a woman."

CHAPTER 7

Early the next morning, Ludwig was in the stable with Frau Kempf.

"You put both hands on the udders and squeeze with your thumb and first finger then with the rest of your hand and pull. You ready to try it?"

Eagerly, the boy put his hands on the warm, soft teats and squeezed as instructed. His effort was rewarded with a white stream tinkling into the blue enameled bucket between his knees. Again and again his motion was enriched with the sound of the warm liquid rushing into the pail and the sweet smell of rich, fresh milk. To Ludwig, milk was an item that originated in aluminum tanks and was ladled out for a fee into customer's pitchers. To be sitting next to a large, live animal and relieving it of its burden of milk gave him a satisfaction he had never before experienced.

He looked up into the face of Mrs. Kempf. She smiled and told him he was doing well. Suddenly her homely face became appealing and Ludwig was overcome with a happiness he had almost forgotten existed. His cheeks suddenly became red and round and his lips widened revealing his even, white teeth. Above all, his eyes suddenly sparkled with a light from within.

"I can do it, see? I can milk a cow."

"You are doing wonderful. Just think, there is another one waiting to be milked. In the spring there are fields to plow and seeds to sow. Then the plants sprout and need tending until they are ready for harvest. I'm sure you would make a good farmer."

"I think I would like to be a farmer."

"How would you like to stay here with me?"

"As long as Sigrit can be here, too."

The mention of the girl stabbed the woman in the chest. She did not want her. A seven-year-old girl was nothing but a liability. She would eat more than she could work. This boy was big for his age and she could expect a man's labor from him. In return, he would eat well, a luxury most Germans did not enjoy these days. She would have to think of something quickly to convince the boy his sister would be better off in Bavaria, while he would be safer with her.

"Travel nowadays is treacherous for young men like you. The military police might think you're a deserter and hang you from the nearest lamppost before you can explain yourself."

At the word *hang*, Ludwig felt as if he had been stabbed with an icicle. He shuddered with cold.

The woman knew the boy's history and saw the effect of her words. She continued. "However, your sister is better off not being here. There is an old man in town who seeks out little girls and entices them to him. He likes to *play* with them. Do you know what I mean?"

"Why don't they throw him in jail?"

"He is very old and they consider him harmless. Now, you and I know what he is doing is wrong, but many people still have the attitude that the female gender is put on this earth for the gratification of men"

Ludwig had parents that loved and respected each other. The idea of men using women just for pleasure was strictly foreign to him. He knew he had a lot to learn, but at the present that was not his priority.

"Besides," she continued, "there is a family in Bavaria with a girl that really needs a companion. Wouldn't you want your sister to live with a family like that?"

"Sigrit has always wished for a sister."

"There she shall have one and you will be safer here with me. You can help me farm. You'll like that. Don't you agree?"

"Yes," he said softly.

"Then that is settled. You stay here and help us to convince your sister that she is better off going to Bavaria with Hannelore."

"I'll do that, but please let us have today together."

"All right, I'll invite Hannelore to stay today."

"Thank you."

"I think you and I will get along very well," said Mrs. Kempf with a big grin.

∽∽∽

Sigrit sat in the train staring out the window. Hannelore Kempf kept her face behind a book, an act that discouraged conversation. Sigrit tried to figure out why Ludwig no longer traveled with them. They started the journey both heading to the same family in Bavaria. It had been explained to her that Ludwig was to stay with Frau Kempf while she had to go on alone. What seemed like an eternity ago, she was a child, secure with a mother and father that loved her. Ludwig was a typical older brother, teasing her and acting like she was the cross of his life. Since her parents died, he treated her in a kind and loving manner.

Then *Tante* Erika took over the role of a mother so readily. Not only did she look like her mother, but her voice was similar. First she was yanked away from Goerlitz and her aunt, then she had to leave Ludwig behind and travel with that cold woman to who knew where? At least the sun was shining. Sigrit hugged her worn teddy bear, an object that had been with her since she was a little baby. She had to make sure she was never separated from that toy. Suddenly she felt a hunger pang like a blow to her stomach.

"Fraulein Kempf, I am hungry."

The woman looked at her wrist watch.

"It's only eleven fifteen, can't you wait until noon?"

"I am so hungry, it hurts."

Reluctantly Miss Kempf took a ham sandwich out of her leather bag and gave it to the girl.

Gratefully Sigrit started eating. Soon the other passengers in the compartment got out their lunch and joined in.

༄༅༅

It was snowing in Munich when the train pulled into the station in early December. Hannelore woke Sigrit.

"Wake up, child. We have to catch another train. Wake up, time to go."

Sigrit was dreaming she was back in her room in Goerlitz, wondering who was telling her to wake up. The voice did not sound at all like Mama's. She opened her eyes and saw a head surrounded by bright light.

"Mama, what did you do to your hair?"

"Come on, Sigrit, we have to get the other train."

Then Sigrit woke to reality. She was not in her room, but in a crowded train somewhere unknown with Fraulein Kempf.

Without saying a word, Sigrit put on her blue wool coat and hat, donned her knapsack, and gave Hannelore her hand. The woman led her onto the crowded platform, almost bumping into a red cap.

"Excuse me, could you tell me where and when I can get the train to Hollstein?"

The man opened his book and informed them that it would be four hours until the next train to Hollstein.

"Come, child, that will give us an opportunity to see a historic site or two."

"What historic site?"

"You'll see."

Outside the terminal, the woman and girl got on a streetcar and rode to the Marienplatz.

"There, child," said Miss Kempf, pointing to a large ornate building with a high tower, "that is City Hall. If we're lucky, we'll see the clock strike the hour."

Sigrit yawned. Sure, city hall was big and fancy, but she would rather be sleeping and dreaming of home. And to feel lucky to hear the clock strike? Some people just did not expect much.

Sigrit became weary of standing in the plaza. She was getting cold and hungry and wanted to go somewhere warm. Then the clock struck the hour of eleven in the morning.

"Can we go now, Fraulein Kempf?"

"Wait, look at the clock."

Sigrit looked at the clock high above the street. That was the first time she noticed the carved figures of a king and queen and court jesters. Beneath them were men holding green garlands above their heads. Then the glockenspiel started and the figures went into action.

The men danced, the jesters marched around while others danced, knights on horses went at each other with lances until the Bavarian knight knocked the Austrian knight down. The show went on for a quarter of an hour while the music played. Sigrit watched with fascination, feeling her mood improve. She wondered how anyone could walk by with a grim expression.

After the show was over, Hannelore led her to a small street. They entered a plain looking building. The odor of stale beer and tobacco smoke filled the air. At first glance the hall did not appear very large until the two kept walking a long way to get to the toilets. After they used the private booths they took out washcloths and soap and freshened up. Feeling somewhat better, they went back into the hall and sat down at an empty table. Men and women of all ages occupied the hall. Many of the men had bandages of recent wounds, while others sat over their beers with crutches next to them. Sigrit wondered what it felt like losing a limb. She hoped to never find out.

A waitress with six, full, liter mugs in each hand came by and nodded to Hannelore. She nodded back and the middle-aged woman set a liter mug in front of her.

"Could you bring a sprudel for the child and each of us a weisswurst platter?"

"Yes Fraulein, in a few minutes."

A short time later the waitress returned with a clear bubbly water for Sigrit and two platters each containing a large white sausage and some bread. Hannelore produced the required ration stamps and paid, then turned to Sigrit with a big smile,

"Eat, child, and enjoy."

"Thank you, good appetite."

Hungrily, Sigrit bit into the smooth white sausage. She had to bite firmly to get past the casing. Once beyond it, the most magnificent flavor exploded in her mouth. It was spicy and mild at the same time. To stretch the time of enjoyment she ate bread between bites of sausage. The bread was light and flavorful without added sawdust.

"This is a specialty of Bavaria," said Hannelore with a gleam in her eyes.

First the clock, now this wonderful meal. Bavaria can't be all bad, Sigrit decided.

"Has anything historic happened here, Fraulein Kempf?"

"Yes, child, our beloved Fuehrer had his early meetings here," she said with enthusiasm. "He came here and gave speeches and organized the Nazi party."

The waitress stopped by and picked up the empty plates.

"Excuse me," Hannelore said to the waitress, "were you here when Hitler celebrated his birthday here in 'thirty-nine?"

"Oh, yes. I'll never forget that night. I stood as close to the Fuehrer as I am to you." She uttered the word *Fuehrer* as if she spoke of someone holy.

"Do you remember where he sat?"

"At the table right across the aisle here, the one with the checkered tablecloth. Hitler sat where the old man with the full beard is sitting, and Eva Braun sat across the table from him. People were constantly walking in and greeting him. And the flowers, you should have seen them." The woman's eyes had a far-off look. "Even I could take some home. I still have them. Dried and dusty, but a bouquet given to Hitler, nonetheless."

Before Hannelore could express her appreciation, the waitress rushed off to a table newly occupied by some men and women. There she quickly sold eight liters of beer.

"Come, child, drink up and you better visit the bathroom again before we go," said Hannelore, gathering her things.

When they stepped outside it had stopped snowing. After walking a short distance, they came to an open air market. Hannelore purchased a pair of sausages and some rolls. The vendor also had some Christmas ornaments carved out of wood. Sigrit was reminded that in a few weeks would be her favorite holiday. She stared at the brightly painted ornaments, thinking of the apartment she had always considered home. She wondered if it still stood empty with all the furniture in it and all their beautiful Christmas ornaments packed away in the attic. The *attic*—the thought of that place brought the memory of that horrible scene to her mind and tears to her eyes.

"Please, let's go, Fraulein."

Hannelore saw the child's distress and was reminded of her parents.

Traitors, damn traitors. I'll teach you, you child of traitors.

"Wait, do you have a small gift for your hosts?"

"No."

"Then we can remedy that. We'll buy some ornaments and give them that. Don't you think that would be a nice present? Pick out a few pieces. You've got money."

Sigrit's eyes were flooded and everything was a blur. She pointed to six ornaments. The vendor wrapped them in newspaper. She put the purchase into her knapsack and pulled Hannelore to go.

"Not so fast. On my way back to Goerlitz I might stop at my mother's. Would you like to buy something for me to give to Ludwig?"

"Good idea," Sigrit said in a falsely cheerful voice. She figured the best way to get away was to pretend she was enjoying herself. She picked up a girl jumping jack and quickly bought it.

"Here, give this to Ludwig with my love."

"That is nice. She will remind him of you. Her dress is the same color as your coat." She twisted the knife by adding, "The one you wore the last time he saw you."

Sigrit looked at the woman and with a bright smile said, "The coat I will wear when he sees me again."

༺༻

The shadows were long when the local train pulled into the station of Hollstein. Besides Hannelore and Sigrit, the only other passenger to disembark the mostly empty train was an old man who appeared to be a local, judging by the confident air about him. Hannelore asked him if he knew where the Wagner family lived.

"Sepp Wagner you want? You go past the church up the street, turn left at the bakery, and walk up the hill to the last house on the right. Just watch the cow plops on the street, Martha doesn't want any in the house."

"Thank you for the help."

"What is it you want from Sepp?"

"We're here from Goerlitz and—"

"Oh yes, you have the children. But where's the boy? Sepp told me he's getting a boy."

"That is a long story." Hannelore pulled Sigrit away and headed toward the baroque church. At a small square, with a fountain carved out of a log representing a man with a shovel, stood a bench. Hannelore stopped, sat down, and pulled the girl face to face with her.

"Sigrit, the story we will tell these people is that Ludwig was drafted by the Home Guard. The military came aboard the train and took him away. That is the story, and if you tell anyone anything else, I will find out about it and Ludwig will be severely punished. Remember, I can get my hands on him. Now do you understand?"

Sigrit looked at the ground. "Yes, Fraulein."

"Look me in the eyes when you speak."

Looking straight into her face, Sigrit said, "Yes, Fraulein Kempf."

"That is better. Now don't forget it. Once I tell the story you will never speak of the incident again."

"Yes, Fraulein.

Sigrit approached the half-timbered house with deep apprehension. This place was to be her home for who knew how long with people she had never even seen a picture of. She felt fate had dealt unfairly with her. What could she possibly have done to be punished so severely? Why was this happening to her? A hunger pang hit her in the stomach with a vicious blow. She longed to be hugged and held and comforted. At the moment she would even be happy to be loved by Fraulein Kempf. She looked up at the homely woman, hoping for a small smile, but saw only a grim determination on her face. Sigrit looked down at the old brown bear and found comfort in his friendly glass eyes. She kissed the toy, took a deep breath, and boldly stepped toward her future.

A woman who looked to be past forty answered the knock on the heavy wooden door. Her brown hair was combed back into a bun even more severe than Miss Kempfe's. Above the right eye was a broad ribbon of white hair. She was dressed in a coarsely spun, black dress accented by a coarse blue apron that had seen many washings and carried the stains of a week of food preparations. The face that had been pretty in youth showed the wear of hard work, worry, and grief.

"Yes, who are you?" she asked in an unfriendly voice with a heavy Bavarian dialect.

"I am Fraulein Kempf and this—"

"Ah, the woman with the children. Come. Sepp, the children are here," she said with her voice gaining some luster.

A man dressed in black leather pants that tied below the knees and a gray knitted sweater decorated with green leaf embroidery came to the door. Unlike his wife, the good looks of his youth had mellowed with age. His blue-gray eyes still sparkled with anticipation that life had its small pleasures to be enjoyed every day. The space between his sculptured nose and small mouth was decorated by a precise mustache that curled up and around before ending in a point. It added the appearance of a perpetual smile to his face.

"Gruess Gott," he said. "Come in, come in. Bring the children out of the cold."

Hannelore and Sigrit stepped into the large kitchen heated by a large, green-glazed tile stove. At a wooden table built to last for centuries sat a girl of eleven with an open book in front of her and a pencil in her right hand. The white paper under her hand seemed to reflect the light onto her evenly featured face inherited from her father. Upon seeing the little girl in the coat the same color of blue as in the Bavarian flag, her eyes lit up with love and anticipation of the surrogate sister she had always wished for. The girl came from behind the table to assume her position for proper introductions.

"My name is Hannelore Kempf and this is Sigrit Lachmann."

Sigrit slipped her right hand out of her mitten and extended it to the man. He took it and said, "I'm Sepp Wagner. This is my wife Martha and our girl Greta."

Sigrit gave her hand to the woman and Hannelore started shaking hands with the man.

"Pleased to meet you," said Hannelore.

"Good day, Frau Wagner, good day Herr Wagner," said Sigrit with a curtsy.

"You can call us Herr Sepp and Frau Martha."

"Thank you."

"And you can call me Greta," said the girl, stepping toward Sigrit and hugging her. "Come, I'll show you to our room."

As the two girls left the kitchen to go upstairs, Sigrit heard the inevitable question of where the boy was. Hannelore sounded very truthful when she answered. Then there was the raising voices of Sepp's reply. Sigrit could not make out all the words, but she did hear about damn Nazis and the waste of fighting a lost war. Such free expression of opinion shocked her, since such words said to the wrong person could result in capital punishment.

The bedroom was large with two single beds, each against a wall. The decor had a masculine look with only a recent touch of femininity like dolls and a large wooden doll house.

"You can have this bed here. I've only recently moved into this room. It used to belong to my brothers. They both were killed in the war this year."

"I am very sorry," Sigrit said.

"Yes, Mother has not been the same since. She is constantly sad. Try as I might, I don't get much affection from her. I make things for her and all she can do is criticize either my embroidery or painting and even my sweeping the floor."

"I would think she would give you twice the love to make up for her loss."

"I thought so, too. I lost two brothers I love."

"And I was separated from my brother and dear aunt shortly after my parents died," Sigrit said, on the verge of tears.

"Forgive me. I don't want to burden you with my problems. Sigrit, that seems like a big name for a little thing like you. Would you like me to call you Siggy?"

A nickname? Sigrit had never had one. Her family was too formal to even consider calling anyone other than by their real names. Some children in school had nicknames and, in a way, she envied the casualness of one. Siggy, yes, she liked the ring of it.

"Greta, Siggy sounds wonderful."

"Good, you can be my little sister, Siggy." With those words the girl gave Siggy an embrace. Sigrit accepted the affection wholeheartedly and returned the embrace, adding kisses to Greta's cheeks and mouth. Two souls, both hungering for affection, had found each other.

CHAPTER 8

It was dawn on the first of December when the train finally arrived at the terminal of Stuttgart. Erika got up stiffly from the wooden seat, put on her coat and knapsack, grabbed her satchel, and left the train. She stepped onto the concrete platform and was hit by water. Looking up, she saw that the curved roof of the dead end terminal had most of the glass missing. Some of the steel girders were broken and twisted. Rain was falling on her.

She walked past the steam engine toward the exit. Passing a snack area she could smell the delicious scent of real coffee.

It's too early to pop in on someone. This place is as good as any to kill time.

All the tables were occupied. Erika spotted an empty chair at a small table. "Excuse me," she addressed the one man and two women sitting at the table, "is this place free?"

"Yes," said the man. "Feel free to sit there."

"Thank you."

"This place is popular because it's one of the few where one can still get a cup of genuine coffee," said a grandmotherly lady wearing a bright red cape accented with black velvet and braiding. "Do get a pretzel here. They are the best."

Erika pulled out her wallet and took out a bread ration stamp. The waitress took her order and soon returned with a cup of steaming coffee and two pretzels. The waitress took the stamp and the money, put it into a leather pouch, and slipped it into the large pocket of her apron.

"*Guten appetit,*" said the old lady in the red cape.

The other woman and man at the table were just sipping their coffee in silence. None of the people seemed to be together.

"Thank you," replied Erika. She slowly sipped the coffee and smiled. "Delicious." Then she picked up one of the soft pretzels and to her surprise found the top sliced a little and real butter on it. She bit into the shiny, brown, baked goods and closed her eyes. "Mmm, I had forgotten how good they are."

"The pretzels of Stuttgart are the best in the world. Believe me, I have traveled a lot and was always happy to get back home to my pretzels. Normally, I get fresh ones every morning and have two for breakfast. Has it been a long time since you have been in Stuttgart?"

"Yes, since the spring of 'thirty-nine."

"Ah yes, that was in the good old days. You will find quite a few changes since then."

"How has it changed here?"

"You will see, but first, enjoy your coffee."

"I beg your pardon, but you don't sound like you're native to this city."

"I am proud to say I was born here, however, in my house we always speak the written German." The lady softened her statement with a smile.

Erika felt reprimanded for having pried into the woman's life. Meanwhile the other two people had vacated the seats. Two well-dressed old ladies rushed for the empty chairs, pushing a gentleman out of the way. They kissed their friend and gave a quick "good morning" to Erika. The women sat down and soon the three women were all talking at the same time. Red cape spoke in high German while her companions spoke in the *Schwabian* dialect. Erika finished her coffee, picked up the second pretzel, and bid the three ladies farewell. The women nodded to her while all three were still talking.

Erika walked down a long flight of steps to get out of the station onto the street. The rain had stopped and the sun was just appearing over the hills. Across the street with numerous streetcar tracks was the Graf Zeppelin Hotel. Erika smiled when she thought of the passionate night she and Rowald had spent there. It was in May of 'thirty-nine when they started the evening by going to the ballet. Then they went to a night club for dancing. By the time the club closed they felt so passionate for each other they did not want to wait for a streetcar and ride for almost half an hour to his brother's house where they had been staying. Rowald and Erika went to the closest hotel and rented a room with a private bath. They even made love that night in the bathtub full of water.

Tears came to her eyes and she wiped them away with her gloved hand. "Oh Rowald, I miss you so much. Please come back soon."

She crossed the street heading toward the King's Plaza. At first she did not realize that the office building she passed was only one wall. Rounding the corner, she could see all the way to the grassy square dominated by a huge column with an angel on top. Where the view used to be obstructed by buildings and shops, there was now only rubble. Walking quickly, she arrived at the plaza in time to see the stucco walls of the palace illuminated in the pink light of the early morning sun. The walls facing the plaza stood, but the rest of the palace lay in ruin. Ionic columns of an office building on the other side of the street still stood proudly, looking like ancient Greek ruins.

"What is happening here?" she asked herself. Erika had never seen such destruction. In Goerlitz there were some bombings, but nothing compared to this. "I should have stayed home." Then she remembered Commandant Schnellhauser and his strong urging for her to leave Goerlitz. She wondered if he really knew of the destruction in Stuttgart.

"Oh well, now I'm here. Hopefully, Lydia is well and their house is whole."

The bells of the church were ringing. She looked toward the sound and saw the two mismatched towers of the sixteenth century *Stiftskirche*. The towers were like a beacon, drawing her closer. She went to the church and found the heavy wooden door locked. Disappointed, Erika turned around when a woman approached.

"I was hoping to go to church," Erika lamented.

"So you want to go to church? We don't use the door anymore. Come with me."

The two women walked around the corner of the building and went into the church. The wall was gone leaving the church open like a doll house.

"The building inspectors don't like us going in here, but I don't care. It's the only church around here. I hope your prayers will be more effective than mine have been."

"Lately I've been asking for little things," said Erika, "and sometimes I got what I asked for."

"I guess I have to start doing that, too. Maybe God isn't powerful enough to grant us big wishes. If He is all powerful and good, how come He lets His house be destroyed? I'll pray for small favors like a cup of genuine bean coffee."

"And after you get done praying, go to the train station for your coffee."

"You mean they still have it?"

"I had a cup just a few minutes ago."

"Thank you for the tip. I tell you, sometimes visitors know more than the locals."

After leaving the church, Erika walked back to the plaza to catch a streetcar to Feuerbach. While waiting, she looked around at the hills. The city was completely surrounded by hills, some covered with trees and others planted with vineyards.

Streetcar number thirteen arrived and Erika got on. Many of the windows were broken and covered with plywood. The streetcar was crowded with mostly women workers commuting to the factories. The air was heavy with the stench of unwashed bodies and human exhaust gas.

Erika rode along, hardly seeing out of the windows. The conductor called out in a deep foghorn voice the upcoming stop. When he called out the next stop to be the Feuerbach Hospital, Erika made her way to the exit. As soon as the electric streetcar stopped, she got off.

She walked downhill on Wiener Street, looking for the Zeller's house. By the time she reached the tall, four-story, yellow brick school, she realized she had gone too far and headed back uphill toward the hospital. When she saw number ninety-four on a house, she again realized she had gone too far and turned around. The next house was numbered ninety. In between was the rubble of a house which had the address she was looking for.

"Oh my God, no!" was all she managed to say as she stood there with her mouth open. The house that used to be two and a half stories was no higher than two yards above the street. It had obviously been hit by a fire bomb, judging by the burned wood.

Erika went to the house next door and rang a door bell. A young woman looked out of a window facing the street. A little child barely tall enough to see over the windowsill strained to see who her mother was talking with.

"Excuse me, I am looking for my sister-in-law, Lydia Zeller. Do you have any idea where I might find her?"

"She should be at home."

"Where might that be?"

"Why, at her house next door," the woman answered, as if Erika was dense.

"I don't know if you have looked lately, but there is no house."

"There might not be a house, but the basement is still there. That's where Frau Zeller is living." With that she shut the window.

Erika went back to the rubble. Most of the houses on the street had small yards running along one side and behind the houses. The doors were on the side of the houses off the yards. Four steps went up to where the house door used to be, but on the other side of the little porch, steps led into the basement. The steps were clear of dirt and rubble. Erika went down and knocked on the steel door.

After knocking loudly three different times, she heard a sleepy voice finally answer. "Yeah, who is there?"

"It's Erika! Is that you, Lydia?"

"One moment!"

While she was waiting, Erika recalled the last time she had seen her husband's brother, Ernst and his wife. The brothers were both good-looking, but did not really resemble each other. Rowald was almost six feet tall, while Ernst barely came up to his shoulders. Ernst's hair was blond like his mother's while Rowald's was dark brown like his father's. Lydia also was blonde and petite. She carried herself as straight as possible and would get up in the morning and completely dress herself, fix her hair, and don jewelry before she had her morning coffee. Her house always was immaculate with nothing out of place.

The two brothers, less than two years apart in age, had both finished medical school in 1937. Judging by the way the two had joked around, a passerby would have thought the two were stand-up comics. Just listening to Ernst give a guided tour of Stuttgart to his brother and sister-in-law, kept the women laughing so hard it hurt. Ernst made up the most outlandish history for every building they saw.

Finally Erika heard the sound of the door being unlocked and slowly opened. A gaunt, pale young woman with dirty, stringy hair, dressed in an old bathrobe, blinked while her eyes adjusted to the light. She could not recognize the visitor shadowed by the bright daylight.

"Lydia, is that you? It's Erika."

"Erika? Erika Zeller? What are you doing here?"

"Didn't you get my letter? I wrote and asked if I could come for a visit."

"No, but I'm so glad you're here." She flung her arms around Erika and started crying. "Oh Erika, my dear sister. I'm so sorry my place doesn't look good. Come in, dear, please come in."

"Gruss Gott, Lydia. How good it is to see you again."

During the hug Erika felt her sister-in-law's swollen belly.

"Come in and close the door, I'm trying to keep the place warm. What time is it? I was still in bed."

"It's ten o'clock, but please get back into bed if you want."

"No, no. You are a reason to get up. As you can see, I'm pregnant. I've been feeling pretty poorly, and then the house got bombed. Fortunately, I was at the shelter that night and not just down here as usual. But we had so many air-raids, I started going to the shelter. My tenants upstairs, Mr. and Mrs. Korwitz, left one day and never came back. I have no idea where they went. I saw them leave with a small bag one morning without notice or anything. I didn't know what I should do with the apartment since they left their furniture and did not pay any more rent. Maybe they'll return. It makes no difference now since all their things were burned anyway. The house got bombed two months ago. It burned and settled for three days while I stayed with neighbors. Then I made this place livable and moved in here. I spend most of my time sleeping. I'm so glad you're here, Erika. You will stay a while, won't you?"

While the young woman was talking like a burst dam, Erika's eyes gradually adjusted to the dim light in the twenty-by-thirty-foot room. The floor was bare concrete. An enameled cast iron stove stood against an outside wall with a smoke stack going out a boarded-up window. Next to the stove on the floor was a pile of coal and wood. A pot of water sat on the stove.

A bare light bulb hung from the concrete ceiling. A scorched wooden table covered with newspaper held a gracious porcelain lamp, mostly intact.

Another small window was boarded up with plywood. A metal bed that had survived the fire stood against the wall. It was evident that the burned paint had been scrubbed off. White blankets hung over the opening that led down into the cellar. Two chairs were piled high with clothes.

In one corner, there stood a galvanized bucket with a toilet seat on it. A small stack of newspapers near it served as toilet paper. Another bucket next to it was half full of clear water.

Against another wall was a chest of drawers with only one drawer missing and on top of that stood a large metal ammunition box painted olive green.

"Yes, Lydia, I'll stay a while. Please relax, we'll have lots of time to talk. Now tell me, have you heard from Ernst?"

"Yes, he is still in France. They are encountering heavy fighting. The Americans are there now. I'm sure he has his hands full taking care of all the wounded. He was home in June for ten days, that's when I got pregnant. It's such a problem getting food nowadays that I just sleep most of the time. That way I don't use many calories. But now that you're here I have to get up more. Will you help me?"

"Of course, I'll help you in any way you need me. Why don't you get dressed while I make us some breakfast?"

"The food I have is in the steel box there," she said, pointing to the ammunition box.

Erika opened it and found a pitcher containing sour milk, three eggs, some stone hard bread and a jar of jam.

"My dear girl, you don't expect to survive on this? Remember you are eating for two."

"Oh dear me, I didn't even ask what you're hearing from your Rowald. Where is he?"

"The last I heard two weeks ago, Rowald was missing on the Eastern Front."

"That's terrible. Oh, my dear Erika, I am so sorry. Let's hope for the best."

"Yes, I hope for the best, too. Now, do you have food ration stamps?

"I have plenty of them, but people start lining up at the stores three hours before they open in the morning. I hardly have anything to wear anymore, and what I do have doesn't fit. I don't want to be seen by anyone, and I can't take standing on the cold street for three hours."

"Now I'm here to do that. What do you have to cook on besides the coal stove?"

"That's it. Oh dear, what are you going to sleep on? Maybe you can find something in the cellar. Look there." Lydia pointed toward the curtain of blankets.

Erika pulled aside a blanket and stepped down into the wine cellar with a stone vaulted ceiling and dirt floor. By the light filtered through a small, dirty window, she saw against one wall a wine rack with several dusty bottles on it. In a corner was a pile of broken wooden furniture.

Against another wall was a potato bed with the dry remains of potatoes. The potato bed was like a bunk bed built out of raw lumber. If Erika could get some help moving it into the main room, it would serve very well as a bed.

"Is there anyone who could help me move the potato bed?"

"Yes, the shoe maker around the corner has a deaf-mute working for him. He will help."

"Good, but first, we have to take care of you." Erika reached into her knapsack and pulled out the pretzel from the train station and some ham from home. She also pulled out a tin of tea. "Now, if you tell me where your dishes are, I'll make breakfast."

Lydia pointed to the chest of drawers.

Erika opened the top drawer and found a few expensive china plates with chips and cracks, some cups, and a china coffee pot. Next to the china was a small assortment of silver-plated flatware and kitchen utensils. She set the food on the table with the lamp, cleared the pile of clothes off the chairs, and held one chair out for Lydia.

"Madam, breakfast is being served."

Lydia, who had managed to dress herself quite decently in a blue knitted wool skirt and green, long-sleeved sweater, laughed and took the seat.

"This is the first time I have laughed in months. Oh, Erika, I'm so glad you're here. You're the answer to my prayers. And all that good food—wherever did you get that?"

"I brought it from Goerlitz." Erika sat down, had a cup of hot tea, and enjoyed watching her sister-in-law slowly eat.

"I know there's a lot to do today," Lydia said. "But I'm going to enjoy this delicious food as long as I can."

"You do that, and then we'll see about getting you and me a bath."

"For that we have to go down to the public baths at the school."

CHAPTER 9

Martha held the corners of her apron full of fresh eggs. She looked at the snow-covered Bavarian Alps brightly illuminated by the more-than-half moon. Glancing at her country house, she saw the yellow light pouring out of the windows. The house at the edge of town, with its white-painted stucco and dark, wooden beams looked cheerful, but Martha's heart felt very heavy.

She raised her face to the moon and said, "Are you shining over my sons? My two dear boys who are lying under the frozen Russian soil?"

Tears welled in her eyes and she rushed into the kitchen. Sepp sat in an oval wooden tub of water, next to the large tile stove.

"I'm almost done. I think the water on the stove is hot for your bath."

"Why should I take a bath?"

"Don't be silly woman. You know it's Christmas Eve."

"Christmas, bah. Two sons we have lost this year and you worry about Christmas. I'm going to ignore the whole thing."

"Martha, stop this. We still have Greta and we'll celebrate Christmas for her. She and Siggy set up a tree and made a fire in the parlor. Then we'll go to midnight mass. It's high time you go to church again."

"I'm not going to church. You take Greta and Siggy. I'll be in bed long before midnight. Have you fed the cows yet?"

"No."

With an exasperated look, she left the kitchen, carrying a kerosene lantern, and headed across the hallway into the stable. She hung the lantern on a nail, picked up a pitchfork, dug into the pile of hay, and filled the nearest cow's manger. When she returned to the hay she was startled by movement.

"Who is in there?" Martha demanded with a firm voice, holding the pitchfork in front of her like a weapon.

Some more rustling in the hay revealed the gaunt face of a young man.

"Please, gracious lady, I mean no harm. Don't hurt me."

"Come out! I want to take a look at you. Breaking into my stable—what is the meaning of this?"

The young man dressed like a peasant in brown corduroy knickers and gray loden cape crawled out of the hay followed by a girl.

"What! Two of you? Who are you?"

The man rose and helped the girl to her feet.

"We have walked here from Nuremberg and are heading for Switzerland. Please, gracious lady, let us stay here and rest for a while. My wife is very tired." His voice cracked with concern.

"You are Jews, are you not?" Martha asked suspiciously.

I've heard Jews are treacherous and trying to sabotage the Fatherland. I remember dear old Frau Schmoll who scoffed at the warning and let a Jewish family live in her house. One night they all disappeared. Rumor has it the Jews killed the old lady to steal her gold.

The girl's lips squeezed tightly together and she grasped the man's hand with both of hers.

"What is the matter with you?"

"I'm in labor."

"You mean you're ready to have a baby? Oh my God, you poor thing. I'll have to get a midwife. Oh my, what will Sepp say? I'll let you come into the house. No, no I can't do that. The Gestapo might have a search. Those *Schweine* do that. Searched here a number of times. They don't care, came the day I learned my Hans was killed. Oh dear, what shall I do?"

"Please, Frau, let us stay here. It is warm. Don't tell anyone outside your house that we're here. I can help my wife. My father was a doctor. I know what to do."

"Okay, I'll spread some hay for you. I'll get some linens and food. Oh dear, I hope I'm doing the right thing."

Martha rushed into the big bedroom where her husband was in the process of tying his leather pants below the knees.

"Sepp, there are Jews in the stable. The woman is having a baby."

"What? We have to get them out of here."

"We can't. Don't you understand? The poor girl is having a baby. We can't throw them out." She clutched him as if her life depended on it. "Please Sepp."

"All right, for you, I let them stay. But if any one finds out about it, I know nothing."

The woman scurried about gathering a wool sheet, blankets, and pillows. She thought the girl probably had no baby clothes. She rushed into the attic and dug in a trunk. There was every garment her children had ever worn. Martha pulled out an armful of baby clothes and squeezed them to her chest.

"Oh Hansi, Seppi how happy I was when you wore this. My dear sons so cruelly taken from us. How proud you looked in your uniforms. And now you are gone. God has forsaken us. The whole world is fighting us. What use to celebrate Christmas? There is no God anymore. Christ, how can you let this happen? Holy Mary, forgive me. Maybe you can talk some sense into them. I better get down there and bring that poor couple this and not forget the food."

She went into the kitchen where Greta was feeding the cat.

"Oh, Greta, quick, get some bread and meat and bring some tea. Now don't tell anyone about this, but there are some people in the stable and we have to make them comfortable."

Greta, carrying the food on a tray, followed her mother. As they entered the stable it was very quiet. Martha felt disappointed. She wondered if the couple had left. Then she saw them by the light of the lantern. Both parents were looking at the baby wrapped in a shawl and lying on a pile of hay.

"Come and see, *gnadige* Frau, we have a son," said the new father.

Martha knelt to see the baby. She beheld the little round head and the tiny perfect hands. The baby opened his eyes and he seemed to smile.

Martha burst into tears. Suddenly she knew what Christmas was about. A celebration of babies, all babies. No matter how doomed the world seemed, as long as babies were born, there was hope for the future. Here in her humble stable, a baby was born like another 1944 years earlier.

Martha thought about her two sons. Suddenly she had fond memories of them and it hurt less. She reached for her daughter and flung her arms around her.

"My dear girl, thank God we have you."

About an hour later Martha stepped into the parlor where Greta was practicing a Christmas carol with Sigrit. Martha was dressed in her regional dress that included a silk shawl with fringe. The silver chain on her bodice hung heavy with silver coins that jingled as she walked.

"What have we here? You have not worn that since the boys left," Sepp said.

"It's Christmas Eve and we're going to celebrate and go to midnight mass."

"You are not going to wear your black dress? What will the neighbors think?"

"Don't worry about it. It's Christmas. Time to celebrate the birth of Christ and all others."

CHAPTER 10

The week after Christmas was the most joyful time in the Wagner house since before the war. The depression Martha had been suffering disappeared for the most part. There were times she was overcome by grief, but instead of crawling within herself, she shared her feelings with Sepp or Greta. Occasionally, she would hug Sigrit who felt like a member of the family. She thrived in this loving family and appreciated the abundance of good food. Everyone called her Siggy. She felt as if the trouble and grief belonged to Sigrit, while Siggy was a carefree Bavarian child. Her life was good. If Ludwig were there, then it would almost be great.

She had written to her Aunt Erika as soon as she arrived at the Wagners. A few days before Christmas two cards came in an envelope from Erika. One was to the Wagners and the second was for Sigrit. This simple postcard became a most prized possession. The girl had also written to Ludwig but received no reply.

The Jewish family named Goldstein was quartered in an attic bedroom. Had there been a search, it would have been impossible to make a quick escape. Everyone hoped for the best, and that the Nazi officials would be more interested in spending the holiday week with their families rather than search for citizens who wanted to leave the country.

Sarah had been a beloved prima ballerina with the Nuremberg Ballet. Ruben was a choreographer and the artistic director with the same company. It was known by everyone that they were Jewish, but being celebrities, no one touched them. The two talented young people were so involved in their art and later in each other, that they did not even realize there were less and less Jews in their city. When they were planning a wedding, they could not locate a rabbi. Not being very religious, they just had a civil ceremony at city hall, followed by a reception in a local restaurant. The guests were mostly people involved in the theater, not only the ballet.

Sarah soon became pregnant. Her physical state forced an early retirement. After she stopped dancing, both of them were notified to report to the Bahnhof Platz with only one small bag for relocation. That was when Sarah and Ruben fled the city. Traveling mostly on small country roads and dressed like farmers, they had managed to slowly make their way to Hollstein where Martha found them on Christmas Eve.

The young mother was recuperating rapidly from the delivery. Her husband stayed with her while she was awake. One afternoon in late December he came into the kitchen with the baby in his arms. Sepp sat at the table, carving a piece of wood, while Martha sat knitting some socks.

"Ruben, come and sit down. May I hold the baby a while?" Martha asked.

"Of course, *gnadige* Frau." Ruben gave the baby to Martha and sat on the bench next to Sepp. Sepp offered the young man some snuff. Fearing refusal of the vile substance would seem unfriendly, Ruben put a small amount on the back of his hand and inhaled it. His nose tickled and he sneezed.

"*Gesundheit*," said Sepp and Martha.

"Have you named him yet?" asked Martha.

"Yes, we'll call him Samuel, after my father. Sarah and I have discussed it and want to ask you, Sepp, would you mind if we give him your name as his middle name? We'd like to call him Samuel Josef."

Sepp considered for a moment then said, "I would be honored to have the boy carry my name. We'll have to drink to that." Sepp extended his hand to the young man who shook it. "Martha, bring the *Enzian* and some glasses."

Martha went to the cupboard, took out a hand-painted ceramic bottle, and set it on the table. Then she set three small glasses in front of Sepp. He poured the precious liquid and, after toasting the baby, all three drank. Sepp drank quickly and poured himself another drink, Martha and Ruben sipped slowly, enjoying the deep, sweet flavor of the liquor and relishing the warm feeling of celebration and friendship.

At the same time Greta and Siggy were outside, building their fourth snowman.

"We'll make this one a bit smaller than the last one and call her Siggy," said Greta.

"And are we going to make a Ruben and Sarah and baby, too?" Sigrit suggested.

"Good idea, but we'll have to hurry to get them all made. Remember, we have a lunch invitation at Oma's today. She is making pancakes."

"I can hardly wait," Sigrit said, feeling her mouth water. "Let's make the other snowmen near the chapel, that way they'll look like a manger." Sigrit's faith in God and Jesus was also renewed by the birth of the Jewish boy on Christmas Eve.

The girls went to the small, but beautifully built chapel on a hill only a few hundred yards from the house. Sepp's father, now called Opa by everyone in the family, had built it some years earlier. The stuccoed white chapel was only large enough to seat a dozen people. On the ash wood altar stood a crucifix carved out of wood by Sepp. Two vases of greenery and flowers decorated the sides of the altar. In the summer, the flowers were fresh. Now in winter, flowers made out of paper and cloth were mixed with pines. The structure also had a small steeple with an onion shaped roof.

Greta and Sigrit quickly made three small snowmen. Then Greta picked two branches of boxwood near the chapel door and went in, followed by Sigrit. Both girls knelt near the altar and each said a silent prayer. On the side of the chapel hung two pictures of handsome young men wearing Bavarian hats. Greta put a sprig of boxwood above each picture, kissed her fingers, and pressed the kiss on their faces. Sigrit remembered Ludwig and ached for his presence.

Suddenly she felt ravishingly hungry.

"Greta, I think I smell pancakes. Come."

"You must have a nose like a fox."

The girls ran down the hill, across the road, and over another small hill to a house standing at the edge of town.

From the distance they saw Opa outside. He waved when he saw them and told them to hurry.

When they approached the old house, Sigrit could not believe her eyes. Next to the house stood a sled big enough to seat six people. It was painted royal blue and richly decorated with painted flowers. Opa was polishing the brass hardware and the bells of the horses harness.

Siggy walked around the sled with her mouth open. She could not remember anything more beautiful.

"May I sit in it?"

"Of course," said Opa and lifted her into the sleigh. "And tomorrow we'll go for a ride."

"A ride? Me, too?"

"You, too, my child. Tomorrow is New Year's Day and our club will go on our annual outing."

"Oh wonderful," said Greta, "I was afraid that it would be canceled."

"No way, there might fewer participants, but it is tradition, and tradition must be honored," said Opa, taking a deep puff of his pipe and stroking his long, gray beard. "Tomorrow morning at seven we will all assemble in town."

Greta, who also was in the sleigh, hugged Sigrit with excitement.

"Oh Siggy, it'll be so much fun. You'll love it, I can hardly wait. We'll have to find you some more of my outgrown clothes. We'll all be wearing our *Tracht.*"

"Are you all going to sit out here and let the pancakes get cold?" called a friendly voice trying to sound stern.

In the doorway stood Oma, wearing a somber black dress and a big smile. Her white hair was tied back in a bun, the traditional hairstyle of the region. Her face was still smooth and pink in spite of many years of hard work. Opa on the other hand had at least one wrinkle for each year of life. Both people had eyes that sparkled with joy and love, both for each other and anyone they came into contact with.

At dawn the next morning, Opa and Oma, with the sleigh harnessed to two large brown horses, stood waiting outside the Wagner house door. Martha was the first out of the house, carrying a large bag of food. She wore a full green ankle length woolen skirt, a black velvet bodice over a long sleeved white linen blouse, with a white silk shawl of the same fabric as her apron. On her head sat a green, velour pie hat.

Greta and Sigrit each wore green skirts and black velvet jackets. On top of that they all wore heavy gray capes decorated with green-felt oak leaves. Sarah took her place in the sleigh dressed in a simple black wool dress covered by a black cape. Her rich brunette hair was tied back in a bun and streaked with white. Her face looked like an old woman's.

The baby was wrapped in blankets and a quilt. Ruben was dressed in leather pants that tied below the knees, and he wore a gray jacket with silver buttons. His hair was also gray and he wore a long white beard made from a cow's tail. He carried a large burlap sack.

Sepp, also dressed in leather pants and a gray jacket with a green felt hat on his brown hair, locked the door.

"Squeeze together some more," Sepp said. "We'll only have to be crowded for a short time. Come on, Siggy, sit on my lap."

Once everyone was aboard, Opa shook the reins and the horses took off, jingling down the street.

In the square near the church were about ten more sleighs. All were brightly painted and some even decorated with green twigs. When the Wagner family approached, people waved and shouted, "Happy New Year."

Sarah and Ruben got some strange looks, but no one asked who they were.

Opa and Oma got out and climbed into a neighbor's sled that had empty seats. Then Sepp took the reins and all the sleds took off in single file, accompanied by the jingles of horses' harnesses.

The sun was still low in the sky when people pulled out bread and meats for breakfast. The meal was washed down with hot coffee, tea, and beer. For dessert, the adults had a shot of liquor or schnapps.

In a sleigh in front of them a man took an accordion out of its case and played. That prompted more accordions to make their appearance. The music was accompanied by song and the rhythm of the jingles. Even the horses had an extra spring in their steps. These were the horses that normally spent their days walking up and down fields in neat straight rows.

About an hour into the ride, they heard music and singing in the distance. The sounds came closer and, at an intersection, another group of sleighs pulled by horses joined the group from Hollstein. The two lines interwove more than doubling the length of the procession.

"These are friends from Geringen," Greta told her little *sister.*

"How often do you do this?" Sigrit asked.

"Unfortunately, only each New Year's Day."

"Where are we going?"

"Wait and be surprised," Martha said. "Having fun?"

"Oh, wonderful fun. I can't remember ever doing anything better. You are so fortunate. I wish…" Then Sigrit became silent and sad. The music played a folk song she had learned from her mother. The next song was light and comical where everyone joined in with words and laughter.

The Wagner's sleigh was near the rear of the procession when everyone came to a stop. There was a gate and a guard house in the road. Beyond it flowed an icy river.

"We are at the border," explained Martha to the young couple and Sigrit. "Siggy, take the baby and play like you would with a doll."

Sarah took the heavy quilt off the baby and put it across hers and Ruben's lap. The gate was lifted and one by one the sleighs moved onto the bridge across the river. When the blue Wagner sleigh approached the guard house, Sepp was glad to see the same guard in charge that had the post for many years. With him were some young Army recruits carrying rifles.

"Froh' Neu Jahr, Hans," Sepp said, handing the man a smoked ham. Hans put it on a pile of other gifts handed to him by other sleigh occupants. "That's to help you and your men enjoy yourselves."

"Thank you. Happy New Year to you and yours." He took a close look at Ruben and Sarah. Both of them held their breath. This would be it, capture and the—the camps. Maybe the baby would escape if no one looked at Sigrit's *doll.*

The man kept staring at them then tipped his hat and said, *"Froh' Neu Jahr Oma* and *Opa.* Now go."

On the other side of the river was the Swiss border. There the guards started out by checking everyone's passports and identification papers. When the Wagner family approached, the two old guards saw only the liter size bottle of Enzian Sepp handed them.

"That is passport enough," one said, laughing. "Go enjoy your party and Happy New Year."

Sepp shook the reins and the horses took off in a lively trot. The horses knew that not much farther up the road would be a house where fresh hay waited.

It was still well before noon when the procession came to a stop at a Swiss chalet. The sleighs were parked in neat rows, the horses unharnessed, and put into a corral. The people greeted each other with hugs and kisses and went into the warm clubhouse.

The Swiss hosts wore their native dress. Everyone had brought a dish or two and the food was spread out buffet style.

Most of the friends had not seen each other for a year, and the dinner was accompanied by much talking. Everyone sympathized over sad news and rejoiced at good news.

While all socialized, about two dozen children got acquainted and re-acquainted. At times they played outside, then they came in again, ate some more, and snuck some sips of beer.

Sepp talked with some men trying to arrange passage to St. Galen for the Jewish family. They had relatives there. It was not long before Ruben and Sarah had an invitation to stay with a Swiss family who might get them to St. Galen in a few days.

"We have to keep you out of sight of the authorities," said the Swiss host, a tall, thin farmer of about seventy. "They're afraid Switzerland will be overrun with Jews and they would send you back to Germany. But don't worry, I like pulling the wool over the government's eyes."

"Sarah and I can't thank you enough," Ruben said, shaking the man's hand with both of his. "And you, Sepp, you and Martha have been wonderful."

"Hey, don't think anything of it. It is you that have done us the favor. Thanks to what happened in our stable, I now have a wife again, not a zombie."

Sepp gave the young man a fatherly hug. Ruben's eyes misted as he hugged Sepp back.

After everyone had eaten, an accordion, zither, and guitar were played in a corner. In a matter of minutes, more musicians joined them and played the old songs everyone knew. Soon everyone who was not playing was dancing. The whole house vibrated in time with a hundred feet. Then the Hollsteiners danced a folk dance for their friends, followed by the folks from Geringen, and then the Swiss.

Unfortunately, the shortness of the day cut the party short. In order to get back to their homes before dark, the guests had to bid farewell in the early afternoon. To prolong the socializing, the people rode in each other's sleighs. When the border guards saw the procession, they opened the gates and waved everyone through. At the crossroads everyone stopped and got back into their own sleighs. After a last farewell and wishes of a speedy end to the war, they continued on to their own villages.

Lying in bed in the dark, Siggy and Greta talked about the events of the day. Greta mentioned a Swiss boy named Anton a few times.

"Anton has become quite tall in the past year. Did you notice his beautiful wavy hair, Siggy?"

"Yes, and I also noticed his forget-me-not blue eyes and the way he looked at you. I think he loves you."

"You really think so? I'll soon be twelve. It won't be too many more years and I can get married. When I do, I want to get married in Opa's chapel."

"Be sure to invite me."

"I will, I promise."

CHAPTER 11

The winter of 1944 to 1945 was cruel in Europe. It was extremely cold with much snow. The Allies slowly gained ground against the highly trained and disciplined German soldiers. Bombings of German cities kept up relentlessly. Pictures taken from the air showed only devastation. Yet daily, people crawled out from the underground shelters, assessed the damage of the last air raid, and proceeded to repair it as best they could. Life went on, one day at a time.

Erika nursed her sister-in-law Lydia through the winter. She fell into the role of caregiver again. As soon as the authorities realized that without her, Lydia would just lie in bed and die, Erika received an official residence permit for Stuttgart. That meant she got her monthly ration stamps.

Jutta had sent her several boxes of her clothes from Goerlitz, along with a few luxury items like her crystal and silver vanity set, and silver flatware. With that, and some old travel posters she had been able to buy, she made the basement of the bombed house almost tolerable.

Occasionally, Lydia received a few letters from her husband in France. His letters were always positive and encouraging. Often there were four or five letters in one mail delivery. After reading them, Lydia would be cheerful for the rest of the day and the next. Soon Erika only gave her one letter at a time. The rest of the time she put one with the mail and told her it had just been delivered. That way Lydia was in a good mood more often.

A pregnant woman was a rarity in those days. Erika felt it was her God-given duty to bring the pregnancy to term with the delivery of a healthy baby.

Erika usually got up early in the morning, made a fire, then took ration stamps and money, and headed to the food stores. If one did not stand in line a good two hours before the store opened, one did not get anything. One day she stood at the bakery, another day at the green grocer, another at the general grocery store, and on the fourth day at the butcher. One afternoon a week, the butcher sold the water in which the sausages had been cooked. When Erika was lucky, she was able to buy a quart. That evening the soup had a few fat eyes on the surface.

Lydia only got out of bed after Erika returned from the store at about ten in the morning. After breakfast, the two women took a walk in the woods. Erika made Lydia get out for fresh air and exercise.

When Lydia resisted, she would remind her, "If you don't want to go for a walk, stay home but let me take the baby."

"Being as we're still attached, I have to come along," Lydia would reply.

Once underway, however, she was glad to be outdoors. The forest was peaceful, especially when covered with fresh snow.

Spring came early and affirmatively in 1945. By the end of March, the days were warm. Some rubble-laden gardens still had fruit trees standing that exploded with radiant blossoms. They were all the more beautiful because they promised continuity in destruction. The darkness of the nights hid springtime's beauty and the sky rained more bombs that found their targets, causing death and destruction.

Lydia had heard from other mothers about "lightening." She was waiting for it to occur at any minute now. She felt heavy and awkward. She wondered if Ernst would still find her attractive or if he would consider her as hideous as she felt. She could not wait to feel light again and knew that once the lightening took place it would not be long before she was relieved of her pregnancy.

"When will I have the lightening?" Lydia asked Erika one afternoon.

"I don't know. Maybe there won't be any."

"I just have to have it. I don't think I can take another day of feeling like I'm carrying a lead cannon ball inside of me. Can't you do something to bring it on?"

"Lydia, you know if I could, I would carry this baby for you for an hour or two. Just think, you have a bit of Ernst with you."

"You're right. I just wish the baby wasn't getting big enough to go to school when it's born. Do you think I'm ugly?"

"No, Lydia, you are beautiful. I wish I was as beautiful as you with a little Rowald in me."

"I suppose things could be worse. They sure would be if you weren't here, Erika. Fate sent you to me last December. I don't think I would have survived the winter without you."

"It is strange that a Gestapo Commandant practically ordered me to come here."

"God works in strange ways. Anyway, tomorrow I have a doctor's appointment."

"Yes, I'll go with you," Erika said. "I wish we could go to a movie afterward."

"Yes, wouldn't it be nice? But the movie houses were bombed years ago."

"We better get some rest. I'm sure we'll have another air raid tonight."

Lydia took off her tent-like dress and carefully draped it over the chair next to her bed on top of her coat. Both of them took off only their outer garments and shoes in order to be quickly dressed when they were awakened by the sirens.

Erika tucked Lydia in like she would a little child. When she bent down to kiss her on the cheek, Lydia put her arms around Erika's neck and gave her a loving squeeze.

Erika felt the vibrations of need, gratefulness, and love. It felt good to be needed and appreciated.

"Good night, Lydia."

"Good night, Sister."

A few hours later Lydia called to her sister-in-law.

"Erika, Erika wake up."

Erika opened her eyes to total blackness.

"Wake up Erika. Turn on the light."

Erika reached for the lamp near her bed and turned it on.

"Anything wrong? I didn't hear any sirens."

"No sirens, but I feel wet."

Erika jumped out of bed and crossed the cold space to Lydia's bed. She lifted the covers and saw a large, pink, wet stain.

"Your water broke. Do you have any contractions?"

"No. But I have a real bad backache."

"We have to get you to the hospital. Come get up."

Erika picked up Lydia's dress to help her into it.

"I can't go to the hospital with water running down my legs."

"No one will see you in this total blackness outside. Come, we must hurry."

The electric light blinked three times.

"Oh, oh, air raid coming," said Erika. Then the sirens started to blare.

"Come quickly. We'll get to the hospital before the planes come."

Lydia got to her feet and doubled over in pain. "I can't walk, it hurts too much."

"You have to. I'll help you. Lean on my shoulders."

"I can't. Let's stay here."

"Then we better go into the wine cellar. Wait here, I'll get a place ready."

Erika spread out some newspapers on the floor in a corner. She put some pillows on it against the wall. Then she helped Lydia walk slowly into the wine cellar and set her on the papers. She helped Lydia take off her underpants, put a warm sweater on her, and covered her with a blanket.

"Lydia, just relax a while, I'll build a fire."

"Open the curtain so I can see you."

"Don't worry. I'm not going to leave you, dear sister."

While Erika was making a fire in the stove, Lydia sat in the corner complaining about the severity of her backache.

"Am I having a lightening?"

Erika laughed. "I believe that you, dear sister, will feel a lot lighter before very long."

"Good. I would hate to have a baby here during an air raid."

The drone of airplanes penetrated the thick walls of the basement. They heard explosions coming closer and closer. Erika took some candles and matches into the wine cellar and brought the one table lamp close to Lydia.

"Let me massage your back, that might help."

Lydia lay on her side and let Erika massage her back. Erika found it inconceivable that the woman did not know she was in labor. She figured that she would not tell her for as long as possible. Lydia might panic and contract her muscles.

From outside they heard whistling then a loud bump and the ground vibrated. Over and over, closer and closer.

"Erika!" Lydia screamed. "Come under the blanket with me, we're going to be bombed again."

Erika crawled under the blanket and hugged the frightened woman. Erika was afraid, too, but she did not dare show it. "Shhh, Lydia, this night too will end."

Then more whistling, closer, and a loud bang. The cellar vibrated and bits of plaster fell on the blanket. The room was in total darkness. Then another loud bang and the ground shook.

Lydia screamed and Erika held her.

"Shh, Lydia. It has passed. That second bomb was on the other side. Don't be frightened."

"It's the pain. I feel pressure and such pain. Turn on the light."

Erika crawled out from under the blanket and lit three candles since there was no more electricity. She lifted the blanket and looked between Lydia's legs. She could see nothing.

"Lydia, I'm going to get a flashlight and look at your vulva. Will you give me permission?"

"Yes. You can help me. You can make the pain go away, can't you?"

"Yes, Lydia, together we'll do it."

Erika got a flashlight and looked up the woman's vagina. She saw what she expected—hair. If Lydia could remain relaxed, she might just pass the baby without any tearing.

"Lydia, your lightening is almost over. Now you have to help me. When I tell you to push, do it with all your might and I promise you will feel a lot lighter."

"Yes Erika, will that help my backache, too?"

"You can bet on it."

Erika put her hand on Lydia's stomach and when she felt the contraction she said, "Now push with everything you've got."

Lydia showed the strain in her face. The baby's head was down to the surface.

"Relax one moment. Now push again."

The head came out and Erika put her hand under the face—the baby cried.

"Erika, what's that sound? It sounds like a baby."

"Yes, you dumb child, you are delivering. Come on, give another push for the body to come out. Do it now!"

Lydia pushed with all her strength and the baby slipped gently into the world of tragedy and destruction.

"You did it. Hurrah, you did it. You have a son."

"Let me see."

"Wait." Erika laid the boy on a small blanket, tied the cord near the baby, and cut it off. Then she wrapped the crying baby in the blanket, wiped off the head and face with a dry wash cloth, and handed him to Lydia. Lydia beamed with happiness. She did not pay any attention to the afterbirth being expelled onto the newspaper along with a gush of blood. Erika wrapped it up and threw it into the garbage. After cleaning Lydia up, Erika pressed on her stomach and felt a hard lump.

"What are you feeling for? Not another baby?"

"No, Lydia, I'm feeling for the uterus. It feels hard and that is the way it's supposed to be. Otherwise we might have a hemorrhage on our hands. You did wonderfully, and things look normal. We'll have the doctor check you in the morning."

Lydia was paying little attention to Erika. She had put the baby to her breast and he sucked hungrily.

"Can you get up and get into my bed? Yours is all wet. Hopefully the mattress will dry quickly."

"I think I can get up. Help me."

Erika took the baby and put him into her bed. Then she helped Lydia up and held on to her as she walked to the bed and got in. The sirens sounded the all clear.

"I need to get some air. I'll be right outside the door."

"Go ahead. And thank you dear, dear Erika."

"Now try to get some sleep. If you need me, just call."

The air in the cellar was still heavy with the miasma of childbirth—the smell of blood and fish.

Erika stepped outside and saw the town burning. The house across the street had been hit and was in flames. People were boldly running in and out trying to save a few precious possessions. They ran out of the house with anything they could grab—a mattress, a table, a lamp, some clothes. They put it on a pile in the street and returned for more.

Briefly Erika considered helping them, but suddenly her muscles felt like spaghetti. Then she realized that she had pushed every time she told Lydia to push. So she just stood there in the darkness, watching the house across the street burn. Soon the flames engulfed the whole structure and there was nothing left to save. Only then did the people stop running in. They stood in the street and watched the fire in silence. Erika looked at her watch. It was almost four in the morning, another two hours until dawn. The sky was so red that dawn would not be seen.

She went back inside and found Lydia crying bitterly. Quickly she went to her and hugged her.

"Are you in pain?"

"No, Erika, not physical pain, but *welt-schmerz*. Just think, in another eighteen years my son will be old enough to be a soldier. Then he will have to go off to war and fight. Not only will I have a husband to worry about, but also my precious baby."

"My dear Lydia, this war will be over soon. Then we will just have to get involved in government and work to ensure that there will never be a war again. Hush, hush, dear girl. Just think, your Ernst will return soon and find you pretty as ever with your little son. Then you will rebuild the house and probably have more children. You will have a good life and will be very happy, I just know it."

"Erika, you're so good. Always looking at the bright side of things. I wish I were more like you."

"You will be. Now sleep. You have just gone through a lot and have every right to feel blue. Sleep, tomorrow will be a good day. Have you decided on a name yet?

"Not yet, I'm too tired now. I'll do it when I have time."

CHAPTER 12

It was a gray and rainy day in early March as Commandant Millard Schnellhauser stood at his office window, watching the skeletons working in the street of Goerlitz. Two SS guards, in black uniforms and carrying rifles, were keeping watch over the dozen or so bony shadows of human beings. These poor creatures were the inmates of a small prison camp from outside town. For over a week now they had been working in the street near Gestapo headquarters, putting up tank barriers.

Millard did not understand how the poor prisoners got enough energy to stand, much less dig holes, put in heavy logs, and then put logs across a barrier. Whoever gave the order for such labor did not have the faintest idea what a tank was capable of. These pitiful barriers would never stop one. Had everyone in authority lost their senses?

But who was he to talk? He was a person of authority, or at least he used to be. Nowadays, he just showed up at the office in the morning, issued travel permits, barked commands at SA recruits because they expected it, and went back to his empty apartment in the evening. Every day he dressed in one of his three suits. When he'd bought them his wife had commented that the fabric would wear like iron. The fabric still looked good, but the man inside was worn out.

Being a policeman was something he used to be proud of. His father had been a policeman and Millard could not remember ever wanting to be anything but the protector of the good people and the enemy of criminals. After returning from the war in 1918, he joined the police force, using all the influence he could muster. Years of walking a beat did not dampen his enthusiasm and conscientiousness. He studied crime solving in his spare time. Should the possibility for a promotion come his way, he wanted to be prepared.

When he walked the beat as a young policeman he turned many a girl's head. There was a cafe on Berliner Street that sold the best pastry. The owner liked for Millard to come in and enjoy a bun, gratis. It discouraged shoplifting. One day there was a pretty new waitress who treated him politely, but did not make eyes at him as the other waitresses did.

She was new in town and single. He asked her out to a movie and she refused, a first for him. She became a challenge. After he learned her full name, Brigitte Mond, he looked up where she lived. Wearing civilian clothing, he took walks in her neighborhood. The third day he saw her coming out of the house struggling with a wheelchair in which an old lady was sitting. Millard rushed to help her get the wheelchair down the steps. She looked at him as if she should know him, but could not remember.

"Fraulein Mond? What a coincidence to see you here. I'm policeman Millard Schnellhauser, I was just taking a walk."

"Ah yes, from the cafe. I would like you to meet my aunt, Frau Mond."

"Pleased to meet you, gracious lady," he said, kissing the air above her hand.

The old lady blushed. "My, my, where has this gentleman been hiding? Brigitte, you never told me about him. I think he likes you, judging the way he looks at you."

"Auntie, please," she said, turning red in the face.

"There, I embarrassed her, good. That child is much too serious for a young girl. What she needs is a fellow to ask her out dancing."

"Madam, I'm just the one to do that." Turning to Brigitte, he made an exaggerated bow and said, "It would be my greatest pleasure to accompany you to a dance Saturday evening. Please consent."

"I guess I better, otherwise Auntie will never let me hear the end of it."

Thus their romance started. A year later, in 1925, they married. They made a handsome couple. His tall straight frame gave him an aristocratic look. She was a head shorter with brunette hair usually put into a French twist. White, pearl stud earrings were usually the only decorations on her head. The large green eyes and rosebud lips needed no artificial enhancement.

In order to continue her duty of taking care of her aunt, Millard moved into her aunt's house. He thoroughly liked the old lady and the arrangement was a happy one. Soon, however, the old lady died and the niece inherited the house.

Millard saw the change in her attitude immediately, but was helpless to do anything about it. One could not buy a house on a policeman's pay. Now she was an heiress with a house who tolerated him and all his shortcomings. She let him know that he was inadequate as a bread winner, a gardener, a handyman, and a lover. When their daughter was born, the list of deficiencies became longer. Even as a father he could do nothing right. She told him to pay more attention to his child, then that he paid too much attention to her. Either he was too strict or too lenient, whatever mood she was in.

But duty still reigned supreme in his life, duty as a police officer, as a husband, and as a father. He would never dream of running out on his vows. As the love for his wife diminished, the love for their daughter, Lotte, increased.

She was a beautiful child with curly, golden hair and large green eyes. Her face came mostly from her mother, but her tall physique and long legs came from her father. Even as small child she was a fast runner.

Finally in 1934 his big career opportunity came. There were openings for advancement in the Secret States Police —GESTPO. Here was his chance to get off the streets and work in a supervisory position in an office. It was too good of an opportunity to pass up. All he had to do to accept was to join the Nazi Party.

His first impression of Hitler and the party was that they were a bunch of radicals. To blame all the ills of the country on Jews was simply ridiculous. True, some Jews weren't too likeable, but neither were a lot of his German neighbors. The only Jew he really knew was his doctor, a fine gentleman. No one would harm people like that. Besides, the Nazis had done a lot of good in the country. Germany went from a defeated and bankrupt people to a proud nation again. Many people believed Hitler to be the greatest man in history. So many people could not be wrong.

The day he learned about his promotion, he received some respect at home. Brigitte hugged and kissed him as she had not done in years. She cooked his favorite foods for the next few days. Best of all, he told her to go shopping for some nice clothes because they would be going to some important functions in the near future. Life was good again, at least on the surface.

In the autumn of 1942 he got a call from his daughter's school principal. Lotte had fallen down a long flight of stairs and suffered head trauma. She was being taken to the hospital at that moment. The man concluded by apologizing. "I tried ringing your wife at home, but got no answer. I therefore took the liberty to call you at work."

"That is quite all right, thank you for notifying me."

He hung up in great distress. Brigitte was probably in the yard. He would swing by on the way to the hospital and pick her up.

When he got to the house he was shocked to see a black Mercedes with a driver waiting in front of the house. He rushed in, reckoning something was dreadfully wrong and expecting to see whoever came in the car to be in the living room. No one was there.

"Brigitte, where are you?"

Silence

He went into the bedroom to go through to the bathroom. The first thing he noticed was the black SS uniform hanging on a hanger on the closet door. Underwear was neatly lying on a chair.

"What is going on here?"

"Millard, what are you doing home at this time?" Brigitte said, suddenly sitting up in bed. She pointed to a man lying in bed and said nonchalantly, "I would like you to meet General Count von Lautendorff."

The man gave a limp wave of the hand.

There were a thousand things Millard wanted to say to her. The words stuck in his throat like a mob trying to escape the police through a small doorway. He felt the blood draining out of his face and the nerves tingle in his forearms. Stuttering something incomprehensible, he ran out of the room. In the living room, he flopped onto the sofa, staring with dazed eyes. He felt totally numb. A short time later the general walked by without saying a word and left the house. He heard the car drive off.

A few minutes later Brigitte came into the living room dressed in a cotton summer dress. She sat in a winged chair on the other side of the room and looked at him in silence. When she saw him get ready to speak, she held up her hand and spoke.

"So you finally found out. You are some policeman not to have realized what has been going on for years. Or were you just a much better actor than I gave you credit for?"

"I had no idea," he whispered. "I trusted you. How can you do this to me?"

"You stupid man," she said sternly. "I have not been doing this to you, but for you." She rose and walked to the middle of the floor. "How do you think you got your present position? By hanging out in cafes on Berliner Street? If it wasn't for me, you would still be walking your beat. I slept with men who could help you. Do you think I always enjoyed it? I tell you, most men are as poor at sex as you. They all think they're a heavenly gift to women."

"Sleeping with a SS general, does that mean I'll get a promotion soon?"

"No, I sleep with him for fun and personal satisfaction. By the way, you did not tell me what made you come home early."

Suddenly a boulder hit him in the stomach. "Oh God, it is Lotte. She fell and is in the hospital. I came to get you."

Without saying a word, they drove to the hospital. Quickly they were led to her small private room. Millard wondered who in the hospital his wife had been sleeping with to rate that.

A dagger went through his heart when he saw the twelve year old girl lying in the white bed. Her skin was almost as white as the sheets, her face highlighted by the red and blue of the bruises. Her head was wrapped in white bandages, not a curl of golden hair could be seen. He wondered if she still had hair or if she had been shaved. A large blue and purple bruise hid her right eye and the left one was closed.

Millard held her right hand and kissed her on the forehead. He felt no response. Brigitte stood on the other side of the bed and appeared carved out of stone.

The doctor entered. "Herr and Frau Schnellhauser, I am very sorry. We did what we could. She has a severe concussion and is in a coma."

"She is just sleeping," Millard said sternly. "Give her a little time and she'll wake up, you'll see."

"She might, it's up to God."

Millard grabbed the old doctor by his lapel. "She'll be well soon. You'd better make her well."

Brigitte pulled her husband off the doctor. "Millard, the doctors here are doing everything they can. Now behave yourself."

"Sorry," he said, straightening the lapel. "Forgive me. Now tell me what the situation is."

※※※

For two days he sat at the girl's bedside. Occasionally she opened her eye—making Millard think she had awakened—only to close it again. Brigitte spent a few hours at the hospital and went home. She came the next day, saw there was no change, and left with instructions for him to call when there was an improvement. Millard was glad he did not have to look at his wife.

On the third day she died. He did not know she was dead until a nurse came into the room to check on her patient. When she told him that his daughter was gone, he did not believe it. He wrapped the body of his daughter in his arms and kissed her on the forehead. Then he sat there, looking at Lotte. Finally Brigitte came and forced him out of the room for the staff to clear the bed.

At home he cried like he had not done since he was a small child. Tears of years of pent-up pain came pouring out. After several hours he composed himself enough to pack his clothes and head to his office. That night he slept in a vacant prison cell in the basement of his headquarters.

※※※

One of the guards of the work crew called time out for lunch. That meant lunch for the guards. All the skeletons could do is sit wearily on the sidewalk and watch them eat. Millard quickly left the office and drove home.

He took every bit of food he had in the apartment and put it into pillow cases. There was bread, butter, cheese, produce, rice, beans, and even some lunch meat. Before returning to the office, he checked the mail. To his delight there was a letter from his friend Sepp Wagner. Sepp and he had been friends since they were boys. They met when his parents vacationed in Hollstein years ago. Since then Millard had seen Sepp only three times, but they had kept in touch with letters.

Sepp wrote how well Sigrit was doing. She was a fairly happy child and doing well in school. Millard felt that at least he had done for that little girl what he could not do for his own daughter—help her survive a difficult situation. He wished the brother was with Sepp's family, too. He felt sorry the boy had been drafted and would most likely become cannon fodder.

Then his thoughts went to the aunt. He wondered how Erika was making out in Stuttgart. He wished she was still in town and he could see her, but figured that most likely she'd be better off in Stuttgart. He had no illusions what could happen in the next few weeks. The Russians had suffered severely at German hands and would be eager for revenge.

When he got back to headquarters the guards were still enjoying their lunch. He went up to them and asked them harshly, "What is the meaning of you taking so long to eat while your work crew goes hungry?"

"There were no arrangements made for them to eat," one soldier answered boldly.

"Then we shall remedy that," Millard said going to the prisoners and handing out the food.

"Here, eat."

The prisoners took the food suspiciously. They sat there looking at the bread. Finally one started eating and told the others that it was good. Soon they were all eating and dividing the lunch meat among themselves quite evenly.

"And the rest I want you men to take back to camp for later." He handed two pillow cases full of food to the prisoners.

"Thank you, thank you, kind sir," they all said.

"You are welcome, and God be with you." Then he whispered, "Stay alive, this will end soon."

The guards looked at each other and rolled their eyes. One drew a circle on his temple with his finger.

Back in his office, Millard looked out of the window again. It seemed to him the prisoners were standing a bit straighter and working a little more lively.

Why is there so much cruelty in the world? Why, why? Is it really necessary to have war and killing and torture? Why can't we all be a little nicer and gentler to each other?

Brigitte, the girl I loved more than life and who I thought loved me, we could not get along and live in harmony. If two people in love can't get along, how can we expect nations with millions of personalities to get along? We just have to learn to respect each other and we have to learn to control the horrible weapons.

Suddenly, his daughter's face flashed before him, saying, '*Papa, I was pushed down the stairs, pushed hard.*'

He reached into his desk drawer and took out his revolver. The Mauser felt natural in his hand. Good balance and quality. He pointed it at one SS guard and aimed.

"Bang," he said. "If it would help, I would really do it."

Then he pointed at the other guard and said, "*Bang,*" like a little boy playing cowboy.

Finally, he put the barrel to his own temple and pulled the trigger.

CHAPTER 13

Ludwig heard artillery fire in the distance as he worked alone in the field, planting potatoes. The deep explosions of tank fire and the higher ratt-tatt-tatt of machine guns were becoming as much part of the sounds of life as birdsong used to be. At night the eastern sky glowed red.

The little school in the village of Eichdorf had been closed since before Christmas. When the regular teacher was drafted three years earlier an old teacher came out of retirement to teach in the one room schoolhouse. Unfortunately, he caught a cold that went into pneumonia and he died. The school board for the region gave the eighth graders a test, which they all passed, and they were awarded their eighth grade completion certificate. The younger children were given an extended vacation.

Ludwig had written several letters to Aunt Erika and was disappointed at never having received a reply. Frau Kempf kept telling him that the mail was very undependable these days. He had always given the outgoing mail to her, never suspecting that she would do anything but bring it to the post office.

One day he was at his new friend Heinz's house when mail was delivered. The family got a letter from someone near Stuttgart. Ludwig quickly wrote a letter to his aunt in Stuttgart, using Heinze's return address. Finally, he got a letter from her at Heinz's house.

Erika was very happy to hear from him and to find out that he had not been drafted as she had heard from Sigrit. She told him about Sigrit and Lydia and her life in Stuttgart. The letter concluded, urging him to remain inconspicuous and just ride out the war. After the war they would get back together somewhere.

అఅఅ

One evening toward the end of April silence surrounded Ludwig and Frau Kempf as they sat in the kitchen, looking at each other.

"No gunfire, does that mean the war is over?" Ludwig asked.

"I don't know what it means."

Before dawn they were awakened by thunderous pounding on the door. Frau Kempf opened the door still wearing her nightgown. Two Russian soldiers burst in with rifles in their hands.

"Alle raus," one soldier shouted, while the other one ran through the house, looking in all the rooms. Ludwig was in the process of getting dressed when his door burst open and the Russian ran in. The soldier motioned for Ludwig to

walk in front of him. When Ludwig passed the toilet he opened the door.

"I have to go," he told the soldier.

The soldier motioned for him to go in, while he held the door open and watched Ludwig.

Ludwig and Frau Kempf, who also managed to get dressed while the soldiers watched, were escorted to the center of town. One Russian officer who spoke German told the women to stand in one area and for the men and boys to stand near the fountain. An army truck stood waiting.

"How old are you?" the officer asked the boy nearest to him.

"Thirteen"

"Go home," the officer commanded.

"How old are you?" he asked Heinz.

"Fourteen."

"Get in the truck." Two soldiers pushed the boy into the army truck.

Ludwig was next in line. "Get into the truck," the officer commanded.

Then the smaller boys started lying about their ages. Some of the fifteen year olds could pass for thirteen. They were sent home.

On the other side of the plaza the women were sorted. Any female that looked appealing was told to go into the church. Within five minutes the truck was loaded with about two dozen boys and men and closed up. A Russian soldier, not much older than the boys he was guarding, sat in the back with a machine gun across his legs. There was one shiny battle medal on his chest at which he looked frequently.

As the truck drove off, Ludwig saw the Russians running into the church. The last sound he heard in Eichdorf was the girls screaming.

A train with box cars stood near another town. The truck drove up to it and stopped. Some Russian soldiers opened the back and spoke in Russian motioning for the men to get out and board the train. As Heinz disembarked the truck, he lost his balance and bumped into the young soldier who had been on the truck.

"Excuse me," Heinz said.

The soldier nodded.

In the boxcar there were some boys from another village. After the boys from Eichdorf had boarded, the train began to slowly move east. The only guard was the same young soldier from the truck.

After the train rolled a few kilometers, the guard started to relax and lit a cigarette.

"Where are we going?" asked Heinz in a language understood by the Russian.

"Siberia," he answered.

Ludwig looked at his friend amazed. "Do you speak Russian?"

"Not Russian, but Serbian, it is close."

"Serbian? I've never heard of it."

"The Serbs of Germany are what you can call a tribe. We have our own customs and language. I learned Serbian before I went to school. Then with Hitler we fell out of fashion and had to hide our ways."

Heinz looked around and saw that no one was paying attention to him. He put his closed fist into Ludwig's hand and whispered, "Take this and hide it."

"What is it?"

"Just take it. When I signal I want you to *find* it."

Ludwig felt metal in his hand. He noticed the Russian was not wearing his medal anymore.

A short time later the Russian touched his chest and cried out in alarm.

"What's wrong?" Heinz asked.

"My medal, it is gone," said the Russian, looking around on the floor and searching the straw. "This is a catastrophe. I have to find it."

"Let me help you look for it," offered Heinz. "Will you reward me if I find it?"

"Yes, anything. I must have my medal."

"I'll tell you what. If I or my friend here finds it, I want you to open the door long enough for us to slip out."

"I can't do that."

"I suppose your medal will never be found. It probably slipped through a crack in the wood."

The young soldier looked thoughtful for a while then said, "No one counted. If medal is found, I suppose I could open the door for a little air."

"Then start opening." Turning to Ludwig he said in a low tone, "Go to the door and get ready to jump. Let him see the medal, but give it to me."

While the soldier was sliding the door open a half a yard, Ludwig showed the precious object to him then passed it to Heinz. Without hardly looking, he jumped off the train and rolled down the embankment into a soft green field. Soon he saw another figure jump off the train. The two boys ran toward each other and hugged.

"We are free, free," shouted Ludwig.

"However free we can be behind Russian lines. We're now between the frying pan and the fire. If the Russians catch us, it'll be Siberia."

"Siberia? Is that where we were going?" asked Ludwig, startled. "Oh, those poor bastards on the train."

"Yes, they don't know it yet. The other problem is, we don't want to get caught by the Germans either. They might think we're deserters and hang us."

"Suppose we just go into the woods over there and think about it," said Ludwig. "Wish we knew the battle lines. Should we go south or west? That is the big question."

The sun was still a long way from high noon when the boys reached a forest with light green foliage. They found a spot hidden by spruce trees and fell asleep.

A few hours later they were awakened by female voices. They lay quietly until they saw two girls of about eighteen come into sight.

They were picking the new light green growth off the spruces.

"What are they doing that for?" Ludwig whispered.

"I don't know, but I bet it's against the law."

Soon the girls sat down and started eating sandwiches. The two boys crawled close to the girls then suddenly stood up. Startled, the girls screamed and jumped to their feet.

"Don't be frightened," said Ludwig. "We mean you no harm,"

"For a second I thought you were the foresters come to arrest us for picking the spruce growth."

"No, no we are just some boys who escaped from the Russians," Heinz said. "We want to beg you for some food."

The girls each tore their sandwiches in half and handed part to the boys. They ate slowly, relishing each morsel.

"Since we are dining together, don't you boys think it would be polite to introduce yourselves?"

"This is Heinz and I'm Ludwig."

"And my name is Olga and this is my sister, Polka."

"Pleased to meet you," Ludwig said. "Polka, that is a most unusual name."

"It's a nickname because I do the dance so well.

"Where are you from?" asked Olga.

"Eichdorf, the Russians arrived this morning and took all the boys over fourteen away."

"They did the same thing in our town yesterday," added Polka.

"What happened to the girls?" asked Ludwig.

"The Russians were very polite to the women. They warned us though that not all the Russians are like them, especially the Cossacks."

"Those must have been different troops than came through our town," Heinz said. "Is there anywhere we can go where we might be safe?"

"I think you should hide during the day," Olga said. "And travel west at night."

"Sister, we better get busy," Polka said. "You boys can help us pick some spruce growth."

"What are you using that for?" asked Heinz.

We make jelly out of it," Olga said. "Fortunately we still have lots of sugar. It sure needs it."

"Why don't you boys stay here and we'll be back later and bring you some food?"

With eight hands picking, the sack was soon full. The girls bid them a cheerful farewell and ran off.

"Do you think they'll be back?" asked Heinz.

"I hope so, I'm still hungry."

CHAPTER 14

The war was unobtrusive in Hollstein. The farmers went about planting their crops as they had done for centuries, plowing their fields with horses or oxen. They milked cows by hand and sold most of the milk to the local cheese factory. The real damage was invisible, the young men who left, never to return.

One day in April that changed. A column of jeeps and trucks rolled into town. They pulled into the square near the church. French soldiers got out and stood with rifles in hand looking in all directions. The commanding officer spoke German and demanded to speak with the mayor.

It took a while before someone fetched the mayor from his field. Then the man went home to change his clothes. Wearing his Sunday suit and top hat, the mayor presented himself to the French colonel.

The colonel explained to the mayor that the town was now occupied and that his soldiers would be billeted with the local population. Also, the town was under curfew. No one was to be outside after eight in the evening. Anyone seen out after dark would be shot.

"Do any of your people own guns?" asked the colonel.

"Yes, some men hunt."

"All guns are to be brought to me immediately. Anyone found to possess a gun after one hour from now will be shot."

As soon as the mayor finished making his speech, some people rushed home to fetch their rifles.

The soldiers assigned to the Wagner house were two Moroccans. They moved into Greta's former room.

"Martha, we have to be good hosts," Sepp said the day they moved in. "We'll cook a special dinner for them. What do you think?"

"We have some real nice smoked ham, I'll make that."

The table in the kitchen was set and the fragrance of the ham spread beyond its walls. The two dark skinned men entered, looking puzzled.

"*Que cette?*"

"What?" asked Martha.

Sigrit and Greta were mesmerized by faces so dark. The two men could have been dipped in ink.

"*Que cette?*" one said, pointing to the ham.

"Oh, *das, das ist Schinken,* ist *gut.*"

"*Que cette Schinken?* Moo-moo?

"Oh no, not moo-moo, is oink-oink. It's *bon,*" said Martha proudly.

"No eat oink-oink," one said while both waved their hands back and forth.

"Oink-oink *bon,*" said Martha using the only French word she knew. "Oh, well." She shrugged her shoulders, trying to brush off the insult of someone refusing her special dish. "Then just eat the dumplings and cabbage if it pleases you."

They all sat down at the table.

Sigrit whispered to Greta, "Do you think their whole body is as dark as their faces and hands?"

"No whispering," Martha reprimanded. "If you have something to say, speak out loud."

Sigrit apologized. "It is not important, sorry."

When the girls lay in bed that night, Sigrit forced herself to stay awake. After she heard the soldiers go into their room she quietly tiptoed to the door of their room and looked through the keyhole. In the dim light she did not see any details, but she knew the answer to her question.

The following evening Sigrit was in Opa's stable helping Oma milk the cows. She sat on the little stool and took the teats into her small hands. Milk shot into the bucket between her knees.

"You do that like you have been milking all your life," said Oma, looking proud. "I taught you well. When you get big, we'll hire you as a milk-maid."

"I am getting big and old, too."

"That's right, in a few days we'll have a double holiday, your eighth birthday and Mayday."

"I used to think it was a holiday because it was my birthday," Sigrit said, laughing.

"I have to look after supper now. You know how hungry Opa is when he gets back from the field. If the full pail is too heavy for you, just leave it here," said the old lady.

"I think I can manage it."

"And don't forget to close the stable door," Oma called from the door.

"I will, Oma."

The old woman left the stable with her bucket of milk. Sigrit enjoyed the rhythm of the milking and started humming a waltz. Before long she was singing the words. When no more milk came she picked up the bucket and headed out the door. Unbeknownst to Sigrit, the cow was following her right through the stable door she had forgotten to close.

Sigrit entered Oma's kitchen with excitement and pride.

"See, I can carry a bucket full of milk."

"That is wonderful. You are such a big help."

"Can I help you cook?"

"You may set the table. Opa should be back any minute now and then you better rush home. It's almost curfew."

"I can make it back after Opa gets here. He owes me a hug."

A few minutes later Opa entered the kitchen. Sigrit ran to hug him but stopped a few feet away.

Opa's brows were close together with three black lines between them. The girl had never seen him angry before.

"Who left the stable door open? Flower is gone."

Sigrit felt as if her heart was jumping out of her chest. "Uh-uh," is all she managed to whisper.

"I better go and find her," said the old man, rushing out the door.

"No Josef," Oma shouted after him. "You can't go out now. It's almost curfew. Come back."

"I must bring her back," he shouted, running toward the woods.

Oma stood in the doorway, watching her husband disappear into the dusk. Sigrit silently stood next to her with large tears running down her checks. Her chest felt as if it was in a vice. She could hardly breathe.

"You better hurry home now."

"No, Oma. I'll stay here 'til Opa comes back."

The old woman looked at the child who suddenly seemed to have shrunk. She stooped down and embraced her.

"It will be all right. Flower has gotten out before and was found pretty quickly in the woods. Opa will find her soon."

Sigrit closed her eyes and saw her parents hanging off the rafters.

Will that horrible sight ever leave me?

She cried silently in the embrace of a person she now loved. When she opened her eyes it was dark outside and Opa was still out there.

Each minute seemed an eternity and dinner stood untouched. Oma and Sigrit sat on wooden chairs, waiting in silence. Sigrit remembered another kitchen in Goerlitz.

Tante Erika read to me while we were waiting for Ludwig to return. At least there we had music and Tante's voice so much like Mama's. I wonder what Oma is thinking. Oh please, God, let Opa return safely, please, please Jesus.

The only sound was the slow ticking of the grandfather clock in the next room. Every fifteen minutes, that seemed like hours, the chimes struck. The night was silent except for some shots heard far away, an eternity after ten. When the clock struck twelve Sigrit thought, *Now it is tomorrow,*

"Come, Siggy, let's go to bed."

They both took off only their shoes and lay on the bed. It was six in the morning when they were awakened by Sepp and Martha standing in the bedroom.

"Oma, what is wrong?" asked Martha. "We were worried when Siggy did not return last night."

The old lady sat up with a start. "It's Josef. He went out after Flower and did not return. Oh, Sepp, go find him."

Sepp rushed out of the house while Sigrit quickly put on her shoes and followed him.

A short distance from the house stood Flower with a rope around her neck peacefully grazing.

Sepp looked at the ground with concern. Then he saw a man lying in the grass. He looked at the child and to his relief she did not see the figure.

"Siggy, go and get Oma."

He turned the girl around and gave her a gentle push. She ran toward the house. Half-way there she saw Oma and Martha heading toward her.

"Oma, Frau Martha," Sigrit called to them waving her arms. "Herr Sepp wants you to come,"

"Did you find Opa?" asked Martha.

"Flower is there, over the hill."

Martha started running while Oma walked faster. Sigrit ran back to Sepp.

While Sigrit was getting the women, Sepp approached the figure lying face down in the grass.

"Father!" he called as he approached the form, hoping for a sign of life. "Father, wake up."

Sepp stooped down and rolled the body over. The body was already stiff and lay there, face up, with the arms above the head and off the ground. Before he could roll the body over again he heard a sound that amplified the deepest human grief and anguish. It was a high-pitched wail that ended abruptly then echoed from the woods as if the trees cried in sympathy. Sepp jerked around in time to see Sigrit collapse like a marionette doll with its strings abruptly severed.

༺༻

Sigrit woke up in Sepp's arms as he was carrying her over the hill. A river of tears wet her cheeks. "I killed him, I killed Opa. It's all my fault. I forgot to close the door."

"Hush, Siggy. You didn't kill him. It was the war."

Sigrit struggled to get down.

I don't deserve to be carried so gently after what I've done. I am bad. Always somebody I love dies. I wish I was dead.

Sepp relented and put her down. Her knees, however, could not bear her weight. Sepp picked her up again and carried her to his house. He laid her on a bench in the kitchen then went and woke Greta.

"Greta, get up quickly and run to get the doctor."

"What happened? Is it Oma or Opa? Are they sick?"

"Opa was shot."

Then Greta heard hysterical wailing in the kitchen.

"Who's crying like that?"

"It's Siggy. I better get back to her. Now hurry and get the doctor."

When Martha saw Sigrit faint she knew that her father-in-law was beyond help. She went to her mother-in-law and put her arms around her. The two women slowly approached the body lying face down in the grass.

"I knew it," said Oma, "I knew it when I heard shots last night at eight minutes after ten."

"We had no idea Opa was out. If Sepp would have known it, he would have gone out, too."

"And gotten himself shot. I'm glad he didn't know."

Slowly the women walked around the body. Oma's face was without expression. She just stared at the corpse of the person closest to her for almost fifty years.

"He was a wonderful man. We were very happy."

"I know,"

The old woman knelt down next to the body and stroked his white hair. Martha saw a wound in his hip and a trail of blood. She followed the trail for over a hundred feet, and there she saw a large splatter of blood. She found a twig near-by and pushed it into the ground while saying a silent prayer. Then she took a deep breath and retrieved Flower who was nonchalantly chewing her cud.

CHAPTER 15

Sigrit had been given a sedative the morning Opa had been found and she slept most of the day. Greta sat in the room in the afternoon, waiting for the little girl to wake up.

"Siggy, you are awake. How do you feel?"

Why is she asking me how I feel? Am I ill? Oh, this bed feels so good, I don't want to wake up yet. I'll just roll over and go back to sleep. Oh no! Opa. He ran out at dusk and did not come back. We waited and waited. Shots. Opa got shot.

Startled, she sat up in bed. "Greta, is Opa dead? Is he really dead?"

"Yes"

"I killed him. It's all my fault, I left the door open and Flower got out. Everybody must hate me."

"No, we don't hate you. Leaving the door open was such a little mistake. I've done it dozens of times," Greta said, trying to comfort the little girl.

"I wish it would have been me who went out and got shot." Then Sigrit's gaze went to the window where bright daylight streamed in. "What time is it?"

"Almost four in the afternoon. Don't you want to get up now?"

"Yes, I'll get up," she said without enthusiasm. "How is Oma? Where is Opa? Can I see him?"

"They are in the chapel. I'll go with you."

The girls went through the kitchen where Martha and several of her friends were preparing food for the funeral. The women were busy cooking and talking and paid no attention to the two girls. Sigrit took it as a sign of being shunned.

No one wants anything to do with me. I'm a murderer. They're going to throw me in jail and then shoot me.

She looked at Greta and saw her eyes red from crying.

I made her cry. Oh, my dear sister, I'm so sorry. I don't want to make anyone sad, especially you.

As the girls approached the chapel an old man and woman came out. The woman was crying and the man blew his nose loud enough to be a foghorn. Neither one acknowledged the children.

"Greta, people don't see you either because you are with me."

"Don't be silly, Siggy. Children are often ignored."

Sigrit suddenly felt hunger punch her in the stomach.

I'm afraid to go in. Opa will lie in the coffin with his hands ready to grab my throat and strangle me. He looked so mad the last time I saw him. Then when he was lying on the grass he had a big hole in his stomach and stuff that looked like white sausages sticking out.

Sigrit stopped. Greta put her arm around her and pushed her along. When entering the chapel, the first thing she saw was a number of green wreaths, some with a few flowers. In front of the altar stood the coffin, completely covered with the blue and white Bavarian flag. A recent picture of Opa stood on the coffin.

Oma, dressed in her everyday black woolen dress sat next to the coffin. When she heard the two girls enter she looked at Greta and smiled.

"Come here, Greta," she said with her arms open.

Greta rushed to the old woman, hugged, and held her, showering kisses on her face. Sigrit stood back a few paces with tears wetting the front of her blouse. The old woman looked at her without expression for a few seconds that seemed to last forever. Then the usual warmth and love returned to her eyes and she extended an arm toward Sigrit. The child rushed to the woman and knelt in front of her.

"Oh, Oma, can you ever forgive me?"

"Get up, child, come sit on my lap."

"I am bad luck. I bring death and bad news wherever I go. First my parents, then Aunt Erika learns Uncle Rowald is missing, and now Opa is dead. I wish I would never have been born."

"Hush, hush, child. It's not your fault. It is the war."

The old woman picked up Sigrit, put her on her lap, hugged, and rocked her like a baby. Greta stroked Sigrit's hair like she would a pet. Sigrit tried to stop crying, but the tears kept coming. These were truly good people. She had to make sure she brought no more bad luck to them.

Shortly before eight, all the visitors at Sepp's house went home. Oma insisted on sleeping in her own bed and Martha went home with her to spend the night. Sepp and the two girls sat in the kitchen which was rich with the odor of food. The two Moroccans were still out.

"I'm going to bed. Good night, Herr Sepp, good night Greta," Sigrit said, heading toward the steps to go upstairs.

"Not so fast," Sepp called. "Don't I get a hug tonight?"

Sigrit spun around and looked at Sepp. He had paid little attention to her all day and she felt he resented her. Now he wanted a hug. Maybe he wanted to wring her neck.

She studied his face, expecting to see resentment. Instead, she saw the same bright eyes and curled up mustache that gave his face the appearance of a perpetual smile. When she saw his small ivory teeth, she could hardly believe that he really was smiling at her.

Suddenly her face lit up. She ran toward the man and dove into his embrace. Tears started anew, but these were tears of joy.

It felt good to be hugged and loved. Sepp loved her without making any demands. She had a terrible secret she needed to share now. Instinctively, she knew the secret would become a barrier in her emotions. After a few minutes she said, "Herr Sepp, I was going to go out tonight and get myself shot so I wouldn't bring you any more bad luck."

"You silly child, now tell me. What good would it do if you get yourself killed?"

"I would stop bringing bad luck."

"You don't bring bad luck. Don't ever think that. What has happened has happened. History cannot be changed, but that doesn't mean we can't go on and enjoy living. If you do a stupid thing like going outside and getting yourself killed, I would be very angry at you."

"I don't want anyone getting angry at me."

"There now, don't even think of doing anything stupid. Nothing is worth killing yourself over."

"Nothing?"

"Nothing. God gave us life, and we live until he calls us home."

"Is it a sin to kill yourself?" Sigrit asked, thinking of her parents hanging in the attic.

Sepp looked over her head at Greta. Greta looked anxiously at her father. Catholics had a definite belief concerning suicide.

"Not everyone believes it's a sin," Sepp replied, dreading the next question.

Sigrit said nothing and kissed his cheek.

The next day the French left the village to go north, farther into Germany. The curfew was over.

The funeral was on Mayday, also Sigrit's eighth birthday. Close to a hundred people attended the service held in the baroque church in town. Opa's body was buried in the cemetery surrounding the church. After the ritual everyone came to Sepp's house. All the women wore simple, long, black dresses and black pie-plate hats. The men wore long, black pants and mostly gray jackets. Earlier in the day people had brought over food and cakes, along with chairs and benches. The weather was cooperative with warmth and sunshine.

People arrived in a somber mood. Many women quickly set up food and drink on long tables. Before anyone could serve themselves, Oma demanded everyone's attention. All eyes were on her when she started speaking in a loud clear voice.

"I want to thank all of you for coming." A murmur was heard from the crowd then she continued, "We have buried a good man today,"

"That's right, we all liked him...he was the best..." was heard from the gathering.

"But Josef Wagner would not want you to keep crying because he's gone. He has always said to me that when we have his funeral, he wants everybody to have a good time. So today we celebrate his life."

She picked up a liter mug of beer and raised it high. "Josef, here's to you, *prost.*" She took a big sip and poured some of the beer on the ground. Everyone else took their drinks and did the same. "Now I have to announce some birthdays," Oma continued. "Maria Krautner has her birthday tomorrow." Oma pointed to an old lady near-by. "Stand up, Maria, if you still can."

Everyone laughed and clapped as the old woman not only stood up, but got on the chair, and waved all around.

"And our little Siggy is eight today. Come here next to me, Siggy."

Sigrit was sitting next to Greta and started to blush.

"Go on, go to Oma," said Greta.

Shyly the girl walked up to Oma while everyone applauded.

"Come on, child, and get your present."

When Sigrit arrived at the table where Oma was standing, the old woman reached under the table and picked up something hidden by the table cloth. Meanwhile Sepp, Martha, and Greta joined them. Oma handed Sigrit a long box wrapped in white tissue paper and tied with a red ribbon. Some flowers under the ribbon added to the beauty of the package.

"Here, sweetheart, happy birthday," Oma said.

Sigrit took the package and stared at it.

"Open it up," Martha said.

Slowly Sigrit untied the ribbon, then she took the small bouquet of flowers and placed it in the bodice of her green, dirndle dress. Carefully, she unfolded the paper from the box, while everyone eagerly watched. Finally, she opened the lid and beheld the most beautiful porcelain doll. The doll had glass eyes that closed; long, brown braids, almost the color of Sigrit's; and wore a meticulously made folk dress of the village. She took the doll out and hugged it then raised it for everyone to see.

"This is from all of us," Martha said. "I got this doll when I was a little girl."

Sigrit hugged and kissed all the members of the family. "Thank you, thank you. I will always treasure it."

While she went back to her place to sit down she heard Oma tell everyone, "Now eat and drink and enjoy. Maybe some of you will even play some music."

CHAPTER 16

The war ended without fanfare in Stuttgart. About the only difference was that the bombs stopped falling. American forces occupied the city and surrounding area. They took over the German Army Barracks of Burgholzhof on the grapevine-covered hill, overlooking both the main city of Stuttgart and the surrounding towns. Some of the residential houses of Feuerbach were also used to billet soldiers. The owners and residents were told to leave.

One by one the German soldiers returned. The lines at the stores remained and, as the men returned, they became longer and the food available less. While Erika stood in line in the morning, she heard the news of who had returned within the last day.

"My neighbor, Frau Klaiber's husband, came back," Erika overheard.

"I bet she's happy. I'm sure the first thing they'll do is have another baby," said the woman next to the first one.

"I wouldn't be too sure of that. Both of his legs were blown off and—" She lowered her voice. "—who knows what else?"

It was close to noon when Erika trudged wearily up the street with a heavy bag of food toward her home in the bombed-out house. She'd had little sleep in the past weeks. Lydia had been very demanding since the birth of the baby. Besides nursing the child, she did very little. She did not hesitate to ask Erika to get her a book from across the room. Or perhaps she'd see a cobweb that needed to be removed immediately.

The baby was beginning to be a night owl. He wanted to be awake and entertained in the middle of the night.

"Erika, would you please keep the baby quiet, so I can get my rest," Lydia demanded one night in early May.

"Why don't you play with him so I can get some rest? You can sleep during the day when I'm doing all the chores."

"You as a nurse should have more sympathy. After all, I'm recuperating from childbirth."

"Lydia, it has been two months now. You had an easy delivery and you're not recuperating anymore, you're lazy."

"How dare you speak to me that way. You're living under my roof, rent free."

"The price of the rent here is very high. As soon as it gets light, I'll look for a place to live."

"Oh, Erika, I'm sorry. Don't leave me." The woman got up and approached Erika in the potato bed. "Please forgive me, I'm horrid. I'll get back to normal when Ernst comes home. Oh, I wish he would get here soon." Lydia hugged her sister-in-law and showered her hair with tears. "Please don't leave me."

"Lydia, stop crying. You know I'm here for you as long as you need me. But please, let me get some sleep."

Lydia did keep the baby quiet that night, but the argument had upset Erika too much to go back to sleep.

Later that morning after a visit to the butcher shop, Erika approached the door to the basement. To her surprise it not only stood open, but she heard laughter from within. She entered the basement and Lydia suddenly appeared in front of her, dressed and groomed like she had been long ago.

"Oh Erika, I'm so glad you're back. Look who's here," Lydia said, pointing to a dim figure sitting at the table.

The figure rose and came toward her. The first thing she noticed as the person came into the light was the army uniform with the doctor's insignia. Her heart skipped a beat. Her first thought was Rowald, but she quickly realized the person in front of her was too short to be her husband.

"Ernst, is it really you?"

"It's really me in person, home at last." He hugged and kissed his sister-in-law. "Lydia has been telling me all you have done for her. We both are—no all three of us—eternally grateful."

"I'm glad to have been of help. Welcome home, Ernst."

Erika busied herself with cooking, while Lydia and Ernst talked and held the baby.

In the darkness of night, Erika heard the springs of the bed squeaking as the two people in love got reacquainted. Suddenly, she too wanted to be fondled and made love to. She prayed for Rowald's speedy return. Then she prayed for the terrible ache of longing to diminish.

Lydia had been right when she said that she'd be feeling normal again as soon as her husband got home. Now she got up early in the morning, dressed and groomed herself close to perfection, tended the baby, made the bed, and kept the one large room with damaged furniture looking as good as possible. Every day she took the baby for a walk in a carriage she acquired with a few bottles of wine. She always returned with a bouquet of wild flowers picked along the way.

Ernst inquired about a job at the hospital where he was eagerly accepted.

"Erika," Ernst said, "the hospital is in desperate need of nurses. Wouldn't you be interested in going back to work?"

"No, Ernst," Lydia said with alarm. "Erika can't go to work. I need her here to help me."

She was already upset because Ernst was going to work only three days after his return.

"Lydia, my dearest, you have to realize we have a country to rebuild. Every person is needed to work. You are quite capable of managing the household and our son by yourself. Remember, this won't be like before where you were all alone. I'll be home every evening."

"I guess you're right, Ernst. I have to do it," Lydia said, taking a deep breath. "I am luckier than many women. You came back with all your limbs." She ran into his arms and gave him a long embrace.

Erika went out into the yard and stood at the street. At the three-story house across the street she saw several people engaged in the summertime evening activity—looking out of the windows and talking with neighbors. On an impulse she walked across the street and stood in front of the house. A pretty woman on the second floor smiled at her and wished her a good evening. Erika returned the greeting and blurted out boldly, "Is there possibly a room for rent in this house?"

"Strange you should ask," said the pretty woman of about forty. "I had a roomer who left yesterday. I'll come down and let you in for us to talk."

The woman, whose name was Kate Huber, showed Erika a room at the front corner of the house. It contained a plain, iron, single bed; a small table, with two wooden chairs; a wooden wardrobe, with a full length mirror; and a stand with a ceramic washbowl and pitcher.

"The rent is fifteen mark a week including the electric. The toilet is down the hall. We bathe at the public baths at the school. As you can see, there is no stove in the room, so I must warn you, should you want this room and still be here in the winter, it will be cold."

"I would like to rent the room."

"Before I agree, let's talk," Kate said.

The two women talked late into the evening. It turned out that Frau Huber had been born in Goerlitz, but left that city as a child for Berlin. After marrying and having one son, she immigrated with her husband and child to America. They lived in New York where she had another son. The family did well in spite of the economic depression that was gripping the world. Her husband was a skilled watchmaker and jeweler who had a well-paying job, she explained proudly.

The more Frau Huber talked, the more she reverted into the Silesian dialect. Her straight back stretched her full height to just under five feet. Up to this point the woman's large blue eyes sparkled with the joy of happy memories. Part of the joy was being able to freely talk again to a person without fear of saying something wrong and being thrown into jail. The Americans were governing the region and, in a way, she was one of them. She reached into a drawer and pulled out a passport.

Erika noticed the faded golden eagle with an olive branch in one talon and arrows in the other. She barely could read, "United States of America." Proudly the woman showed her the picture of herself and two young boys fused into its pages.

"Those are my sons Herbert and Walter. Walter hasn't returned from the Eastern Front yet. My Herbert was too young for the army. They tried drafting him at the end, but he was smart enough to escape and come back home."

"Excuse me, Frau Huber, but if it's agreeable with you, I would like to sleep here tonight. I'll just have to go across the street and get a few things, then finish moving in tomorrow."

"Yes, that's good. It is getting late. Let me give you keys for the house door and apartment and you can come and go as you please."

"Thank you, and maybe tomorrow you can finish telling me your story."

"Ah yes, you might have to remind me that I stopped with me living in New York with my husband and two little boys. Yes, I will tell you what happened next. I could write a book," Kate said, clapping her hands and acquiring a far off look. Then sadness brushed her face, starting with her eyes and wrinkling downward from the corners of her mouth on the otherwise smooth face.

Her face quickly lost its sadness when a little girl about five entered the room, ran toward the woman, and hugged her legs.

"Mama, Papa and I are home."

"I see. Did you have a nice visit with *Tante* Berta?" asked the mother, kissing her child.

"Yes, *Tante* had cake to eat."

"Wonderful. Say hello to Frau Zeller. She will be living here. Frau Zeller, I want you to meet my daughter, Caroline, that's spelled with a C, the English way."

The girl shook hands with Erika and made a deep curtsy.

"Now go and get your nightgown on. It's past your bedtime." Turning back to Erika, she said, "Come into the kitchen, Frau Zeller, I'll give you the keys and you can meet my husband."

At the kitchen table sat a man of about fifty. His gray hair was cut short, appearing like a fringe around his bald head. His hazel eyes were focused on some old photographs in front of him. His nose was prominent and symmetrical, his narrow lips clamped tight in concentration.

"Karl, I want you to meet Frau Zeller. She's our new roomer."

The man looked up at the young woman and his face lit up in a friendly smile.

"Welcome, Frau Zeller. Kate, I'm surprised you rent to such a beautiful woman. Don't you fear the competition?"

"With you, Karl, I have nothing to fear."

"You're right, besides you are just as pretty."

The woman gave him a loving smile then turned and took two skeleton keys off a board and handed them to Erika.

Early the next morning Erika went to the hospital and applied for work. She was hired and asked if she could start working that day. When Erika told the administrator that she did not have any white nurse uniforms, he said that there were some in a storage room which she could borrow. Wearing a uniform that was too large for her, she started working on a floor, caring for several rooms containing three beds each.

At six that evening she got off, went directly to Ernst and Lydia's house, and took the rest of her things. With the help of Ernst, it took only one trip across the street to finish the move. Frau Huber met them at the door, being eager to meet her neighbor, the doctor.

"It's a pleasure meeting you, Dr. Zeller. To think that such a handsome young man as you is a doctor," she said with awe. "While you are moving in, would you like to hear the rest of my story, Frau Zeller?"

All Erika really wanted was to get her clothes hung up, get the uniform off, put on a robe, and relax with a book. But the little woman seemed so eager to tell her story and Erika did not want to disappoint her.

Ernst sat down on a chair in Erika's room, giving Frau Huber his full attention.

"Now yesterday I left off while my husband and I were living in New York City with our two boys," she said. "Walter was seven and little Herbert was three. It was July and I went with the boys and their Sunday school class to the beach. I remember being angry that my husband did not want to go. When we returned in the evening, my husband lay in bed in great pain. His stomach was swollen and he writhed around moaning.

"I called an ambulance and we rushed him to the hospital. They operated immediately."

"It was a burst appendix," Ernst said.

"That's right. Gosh, you are a good doctor. Anyway, it was too late. The poison had gone through his body and he died."

"I'm very sorry to hear that, Frau Huber," Erika said.

"Yes, that was a tough time. I had to get a job, worked in a cafeteria. What slave drivers they were. We could never work fast enough. I had to leave the boys with a friend all day long."

"When did Mr. Huber come into your life?" Ernst asked.

"I was moving and Karl was a moving man. We did our dating as a family. On Sundays we would all go to the park or the beach, sometimes a movie or Coney Island—that is a beautiful beach with a big amusement park. He liked the boys and the boys liked him. After two years of seeing each other, we got married."

"What brought you to Germany?" asked Erika.

"We came for a visit in 'thirty-nine and while we were here, I got pregnant. Karl was so happy to have his own child, and the doctor advised me not to travel. I must admit, being pregnant at forty is a lot harder than when I was in my twenties. We decided to go back to America after the baby was born, but then the war broke out and it was too late. You see, I am an American citizen, but Karl is still a German national. Now you know the story of my life."

"You are right, Frau Huber, you should write a book," Erika said, trying to look bright-eyed. "If you would allow me, I would like to get comfortable and read for a while."

Ernst hugged her. "You must be exhausted, dear sister-in-law. I'd better get home. Would you like to join us for supper?"

"No, thank you. I'm too tired."

"I can bring you a bowl of bean soup," said Frau Huber leaving the room before Erika could protest.

Erika kicked off her shoes and lay on the bed. She never heard the landlady setting a bowl of soup on the table.

CHAPTER 17

Sigrit saw the grandfather running toward her with both hands, full of white intestines, clutched against his stomach and his eyes wide with shock. She turned and ran away, but it was like running against a hurricane. She screamed, "Help, help me, help Opa."

She felt something clutch her shoulders. She screamed again.

"Siggy, wake up, wake up. You were having a nightmare."

Slowly, she returned to reality. Greta was hugging her and trying to comfort her.

"My dear Siggy, you were having a nightmare. You shouted to help Opa."

"Yes, Opa was chasing me with his terrible wound. I know it's my fault he got killed. Will he ever forgive me? Will anyone forgive me?"

"Shush, it wasn't your fault. The French shot him. It is the war's fault. You have to forgive yourself."

Greta held her in a tight embrace and rocked her, speaking softly until she finally fell asleep. The next day in school the assignment was to write a letter to someone. Sigrit wrote in neat cursive:

> *Dearest Aunt Erika,*
> *Thank you for your letter from Stuttgart. I am really trying hard to be a good girl. The Wagner family is very good to me in spite of what I have done.*
> *I miss you very much. Now that the war is over, I hope to see you soon.*
> *Much love,*
>
> *Sigrit*

༺༻

When Erika came home from work her landlady gave her the envelope addressed to her across the street. She read the letter over and over, trying to read between the lines. What bad thing had Sigrit done? Over supper with Ernst and Lydia, the girl was the only subject of conversation. Lydia suggested that Erika simply had to go to Hollstein on her next weekend off.

It was a warm Saturday morning as Erika boarded the train. She was surprised by the number of people traveling, most with empty bags and knapsacks. In the train compartment the seats faced each other and the man opposite her had a little boy on his lap.

"Where is everybody going?" she asked the father.

"We are going hamstering."

"Hamstering?"

"Yes, we go to farmers and try to buy, beg, and barter for food."

"Are you successful at it?"

"Usually when they look at my little boy, they give me something. Even just a few potatoes helps us get by."

It was late afternoon and Sigrit was washing the windows on the front of the house. She saw a stranger walking up the street. The figure looked somehow familiar. Could it really be? She looked again, gave a shout of joy, and then ran toward the woman. She stopped a few paces from her to see how Aunt Erika would react upon seeing her. The woman's face lit up.

Without a word she opened her arms and Sigrit ran into her embrace. The two hugged, trying to make up for the months of separation. The pain and suffering they had both experienced in the past six months suddenly seemed less intense. For two souls who loved each other, now being able to touch brought peace and joy to both of them. Neither one could hold back the tears. They were tears of joy.

Sigrit led her aunt into the house. They walked down the corridor, separating the living quarters from the stable, into the large kitchen at the back of the house.

"Look, Frau Martha, who is here, my *Tante* Erika."

Martha wiped the flour off her hands and extended her right one to Erika. "I am very pleased to meet you. Siggy has told me so much about you." She pointed toward Greta who was helping her mother bake bread. "And this is my daughter Greta."

Greta shook Erika's hand and made a deep curtsy. *"Gruess Gott,* Frau Zeller."

"Gruess Gott. Greta, you can call me Erika or Aunt Erika, whichever."

"My husband should be back from the field in about an hour, we will have supper then. If you are really hungry, I can give you a piece of bread to tide you over."

Erika had not eaten since she left home, but said, "Thank you, I can wait."

"Siggy, why don't you show your aunt the guest room where she can sleep."

Sigrit took her aunt upstairs and showed her the room she shared with Greta. Then she opened the door to another bedroom that contained two single beds both against a wall with a small window between them. The ceiling was low, just barely above Erika's head. A calico cat was sleeping on one of the beds.

"That is Katzi. She must have come in through the window. Out Katzi," Sigrit said, clapping her hands.

"Let her be." Erika reached out to pet the cat. "She is so soft and pretty and look, she has six toes. Her paws are like little hands."

"Frau Martha does not want her upstairs, but sometimes Katzi sleeps in my bed. I like that."

Erika sat on the bed and pulled Sigrit next to her. "Now Siggy, tell me about the letter you wrote. What bad thing have you done?"

Sigrit folded her hands in her lap and looked at the floor. Tears ran down her cheeks and she could not speak. Erika waited, while putting her arm around Sigrit's shoulders.

Several minutes went by before Sigrit spoke. "It's my fault Opa got shot."

"What happened?"

"I forgot to close the stable door and the cow got out. Opa went looking for her. The French had a curfew after dark and Opa was still out there. He got shot and died. Oh please, *Tante* Erika, take me home with you. I love Greta and Frau Martha and Herr Sepp, but I feel so guilty. They are still nice to me, but I don't deserve it. I'm such a bad person."

"No, you are not bad. If you were bad, you would not feel guilty. It sounds to me like it was an accident. You certainly did not mean for anything bad to happen." She held the girl close while her shoulders were washed with tears. *Oh Lord, what can I do to make her feel better?*

"Please take me with you. Let us go home to Goerlitz together."

"From what I hear things are not good in Goerlitz. The Russians are there and people are fleeing to the West."

"What about Ludwig? Have you heard from him?" asked Sigrit.

"No, I don't know where he is. Neither have I heard from your Uncle Rowald."

From the bottom of the stairs they could hear Greta calling that supper would be on the table in five minutes.

"Now, sweetheart, wash your face, put on a smile, and come downstairs with me."

To Erika, the simple supper eaten off the large kitchen table was a feast. They had potatoes, spinach, and beef with gravy. Fresh strawberries with cream topped it off. They ate the meal mostly in silence. Greta was clearing the table with Sigrit's help when Sepp said, "Frau Zeller, it is such a pleasure to finally meet you. Siggy has talked about you often. Before you say anything, I just want to tell you that we enjoy having her here."

"Thank you, and please call me Erika."

"And just call us Sepp and Martha."

"Thank you, I appreciate you letting her stay with you. I would like to offer to pay you for her keep."

"Ugh, money, that stuff is worthless nowadays. That little bit of food she eats…and Greta is happy to have a little sister. That war was terrible for so many people. We lost two sons, and what good has it done for our country?"

"Nothing, nothing good at all, just a whole lot of destruction and lost and broken lives," Erika said. "My husband is missing and I have no idea where my nephew is. I pray they both return soon, along with all the other men and women still unaccounted for. Right now I am living in a single room with one bed," Erika continued. "The housing shortage in Stuttgart is critical. Every day more refugees come from the East. If you can keep her a while longer, it would really be helpful. I am her closest relative, and eventually, I hope to get legal guardianship of her."

"Like I said before, we like having Siggy with us. I am sure she told you about Opa," Sepp said.

"Yes, she feels terribly guilty."

"I have to tell you something that Opa kept a secret. The man was suffering from cancer. He was often in pain, but being a stoic Bavarian like he was, he kept it to himself. Only I and his doctor knew about it." Looking at Sigrit, he continued. "Actually, my dear, getting shot saved him from a slow and painful death."

Sigrit's face lit up. "I wish you would have told me before."

"At the time I forgot about it."

Erika looked at Sepp and he winked with one eye. *I know he's lying, but a lie that makes a person feel better is not a sin.*

Martha, who had hardly spoken all evening gave a deep sigh. "Sepp, you are terrible to keep such secrets from your wife."

"Had I told you, it would not have been a secret any longer, and you know what a private person Opa was."

"Well, you better tell that to Oma before church tomorrow. Erika, I hope you and Siggy come to church with us in the morning."

"We will be happy to." Erika felt the invitation was a command. Being Lutheran she was unfamiliar with the Catholic service. She figured she would just do what the others did.

"Frau Martha, may I sleep in the guestroom tonight with Tante Erika? You won't mind, Greta, or do you?"

Consent was given by both of them.

The family spent the evening sitting outside in the grape arbor. Sepp enjoyed his beer, Martha was knitting socks, Greta and Sigrit played checkers, and Erika absorbed the peace and harmony over a glass of white wine. No more air raids, no more gunfire, and a full belly. Life was good again for the moment. She tried putting the *if only* out of her mind and enjoyed the moment.

Sunday afternoon Sigrit, Oma, and the whole Wagner family accompanied Erika to the train station. It had been decided that Sigrit would stay in Bavaria at least until the school year was over. She was doing very well in second grade.

That morning in church Sepp had the opportunity to have a quick word with the doctor and told him about the lie he'd told about his father. The doctor agreed to back him up, in case Oma had questions about it. Sigrit had really perked up to become a much happier child.

Erika boarded the train and found a window seat. She opened the window and Martha handed her a fabric bag filled with food. In it were homemade breads, bacon, smoked sausage, potatoes, cheese, and apples.

"Thank you, thank you for everything. I cannot thank you enough. *Auf Wiedersehen*, I love all of you."

As the train pulled out, Erika reached out of the window and waved her handkerchief until the people were out of sight.

When she entered the apartment house to go to her room it was well after dark. The landlady rushed out of the living room, looking very excited.

"Frau Zeller, there is someone I want you to meet. Please come into the living room."

"Please, Frau Huber, let me put my bags away and wash my hands. I'll be right in."

"Please, don't be long."

A few minutes later Erika entered the living room. The Hubers were sitting around a table with their son Herbert and a strange young man. They each had a wine glass in front of them and were snacking on nuts.

"Frau Zeller, this is our son Walter," said Frau Huber. "He returned from the Eastern Front this morning. Walter, meet Frau Zeller."

Walter rose and walked toward Erika extending his hand. "Very pleased to meet you. Mother told me about you."

Erika reached out her hand which he took and held. His hazel eyes looked at her intensely, his smile revealing even white teeth. His brunette hair was combed straight back.

What a handsome man. I wonder if he has all his limbs. Bad girl! Remember, you are a married woman.

"Do you dance?" he asked.

"Y—y—yes," she stammered.

"Come, Frau Zeller, join us in a glass of wine," Herr Huber invited.

"Thank you, but let me bring something to the table."

Erika rushed to her room and came back with some bread, sausage, and cheese. The five people spent the evening drinking Rhine wine and enjoying the treats from Bavaria. Conversation flowed easily, spiced with many laughs. They all were optimistic that the future would be brighter than the past.

Erika felt the joy of one family being reunited after many years of cruel separation. One family, where everyone not only survived, but had all their limbs and, seemingly, their sanity. She felt hopeful that the good fortune of the Hubers could rub off and her husband was on his way home, too.

Please, dear Lord, bring my Rowald home, too. Please let him be knocking on the door of the apartment in Goerlitz this very moment. Oh, Lord, I pray in Jesus name. Amen.

CHAPTER 18

Early one morning Jutta was awakened by pounding on the apartment door. She put a robe over her nightgown and yielded to the demands of whoever was out there. Anxiously she opened the door and beheld a tall skinny figure dressed in rags. Fear clutched her heart until the figure spoke in a calm voice.

"Excuse me, gracious lady, I was sure I was at the apartment of my Aunt Erika. Could you tell me if she still lives in this house? I am her nephew Ludwig."

"Oh, Ludwig, please come in. I've been expecting you."

Surprised, Ludwig entered the foyer of the apartment.

"You must be wondering who I am. Well, the day Erika took you and your sister to the train station she rescued me and my two little boys. We were refugees from near Breslau and she was so kind to take us in, for we had no place to go. I am taking care of her apartment while she is in Stuttgart. She will be so glad to hear from you and to know that you are alive. Oh, here I go rambling on. You look exhausted.

Go to the bathroom and wash up and I'll get you some clothes."

A half hour later a clean young man dressed in his uncle's clothes, entered the kitchen where a pot of oatmeal was sitting on the stove. The woman and two small boys sat at the table eating.

"Good, you made it while the food is still hot." She got up, filled a bowl, and put it on the table. "By the way, my name is Jutta and that is Maxi and the little one is Fritzi," she said, pointing to the two, tow-haired boys.

"You will have to tell me all about where you have been. Your aunt will be so happy when she gets my next letter. I don't know what she will do—if she's coming back to Goerlitz or will stay in Stuttgart. There has been no news about your uncle, Dr. Zeller. When I first saw you I thought you might be him. If he should come back, I would look for another place to live. Here I go again, not letting you get a word in edgewise. Now please tell me where you have been."

Ludwig took a deep breath and began his tale.

"...and after we escaped from the Russians my friend Heinz and I traveled mostly at night. We begged and stole food from farmers and wherever there was something to eat. One time I was fortunate to find a pair of dirty shoes sitting outside a barn. They just happen to almost fit me, so I left mine in their place. On mine, the soles consisted of a hole with a little frame of leather.

"When we got near Eichdorf, Heinz went home, and after a day of rest, I left. I did not wish to run into Frau Kempf again. Whenever I saw Russian soldiers I hid. I did not want to take the chance of being sent on a Siberian vacation trip.

When I think of the poor kids on the train, my blood runs cold. Who knows if anyone will ever see them again?"

"The Russians here have been pretty nice," Jutta said. "Just last week they had a big festival for the children in the park where all the children got milk and cookies and even some chocolate for them and the mothers. I must say, there were some wild soldiers when they first came, but for the most part they are well behaved."

"Do you think it will be safe for me to walk on the street?"

"I think you will be all right. You should really go to city hall and see about getting some ration stamps. You can stay here, since this is your aunt's apartment. I suppose she is still paying rent since no one tried to evict me."

"Thank you, if you don't mind, I could really use some sleep."

"The boys have been sleeping in the second bedroom, I'll just have them sleep with me and you can have that room."

Before Jutta had a chance to change the sheets, Ludwig had removed his shoes and flopped into bed. Just a few months earlier he'd had no concept of how luxurious a bed could be. There was so much now he would never take for granted. In a matter of seconds, he was asleep.

※

When Erika received the letter from Jutta she was overjoyed. It felt as if a boulder had dropped off her heart.

What a relief to know Ludwig is alive. Now, good Lord, let me hear from or about Rowald. It would be better to know that he is dead than not knowing. I have to get Ludwig to come here. That's what I'll do, send him some money to get here. Sigrit needs to see him. Yes, that's the answer. Ludwig needs to see his sister.

She quickly wrote a letter to Goerlitz and enclosed some money for train fare.

It was a Friday when Erika returned from the hospital after a long hard day. When Walter heard her entering the apartment, he intercepted her before she could reach her room.

"Frau Zeller, you look like you could use a little fun."

"What kind of fun do you have in mind, Herr Huber?"

"Dinner and dancing. I would like to take you into the city to a restaurant where a band is playing nice dance music. I realize you are married, but what harm would it do to keep a friend company?"

"If we are friends, Herr Huber, then you might as well call me Erika. But I had a hard day at work—"

"If you are too tired to dance, maybe we can just eat. We do need to eat, wouldn't you agree?"

Seeing the pleading look in his eyes, she reluctantly said yes. An hour later they were ready to disembark from the streetcar at a restaurant in downtown Stuttgart. Most of the building was a ruin, but a large elegant dining room and the kitchen had been salvaged. A three piece band in one corner was playing romantic music. A few couples were on the dance floor.

They ate their meal mostly in silence. Both of them had so many questions they wanted to ask, but were afraid to. Erika looked at the gold band on her right hand and thought of Rowald. Maybe she was not a wife any more, but a widow. If she was a widow then it would be all right to be with another man.

Oh God, please let me know, am I a wife or a widow?

"They are playing a nice waltz. Do you have the energy for a little spin on the dance floor?"

"Just one dance, Walter."

The music, in combination with being held by a man and moving in time with the melody, gave Erika renewed energy. After the waltz, Walter showed his skill in a fox trot. He led the dance so skillfully she could follow him as if they had been dancing together for years. One dance after another. Time became meaningless. The moment was now and the present was good. Between dances, they enjoyed some wine, but quickly went onto the dance floor to burn up the alcohol.

"Six in the morning will come way too soon," Erika said as they parted outside her room door. "That's when I have to get up,"

"That gives you four hours. You just have to sleep fast."

"Good night, Walter, sleep well."

"Good night, Erika, I thoroughly enjoyed myself. I have a lot of years of fun to make up for. Will you honor me with your company again?"

"Thank you, I would like that."

His lips came close to hers, then he abruptly turned, walked away, and went into his bedroom.

Erika lay in bed with the music still playing in her ears. She felt tired and energized at the same time. *I'll just lie here in the dark and let my body rest.*

She fell asleep with Walter's smiling face swimming before her.

The next evening Erika went into the kitchen to heat up some soup she had brought home from the hospital. Frau Huber greeted her cheerfully.

"Good evening, Frau Zeller. Did you and Walter have a good time last night?"

"Yes we did. He is a very good dancer."

"That I know. He was dancing before he was born. When I was pregnant and heard music he would kick in time. He certainly is making up for the war years, has already left for the evening. I saw him get on the streetcar with a girl that lives down the street."

Erika felt a stab to her heart. *No, you can't be jealous. He has a right to see other girls. Besides, he is younger than you. Behave, Erika.*

"That is nice," she said cheerfully. "I'm sure they will have a good time."

Caroline entered the kitchen wearing a light blue cotton dress. "Mama, look it fits. Good evening, Frau Zeller," she said shaking her hand and making a curtsy. "This dress is the prettiest one."

"We got a package from America today," Frau Huber said. "I still have friends in New York and my one friend has a daughter. She sent some outgrown clothes and some other things like peanut butter and shortening—"

"Yes," interrupted Caroline, "the big yellow post coach was loaded with packages and the postman had one for us. I even got to pet one of the horses. Mama held me up to pet the neck."

"When things settle down, we want to return to America," Frau Huber said with sparkling eyes. "I have more good news. Walter got a job working for the Americans as an interpreter."

"That is wonderful."

"Yes, both Karl and Herbert are working for them at the railroad, using their English skills. I told some soldiers I would wash their laundry. They give me wonderful detergent and pay me with cigarettes. I have never been so well paid."

Erika spent the rest of the evening in her room, lying on the bed and reading. She had a hard time concentrating on her book and thought of Walter dancing with the girl down the street. She fought feeling jealous. It was well after two in the morning when she heard Walter quietly enter the apartment and go to his room. Only then did she settle down to sleep.

Sunday she got off from work at two in the afternoon. Upon entering the apartment, she again was intercepted by Walter.

"Erika, good, you're home early. It's such a beautiful day and if you are game, we can go and watch soccer. We can sit on the hill overlooking the soccer field and enjoy lunch. I made us some peanut butter sandwiches. I hope you like it."

"I have never eaten peanut butter."

"Well in that case, you are in for a new adventure."

Erika quickly changed into a flowered summer dress and the two walked to the soccer field. Walter carried a wicker basket with the refreshments. They watched the game for a while, but neither one found it particularly interesting. The teams consisted of very young players and veterans just playing again after many years.

"Erika, there are too many people around here. Let's go into the forest where we can talk and not have people watch us eat."

They walked deeper into the forest to a clearing with a large oak tree in the middle.

"My favorite tree. I'm glad it's still here. I spent many an hour sitting under it when I was a boy, daydreaming and watching squirrels chase each other through the branches. A perfect place for our picnic, don't you agree?"

"Yes, it is lovely here."

"And no one around."

They sat on a large towel and ate their sandwiches washed down by wine. Then Walter lay back and looked up into the branches with a contented look on his face. Erika expected that he would try to make advances at her and she would have to discourage him. His total lack of interest actually intrigued her.

"Walter, how old are you, if I may ask?"

"I'm twenty-two, is that too young for you?"

"No. I'm twenty-six, is that too old for you?"

"No. But the fact that you are possibly married is a problem."

"What do you mean by possibly married?"

"You have not heard from your husband in how many months now? You say he was on the Eastern Front. Well, I was on the Eastern Front and I know what it was like. I am more than fortunate to have not only come home, but to have come home in one piece. I hate to say this, but there is a very good chance you will never see your husband again."

Big tears rolled down Erika's cheeks.

"I'm sorry. I did not want to make you cry. Please forgive me."

He took her in his arms and, gently rocking her, kissed her cheeks. She returned the tenderness by kissing him on the cheek. A slight turn of his head landed her third kiss on his lips. The next kiss was delivered by him, only not just on her lips, but with his tongue pushed deep into her mouth. His tongue moved and spoke volumes to her without words.

When they separated, he looked deep into her eyes and said, "Erika, I love you."

"Walter, even though we've only known each other for a few days, you bring out feelings I have not felt in years. Oh, Walter, keep hugging me."

Again they kissed, a long deep kiss that tasted so good. Passion surged through their bodies. Erika felt she was the little boy with a finger in the dyke trying to keep the water out.

The hole got bigger and her whole fist could not keep the flood away. She unbuttoned the front of her dress and exposed her breasts to him. His hands gently stroked them, then his tongue tickled her nipples. She groaned with pleasure.

"Yes, please do it, do it now. It has been years since I have had a man. Oh, Walter please…"

Afterward, they lay on the towel in each other's arms, wearing satisfied grins.

"I had almost forgotten how good a man could feel."

"I have had a woman on occasion, but this has been very special. There must be love involved. You are a very special lady and I hope we can go out often together."

"Yes, I'll post my work hours in the kitchen so you know when I am free to go out with you. I hope to go dancing with you again."

"We will make it happen," Walter assured her.

They walked home, holding hands. Whenever a young woman approached them, Erika could see jealousy on their faces. There were so many women who would never find a husband and so many men that returned with broken bodies and spirits. Erika felt lucky to have such a handsome and healthy man walking beside her.

CHAPTER 19

Sigrit and Greta stood at the train station waiting for the local 3:15 to come in from Munich. They were expecting Aunt Erika who had written that she would be coming for a visit and had a big surprise for Sigrit.

"How much longer before the train gets here?"

Greta looked at her wrist watch, a present she had gotten for her twelfth birthday.

"The train is supposed to arrive in seven minutes."

"That long? Do I look okay? I'm lucky you have such nice, outgrown dresses."

"You look very pretty," Greta assured her. "And those red ribbons look wonderful in your dark braids. They are almost to your waist now,"

The minutes dragged by until finally the anticipated black steam engine pulling the train slowly came around the curve. Once it stopped at the station, people emerged from the train until finally Sigrit saw her beloved aunt. Then her eyes widened. Could it really be? She let out a scream of joy and ran toward them. Ludwig stooped down with arms extended ready to scoop his little sister into them. She slung her arms around his neck and cried.

It was a good minute later before she could finally speak and all she managed to say was, "Ludwig, oh my dear Ludwig. I'm so happy to see you."

"Good to see you too, little sister. You have really grown."

When he stood up, she looked at him with awe, "I can't believe how tall you are." She turned to Greta. "And this is my *big sister* Greta. Greta, meet Ludwig."

She extended her hand to him and with a shy smile said, *"Gruess Gott,* it is a pleasure to meet you."

He held her hand while he looked into her eyes and his face lit up even more. "Aunt Erika told me about you. It is my pleasure meeting you, Greta."

"Come, my parents are curious what the big surprise is. It's not far to our house."

When the four entered the big kitchen, Martha washed the bread dough off her hands and gave Erika a big hug. When introduced to Ludwig, she smiled. "Young man, welcome to our house. Do you want a job? We certainly could use your help around here. Do you know anything about farming?"

"As a matter of fact, I do."

"I bet Sepp will offer you a job, but let it be a surprise when he makes the offer." Looking at Erika, she said, "You know how men are. They think we women have no sense."

"Not all men, Martha, but I realize Bavarian men feel that way," Erika said with a conspiratorial smile. "I was fortunate to get some oranges to bring along."

She laid six oranges on the table. Greta and Sigrit each picked one up and smelled it. Neither girl had ever seen an orange before. Both tried biting into it like an apple.

"No, you have to peel it like this," Erika explained.

"Where did you get this?" Martha asked,

"From the Americans. My landlady does their laundry and they pay her with cigarettes and food items. She gave them to me."

When Sepp arrived from the field, he too was delighted to meet Ludwig and soon offered the young man a job.

Ludwig pretended to mull over the offer, then said, "I think working for a while will be good. I have finished eighth grade and really am not inclined to follow academia. Working on a farm will be good and to be here with my little sister, I could not ask for more."

"That is another thing we need to discuss," Erika said. "Eventually I want to become her legal guardian. Right now things are not good in Stuttgart or any other city. Housing is very scarce and there is a great food shortage."

"We know," Sepp said. "We get our share of hamsters. Siggy can stay with us until the situation improves. She seems happy here. Speak up, child. Do you want to stay here a while longer?"

"I would like that, especially with Ludwig here," Sigrit said, looking very happy.

"There, that is settled. Martha, are we eating soon?"

"In just a few minutes. Girls, please set the table."

Knowing that Ludwig and Sigrit were happy and well taken care of for the time being gave Erika great peace of mind. Her job kept her occupied five to six days a week. Occasionally Ernst and Lydia invited her for dinner and she could enjoy her new nephew. They were searching for a better place to live, but so far nothing was available. Her greatest pleasure was going out with Walter. Dinner and dancing occupied the evenings frequently, and when Sunday was nice, they went to the soccer games. They were surprised how private the clearing in the woods remained. After their first love making, they used protection, but a little voice kept telling Erika, *You are closing the gate after the horses got out.*

Toward the end of summer Erika made an appointment with a gynecologist. He confirmed what she already knew. That evening she asked Walter to go for a walk with her. While they were walking on a path going through fields ripe with grain Erika said, "Walter, I have something to tell you."

"What is it?"

"I am carrying a baby, and it's yours."

"Are you sure?"

"Of course, I'm sure. You are the only man I have been with since my husband two years ago."

"No, I meant are you sure you are pregnant? We have been careful."

"Except for the very first time, and that did it."

"Wow, that means I will be a father." He hugged her, lifting her feet off the ground and swinging her. "We will just have to get married right away."

Getting down on one knee he took her hand and said, "My dear Erika, will you do me the honor of becoming my wife? I love you now and always will."

"I love you too, Walter, but I might still have a husband."

"Then we will have the military search for him, and if they can't find him, they can declare him dead."

"Then there is another complication. I have a niece who is eight and I am her closest relative. I need to become her guardian."

"That means I would be a double father. That would be fine. Another thing, I want to return to America and live there. Would you be willing to go with me?"

"I would be willing to do that. Any more complications to us getting married?"

"I can't think of any at the moment, but I'm sure that is not the end of it. I love you, Erika, and I think we can be very happy together." He took her into his arms and gently kissed her.

"Come, let's go home," he said. "And tell the family our plans. I'm sure they will be delighted."

Later that evening Walter and Erika told his parents.

"Pregnant? How can you let yourself get pregnant?" Frau Huber shouted. "You are a nurse. Don't you know about these things?"

"Please, Kate, keep your voice down. The neighbors will hear you," Karl said in a calm, quiet voice. "I could see from day one that those two were in love and things like that happen. It would have been nice if they could have married first, but the young people have all the lost war years to make up for." He walked over to the two and gave

Erika a warm hug. "Let me be the first to congratulate you and welcome you into our family."

"Forgive my outburst. Karl is right," Kate said, giving each a hug. "I too wish you both all the happiness. Just think, Karl, that will make us grandparents. Come, we have to celebrate. Karl, please get the bottle of wine we saved for a very special occasion. A grandmother, me a grandmother, Karl, do I look like a grandmother?"

"Not at all, you look like a young girl."

※※※

The rest of the summer went by swiftly. The bureaucratic search for Rowald produced no evidence of him being alive. In early November Erika received a document declaring her a widow.

The wedding was a small celebration. The nuptials took place in city hall and then the celebrants had a small reception in the Huber's apartment. The Huber family was present along with Dr. Ernst and Lydia Zeller and Karl's sister Berta and her husband Gerald. Part of the celebration was to move Erika's bed into Walter's room that had a stove. The feat was done with much singing and laughter. While Dr. Ernst was making another toast to the new couple, he also mentioned that he would soon start rebuilding his house.

"Dr. Zeller," Berta said, "where are you going to live while the construction is going on"

"They are converting the underground bunkers into apartments," Ernst said to Berta and Gerald, who stood next to his wife. "We'll just have to endure living in one until the house is ready. It can't be too much worse than our basement. Who knows? It might even be better."

"I have a solution," Gerald said. "We have an extra room in our house. You and your family can occupy it until your house is ready."

"Oh, Herr Hahn, that would be wonderful. How could I ever repay you?"

"That you can do by hiring me to draw up the plans for the house and supervising the construction. I am an architect, you know."

"You have the job."

Catching Lydia's eye, he motioned her over and told her the good news. He announced it to everyone in the room and received happy clapping and shouting.

Then Karl announced, "Now that we are all family, let's drop addressing each other in the formal way and use first names. We shall drink to friendship."

They all raised their glasses, then one-by-one interlocked arms and drank a sip, and sealed the relationship with a small kiss.

It took quite a while before they all drank with everyone else. Caroline was the only child in the room, and she welcomed the new *aunt* and *uncle* into her life with happy claps and laughter.

To have new relatives living across the street was the best part of the wedding.

Kate had managed to scratch up quite a feast. The celebrants squeezed around the dining room table to enjoy sandwiches and salads and even some cake.

Walter stared at Erika who looked radiant in a white silk blouse and dark blue skirt with one white rose in her brunette hair.

"Happy?" he asked.

"Yes, very. I love you so much and your family, too.

"We'll have a good life together."

"We'll *make* it a good life together," she said kissing him on his lips.

CHAPTER 20

1948:

"Wake up, Sigrit, wake up, get dressed quickly. Come, you have to see this."

"What is it?" Sigrit asked in a sleepy voice.

"We will be passing the Statue of Liberty soon," Erika answered. "Come, you'll want to see this,"

It had taken three years for Walter and Erika to get all the proper documents to enable them to come to America. The other Huber family had already emigrated a year earlier and settled in Baltimore. They were able to sponsor Walter and Erika, along with Sigrit and two year old Conrad to come to the States.

Ludwig, now eighteen, had remained in Bavaria with the Wagner family. They treated him like a son and Greta considered him her surrogate brother.

Just before Walter and his family boarded the ship to go to America, war clouds again threatened. The Iron Curtain divided Germany and the Russians blockaded Berlin. No one expected that West Berlin could survive as an island of freedom in the Soviet Block. Had it not been for the Berlin Airlift by the Allies, the city surely would have fallen. Erika doubted that she would ever see her hometown of Goerlitz again. She gave all the apartment contents to Jutta, who had gotten a job in town. Occasionally, she received a friendly letter from Jutta written on poor quality paper.

For Erika, life was good. She and Walter were deeply in love. Sigrit, now eleven, seemed happy with them and little Conrad was a beautiful and healthy little boy. They all were optimistic and eager to start a new life in the United States. Erika had been studying English for two years before they left Germany and had almost mastered the language. Sigrit had only been living with them in Stuttgart for two months and was only starting to learn it.

The ship docked in Hoboken and soon the passengers could disembark. Beyond a barrier, people were waiting to receive their loved ones. There was Karl and Kate with Herbert and Caroline. The newcomers had to wait for all their luggage to be unloaded before they could pass through customs and finally hug their loved ones. Kate was crying tears of joy while the families were hugging. Sigrit felt like a stranger. She had only met the Hubers once while she was in Bavaria. But Kate and Caroline made her feel welcome with presents of jewelry from a dime store.

That afternoon they took an air-conditioned train to Baltimore. When they emerged from the train, the Baltimore August heat and humidity took their breath away. Never before had Erika and Sigrit felt such heat.

Once over the shock, Erika smiled and said, "One thing is sure, we are not going to freeze today."

Everyone laughed. "That's for sure," Karl said. "Now we'll take two cabs to get us home."

The taxis stopped in front of a two-story, brick row house. Kate, along with Herbert and Caroline, got out. "We'll have supper ready in about an hour. We'll see you then. Karl will show you the house we rented for you."

Karl got into the second cab and they drove to the next block.

"Here we are. Come in. We hope you like the house."

Erika and Walter emerged from the taxi and looked at the house with amazement. The brick house was freshly painted and, not only had the bricks been painted, but the cement between the bricks was painted in straight white lines. The three steps leading to the front door were clean white marble.

The door opened into the living room. It was sparsely furnished with wicker outdoor furniture.

"We were able to get some bare necessities at a goodwill store nearby. When you replace it, you can always use it in the backyard," Karl said.

The dining room had an old wooden table and four chairs. The little kitchen had a door leading out into a narrow, dirt back yard.

"That is a huge refrigerator," Erika commented.

"That is a standard size in this country. You will need it for sure. It comes with the house."

"You have done so much for us. We hope to repay you real soon," Walter said with an undertone of worry. "How much is the rent?"

"Forty-five dollars a month. When you start getting paid, you'll be able to reimburse us in no time. By the way, didn't I tell you? You have a job waiting at the same place I work."

"That's great. When can I start?"

"This coming Monday. That'll give you five days to get settled in."

Erika started walking up the narrow staircase to inspect the second floor, followed by Sigrit. One room contained a double bed, the other room a single bed and wooden dresser.

"Who will sleep in that bed?" asked Sigrit.

"We'll get more furniture soon. Don't worry, dear." Opening another door revealed a small third room, totally empty. But finding the bathroom with a tub brought shouts of joy—no more public bath houses.

After the inspection, the five people walked to the other house. It was early evening and, on the shady side of the street, people were sitting on the steps visiting with their neighbors. Karl was acquainted with many people by now and introduced his son and family to them. Erika thought it quite strange that only first names were used, and such short names at that.

"Doesn't anybody have a long name? All those Bob, Ted, Dick, Dot, Stef. Only few people have real names."

"Their names are Robert, Theodore, Richard, Dorothy, and Stefany, but people like their names shortened. That's just the way it is."

"Everybody seems very friendly," Walter said. "I was afraid we would find people prejudiced because we are Germans."

"You will find some prejudice, but many of these people are second generation Americans and they remember their parents telling them of coming over from Europe. Just remain friendly, kill them with kindness, and you'll do okay. Here we are. I'm getting hungry, how about you?"

"I could eat a horse," Walter said as they entered the house.

The table was covered with a cold supper: bread and rolls with a variety of lunch meats and a tossed salad. They had iced tea and coca cola to drink. Sigrit had never drunk a soft drink before. She was eager to try Coca Cola. She took a sip and made a sour face.

"Ugh, this is sickeningly sweet. Why do so many people like this?"

"That's the American way. You'll get used to it," said Kate, who was referred to as Oma by Sigrit. "Now today we speak German at the table, but starting tomorrow, we speak only English. Sigrit, it won't take you long to learn the language. Caroline had it mastered in about six months."

"Yes," interjected eight-year-old Caroline. "When I went to school, they had an English class for kids that had just come to America. There were kids from China and Italy, Holland, and Russia. I made friends with the Russian girl. She lives nearby."

"And tomorrow I'll take you girls shopping," said Kate. "Nothing makes you look more like a greenhorn than the old clothes you are wearing."

"But I don't know if we can afford it right now," Erika said.

"Your first dress is a gift from us," Karl told her. "You'll be surprised how cheap the clothes are here. You girls will have fun shopping."

※※※

That night Sigrit was invited to sleep with Caroline in her room. The girls settled into a bunk bed, Sigrit on the bottom and Caroline on top. The room was hot, being directly under a flat black roof. Even after dark the air was hot with no breeze. The girls had a chance to talk and start getting really acquainted. Caroline's German was stiff.

"I hope you don't lose your language," said Sigrit.

"I don't get a chance to practice it anymore."

"We'll have to speak German together in secret."

"Talking about secret, do you know what your name means in English?"

"No, what"

"Geheimnis."

"Really? My middle name is Elisabeth. Would that be better?"

"Yes, then they would call you Betty or Liz or even Elli."

"Which name sounds the most American?"

"Either Liz or Betty."

"I'll have to think about it. I like the sound of Betty, maybe I'll call myself that. Good night."

"*Gute Nacht,* Sigrit.

Next day the women of the family took a streetcar to Howard Street where one store was next to the other. The big department stores exhibited their merchandise in artistic window displays.

"Those are the stores we look at, down the street are the stores where we buy," Kate said.

They went into a store where the windows were jam packed with merchandise. On the third floor was the children's department where Sigrit got a summer dress and a bathing suit. One floor lower had ladies dresses. Erika had never seen so many pretty dresses in one place before. She had a hard time deciding which dress she wanted.

"Kate, why don't you just pick one for me? I like them all."

"How about this blue shirtwaist? It emphasizes your lovely figure."

In the housewares department, Erika bought some household essentials. Then they went to Lexington Market where fresh meats and produce were available. The newcomers had never before seen such an abundance of food. Erika remembered the long lines she used to stand in at the grocery stores. Now there were mountains of food with merchants eager to make a sale. They all smiled and thanked the customers graciously when they took the money. Everybody had their hands full of paper shopping bags when they emerged onto the street again.

"We have too much to carry to wait for a streetcar," Kate said. She raised her arm and a cab pulled up. "Get in. We'll ride home."

That afternoon Kate and Erika were cooking with the help of Sigrit. Karl and Herbert were at work. Walter was at a playground with Conrad and Caroline. That evening both families sat at the dinner table, speaking English. Sigrit was eager to speak, and when there was a lull in the conversation, she said in halting English, looking around the table, "I need your help."

"How can we help you? asked Kate.

"I need—"

Then she looked at Erika, who said, "I need," mouthing the rest of the sentence with a nod.

"I need a new name."

"What is your middle name?" Herbert inquired speaking very slowly while brushing a wave of dark brown hair out of his face. He was the taller of the two brothers with a height of over six feet.

"Elisabeth, I want to be Betty."

"No, Betty won't do," Herbert said. "The girl I'll marry is called Betty."

"What? You have a girlfriend? Kate asked. "Now that is news to me. Where do you know her from?"

"From work. She works at the factory and we meet in the cafeteria for lunch." He proceeded to pull a picture out of his wallet. "Here, you can look at this picture," he said, handing it to his mother.

She looked at it and handed the picture to Karl. "Pretty, she looks Jewish. Is she?" asked Kate.

"I don't know, and if she is, it won't make any difference. I love her. She doesn't know it yet, but she is the girl I'll marry."

"Well, I hope to meet her soon," said Karl. "You really should ask her out on a date."

"That's exactly what we're doing Saturday night. Dinner and a movie."

"If I cannot be Betty, then I keep my old name." Sigrit said, with resolve in halting English.

"Sigrit is a pretty name," Kate said. "It means sweet victory. "Siggy sounds quite American, too." Kate raised her glass of iced tea and everyone followed suite.

"To Sigrit, our dear Siggy" They shouted and drank their tea, then clapped their hands. Even little Conrad clapped his hands and banged at the tray on his high chair, sitting at the table next to his mother. Sigrit blushed and looked down, but she felt warm and wanted in the circle of this family. She missed her brother, but she knew he was happy with the Wagner family in Bavaria.

Four years ago she never would have imagined she would be in America now. This was a new adventure, and she was eager to meet it. The horror of finding her parents hanging in the attic still haunted her. What used to be a constant vision had slowly faded into a shorter episode arising several times a day. There was a time she thought that she could never be happy again, but now she found herself laughing more. When that horrible vision came up, she would think of beautiful mountains or walking in a lovely meadow, picking flowers. She decided she was a survivor and would relish the joys and deal with the pains life offered. At the moment, life was good.

CHAPTER 21

Saturday dawned hot and sunny, filled with excitement in the Walter Huber household. The Goodwill truck pulled up with furniture for delivery. Everybody now had their own bed with used, but sanitized mattresses. Walter and Erika were ecstatic to be able to set up a household of their own. The little money they came with was almost worthless. Their parents lent them one hundred dollars to get started with. Erika counted the few dollars that were left after the purchases had been made.

"We have thirteen dollars and eighty-nine cents left to last until you get paid, Walter. Do you think we'll make it?"

"We have a refrigerator full of food. If I get paid in a week, we will make it."

"It would really help if I could get a little job, too," Erika said. "I wonder if your mother would be willing to watch the children for me to find any kind of work."

In the afternoon Karl and Kate came over with Caroline to see what Walter and his family had done to the house.

There were curtains on the windows and four additional chairs spread throughout the house that could be squeezed around the table. They also added another chest of drawers and an upholstered easy chair.

"Nice, very nice," said Kate. "Erika, you know how to stretch a dollar. Good for you."

"Thank you, Kate, I want to ask you. Would you be willing to watch the children if I get a job? I was thinking I might be able to get a part time job, then we could pay back the money we owe you. I also don't expect you to babysit for nothing."

"I'd be happy to watch my grandchildren. We can discuss pay if you make lots of money."

"Thank you, thank you. I'll start looking for work on Monday."

"Do you have any plans for tomorrow?" Karl asked.

"No, you got any ideas?" Walter pondered.

"Kate, go on, tell them what we are doing."

"In the morning we are going to church. There is a Lutheran church that has service in German. It would be nice for Sigrit. The church is within walking distance. Then we'll come home, grab our picnic lunch, and take a bus to the beach. We hope you can join us."

"Going to church, we can do, but I don't know if we can afford the beach."

"I'll tell you what," Karl said. "This week we'll take you to the beach, next time you can take us."

"Sounds like a deal to me," Walter said. "Siggy, you get a chance to try your new bathing suit."

Sigrit was not quite sure what Walter said to her in English, but she knew it was good so she smiled and clapped her hands.

Sunday morning all the Hubers, dressed in their Sunday best, walked to Zion Church located near city hall. The men wore suits and Erika and Sigrit wore their new dresses. The red brick church building dated back to 1800. The newcomers took the age for granted until Kate pointed out that such age for a building made it a historic landmark. Herbert was already on his way to the beach. He planned to pick up his girlfriend and save a picnic table at the beach for everyone.

The church service was held in German. Erika noted that there were almost as many men in church as women. In Germany the church was attended mostly by women. After the service the pastor greeted all the people as they left—something else she had not seen in Germany. The par- ishioners were friendly and gave the newcomers hugs. It gave Erika and Sigrit a very warm feeling, and both decided that coming to America was a wonderful choice. They were invited to stay for coffee after the service, but Kate declined. She promised they would stay next time.

At home everyone changed their clothes, grabbed the lunch, and hurried to the bus stop to catch the bus to Bay Shore Beach. Since it was such a hot Sunday, the beach was rather crowded. It took them a good ten minutes searching among the many picnic tables to find Herbert. He was engrossed in talking to the pretty young lady sitting with him. She had dark wavy hair and a slim sun-kissed body. The red bathing suit she wore emphasized her narrow waist and ample curves.

"There you are. We were expecting you to look up and wave at us," said Kate.

"Mom, Pop, I would like for you to meet Betty Burger. Betty, meet my mother, father, my brother Walter, his wife Erika, their son Conrad, my little sister Caroline, and Erika's niece Sigrit."

Betty shook hands with everyone as they were introduced. "It's a pleasure meeting all of you."

"We are happy to meet you, young lady," said Karl.

"Burger, is that a German name?" asked Kate.

"My father is a Russian Jew. He married my mother who is a Catholic."

"What does that make you?" asked Karl.

"Betty is a Catholic," Herbert said assertively. "I hope you don't have any problem with that."

"No, no, not at all," Kate said quickly. "Now let's get changed and go into the water, then we'll eat."

They wove their way through all the people sitting and lying on the sand then entered the Chesapeake Bay, walking on the sandy bottom. Betty, Sigrit, and Caroline held hands since they could barely swim. The water was shallow for a long way making it a friendly beach for non-swimmers. Sigrit had never been to a beach before. Caroline felt like an old hand having been there a number of times.

"You know, Siggy, you have to do what I tell you since you are my niece," Caroline said.

"Yes, Aunt Caroline, but you better not tell me to do anything bad."

"I want you to stand with your legs apart so I can swim between them."

"I thought you could not swim?"

"I swim a little. This is fun. Betty, let me swim under yours, too." Sigrit and Caroline both swam between legs of anyone who would stand still. Soon other children joined them. That game went on until they were fetched by Walter to come and eat.

After lunch Herbert and Betty went for a walk along the water's edge. Karl and Kate found a shady spot under some trees and lay down on a blanket. Walter and Erika helped the three children construct a sand castle. Walter anxiously watched the gathering of cumulus clouds.

"We better go into the water for a quick swim and then get ready to go home," he said. "This looks like a bad thunderstorm coming."

After about five minutes they joined Karl and Kate at the blanket.

"Mom, Pop, look at the sky. We better get ready and catch the bus. There is some real bad weather coming."

"You're right. I hadn't noticed," Karl said. "Those thundershowers can get vicious. Where's Herbert?"

"Last I saw they were walking that way," answered Erika with a wave of her arm. "Siggy, go and find them, tell them we are leaving, and come right back."

"*Ja, Tante.*" She ran off in search of her uncle.

A few minutes later she returned. "They said they don't want to leave yet. Herbert will be home after he takes Betty home."

At the bus stop, a bus was waiting. The driver was reading a newspaper. Only one young couple was sitting in the back.

"You folks have enough of the beach already?"

"We don't want to get caught in a thunderstorm. When is the bus leaving?" Karl asked.

"In twelve minutes."

Several families got on the bus before it pulled out. They were about half-way home when the sky opened and water came down in buckets. The wind rocked the bus and visibility was almost zero.

"I'm worried about Herbert and Betty," Kate said. "I hope they are okay."

"I'm sure they have enough sense to get in out of the rain," Walter assured her.

Before the bus reached the stop near their home the rain had stopped and the sun came out more intensely than ever. The rain cooled only briefly, but the humidity rose as a result.

Later that evening the Hubers were all at the senior Huber house playing cards when Herbert arrived.

"You were smart leaving when you did," he said. "Soon the wind came up and blew the sand. We all got sandblasted. People rushed for the shelter where the tables were and a few got hit by lightning. Ambulances came to rush them to the hospital, but rumor has it that one person got killed. When Betty and I got a bus it was so crowded that we had to stand all the way into town." He paused for a breath. "Well, how do you like Betty?"

"She seems very nice…She's pretty…I like her…" were the comments from the family.

"She likes all of you, too. That is good, since we are now going steady."

"Going steady? What exactly does that mean?" Kate asked.

"It means we will only date each other."

"But Herbert, you are so young, and she is your first girlfriend," protested Kate.

"I *am* twenty-one. She might be my first girlfriend, but she is everything I want in a woman and I love her. As soon as I get some money saved up, I plan to marry her." Having said that, Herbert went upstairs to take a shower.

⁐⊰⊱⁐

The sun was just starting to show its first rays when Erika handed Walter a brown bag with his lunch in it and walked with him to the front door. Once outside, she kissed him and he headed toward his stepfather's house so they could walk to work together. When Erika turned around to go back into the house, she saw it. The picture gave her a stab through her heart. The good feelings she had from the last few days were suddenly obliterated.

Her first thought was that she did not want her niece to see it. She was afraid the nightmares might return. The symbol of so much suffering in the young girl's life was now painted on the newly painted green door. She had to get rid of it. She got a bucket of water and a brush, but scrub as hard as she might, she could not erase the large white swastika.

After seeing that both children were still sleeping soundly, she rushed to her mother-in-law's house. Her frantic knocks were answered by a still-sleepy Kate.

"Mom, there is a big white swastika painted on my door. What should I do about it? Has that ever happened to you?"

"No, it hasn't, thank goodness. Can you scrub it off?"

"No, the paint is dry."

"Maybe the landlord, Mr. Petucci, has some matching paint and can paint over it."

"I'm just so worried that Siggy will see it and get really upset. That poor child has suffered so much under the Nazis."

"I'll tell you what, after the children get up and eat breakfast, you bring them over here. I'll take them to the playground. You can call the landlord from the drugstore."

"Thank you, I'll do that."

Later that morning, Mr. Petucci drove up in his navy blue Cadillac. He was an old man who spoke with a strong Italian accent and many hand gestures.

"That's a terrible thing someone did to you. Have you called the police?"

"No, should I?"

"Yes, that's vandalism. We don't take kindly to that. Tell You what. When I get home, I'll call them to report it. I've got some paint in the car and I'll paint it for you right now." Saying that, he proceeded to paint the door.

Some of the neighbors came by and expressed outrage. "Probably some teenagers with nothing better to do," was the general opinion. "We'll keep an eye on your house. We don't want that to happen again."

Another person approached Mr. Petucci and gave him some money. "Here is the rest of the rent I owe you. Thank you for giving me more time. I promise to have next month on time."

"Thank you, Mrs. Dorsey. Mr. Dorsey all recovered?"

"Yes, all well, and he's back at work."

Another neighbor came up carrying a plate of cupcakes. "Erika, I just baked these cupcakes. Welcome to the neighborhood. These are for you and your family."

"Thank you," Erika said with tears in her eyes. "You can have one too, Mr. Petucci. You must own a lot of houses around here."

"I have eight. The rent is my retirement income."

"Mr. Petucci, do you know any place I could get a part-time job?"

"What can you do?"

"In Germany I worked as a nurse. But I understand to work here I need to take some classes. For the time being, I am willing to do most anything."

"Have you ever waited on tables?"

"Only on my own table, unless you want to count waiting on beds."

"My son owns an Italian restaurant and he could use a waitress. The restaurant is not far from here. If you are interested, you can call him and make an appointment."

"That would be great."

The old man handed her a business card. "Speak with Tony and tell him that his father recommends you. There, the door is as good as new. Now I'm ready for the cupcake you promised me."

"Come in, I'll also give you something to drink. Please don't call the police. I don't want to take the chance that my niece will see them here. I'm afraid she would get very upset."

"I'll just make a report that it happened so the cop on the beat can keep his eyes open for such vandalism."

After Mr. Petucci left, Erika made an appointment with Tony for the next morning. Then she went to the playground. Kate was knitting while the children were on the swings and jungle gym.

"Good news. The door is painted and Mr. Petucci is a wonderful man."

"I know. He is our landlord, too. When something needs fixing, he is right there."

"I have a job interview for tomorrow morning at an Italian restaurant," continued Erika. "In spite of the bad start this morning, this is turning out to be a good day after all."

CHAPTER 22

It was a Saturday evening. Conrad was sleeping in his room and Sigrit was in her room with the door closed. She was writing a letter to Bavaria while her radio was softly playing popular music.

Erika and Walter were sitting in the living room on their wicker loveseat. The radio played soft music and three candles gave the room a romantic mood. They were drinking California wine and talking.

"Walter dear, can you believe how far we have come in the past few weeks. I can't believe that only six weeks ago we boarded the ship in Hamburg."

"Yes, that passage was a nice vacation after the stress of getting rid of the apartment and selling the furniture. Too bad the money got changed then, and the old money we received from the sale of the furniture had become practically worthless. It seems like overnight the stores were stocked with merchandise, but now no one has any money."

"Yes, there's going to be a big change in Germany," continued Erika. "But what do you think will happen with the Russian zone? I never expected the blockade to go on this long."

"I'm glad we're not living there," Walter said, taking a sip of wine.

"Thank God for the airlift, otherwise those poor people in Berlin would starve to death."

"That all seems so far away, Erika. Here we are and we have a whole house for our family. I felt like a little boy living in my parents' apartment, even after we got married and had Conrad."

"I too had to walk on eggs to keep peace. Your mother could be quite trying at times."

"Yes, I know. She gets high strung, but she seems less stressed now. I suppose we can blame it on the war and the lack of food. It's a wonder more people didn't end up in the looney bin."

"Walter, I want to tell you that I am real proud of you. Not only do you have a job, but you already got a promotion and a raise."

"I hope Pop didn't get jealous. He is just a machine operator like he has been, but I was promoted to A-1 machinist. Those classes I took in Stuttgart did pay off."

"And the job I have at the restaurant is not only fun, but coming home with money every day makes it especially rewarding," Erika said, putting her head on his shoulder. "I could make more money in the evening, but then I would miss being home with you. Doing lunchtime service is just right. Kate has a chance to be alone with Conrad while the girls are in school and I'm home when Siggy gets home."

Walter gently embraced her. She could feel the vibrations of passion. He kissed her lips and visions of the clearing in the forest came to her mind.

A baby, are we ready for another baby?

The gentle petting became more intense. His lips and tongue played over every part of her body. Neither one wanted to stop to go upstairs where the contraceptive was located. Their passion played out on the living room floor. Not once, but again and again. Long after the children were asleep, they climbed the stairs and went to bed.

By the time they got up next morning, Sigrit had already given Conrad breakfast and was eating an egg and toast. The radio was still on from the night before. The music sounded very familiar to Erika and Walter.

"It sounds like they are singing in German," Walter commented.

Sigrit only smiled. Then the commercial came on. The announcer was speaking German. Walter turned up the volume. In the time span of an hour they learned that Baltimore had German bakeries, butcher shops, and delicatessens. Also there was a German *Haus* where clubs met and had social events.

"Walter, it would be nice to go to some of these functions."

"Erika, we are now in America. We'll have to find American social events to attend."

"Until we get your parents paid back, we better just amuse ourselves at home. If we continue as we have been, that should be about two months. Then we can start going out."

"Well, maybe a little going out. We should start saving for big purchases."

"What big purchase do you have in mind, Walter?"

"A car. Wouldn't it be nice to have a car? There are so many places to explore where buses and streetcars don't go to. Here we are living thirty miles from the nation's capital and we haven't been there yet."

"Your parents took a bus there once and walked around. They said it is very impressive. A car would be nice to have. How about a television?"

"Eventually. We have to set our goals and work toward them. Is it agreed, a car comes first?"

"Agreed," Erika said, giving him a kiss on the cheek. "What do you think, Siggy? Would it be nice to have a car?"

"A car. Yes, I would like that."

Sigrit was in sixth grade. In the morning she attended an English class and after that she walked to another elementary school for the afternoon session. She had made friends with some German children her age in the English class, but found herself withdrawn from the classmates in her regular school. She struggled with composition and American history, but math was a breeze for her. She had always liked the subject and had done much harder problems in school in Germany.

Sigrit found joy and comfort going to the library. She was in awe of all the knowledge contained in the pages of books, free for the taking. One of the librarians took a special interest in her and would guide her to books that she could understand and get valuable information from. Lack of playmates did not bother her. Books became her best friends. The library was a frequent stop on her way home from school.

Caroline was in third grade at the same school and they would walk home together. One rainy day in early November a car pulled up and parked at the curb near the two girls. A young man opened the driver's door and called to them.

"Girls, look. I have something to show you."

Curious, the girls walked closer to the car and there sat the man exposing himself. Caroline sucked in her breath audibly and gaped. Sigrit, on the other hand, had seen animals mate. She had heard that she might encounter such behavior.

Very matter of factually she simply said, "Mister, you have nothing to brag about. My Chihuahua dog has a bigger thing than that."

Shocked, the man closed the car door and drove off. Sigrit saw his license plate and wrote down the number. Next day she told her teacher who notified the police.

The police came to the school to speak with her. There they found out that other children had suffered the same experience. When asked why they told no one, one girl said that she told her mother, but her mother accused her of making it up. With the license number and a description of the car and the man, the police were able to find him quickly and arrest him. After that, Sigrit suddenly became popular. Everyone wanted to be her friend. She received invitations to come to parties, sleep overs, and just to come and play. Too many invitations at one time. She accepted some, and other times she used the excuse that she had to watch her little brother. To simplify her family life, she called Erika, Mom, Walter became her Dad, and Conrad her brother.

When people commented that Walter looked too young to be her father, he simply said, "I look younger than I am."

One day at the end of November Walter was all excited when he came home from work.

"Erika, Siggy, I saw a car for sale on the street. I stopped at the drug store and called the owner and he is coming by to show it to us this evening."

"How much does he want for the car?"

"A hundred dollars. We have that much, don't we?"

Erika ran upstairs to count the money lying in her dresser. She also had a bowl full of uncounted quarters. While she was counting them, someone knocked on the door.

Walter and Sigrit along with little Conrad, went outside to inspect the black 1937 Ford. When Erika joined them with the good news that they had the hundred dollars, everyone hopped into the car, and Walter took them for a little drive.

"She's a solid little car," said the owner who sat in the front seat, lighting a cigarette.

"Why are you selling her?" asked Walter.

"I'm buying a 'forty-nine Ford. Have you seen the futuristic design of those? Long and sleek with a big trunk. I had a good job during the war and saved my money. I don't need two cars. My wife doesn't drive."

"Come into the house with the title and we can finish the deal," Walter said.

That night there was a celebration over the supper table in Walter's house. Then, after eating, they all hopped into the car and drove to the next block to their parents' house where the purchase was greeted with a lack of enthusiasm.

"Now that you have a car, you'll always be taking trips and we'll hardly see you," Kate said.

"No, Mom, you'll still see us," Walter, assured her. "And the backseat is big enough for you and Pop, provided you let the children sit on your laps."

"I've got an idea," Erika interjected. "How about we get Mrs. Dorsey to come over and stay with the children, and just us two couples go out to a dance?"

Kate's eyes lit up. "Karl, what do you say? Wouldn't that be great, to go dancing with Walter and Erika? Where could we go?"

"How about we try Willy's Farm?" suggested Erika. "The place that advertises on the German hour. One does need a car to get there. What do you think, Walter? Wouldn't that be fun?"

Walter saw the animation of joy in the two women. All he could say was, "Great idea, we'll do that. Caroline can sleep over with Sigrit and we'll pay for the sitter."

Karl and Kate, along with Caroline, walked to Walter's house. Mrs. Dorsey was already there, reading a bedtime story to Conrad. Karl wore a dark gray suit and Kate had on a navy blue dress with a full A-line skirt.

"You both look elegant," Walter said.

Erika came down the steps wearing a new red dress with a full skirt. Her shoulder length brunette hair surrounded her face with large curls. Walter's loud wolf whistle lit up her lovely face with a big smile, showing two dimples below her cheeks.

"Hello, Mom and Pop. I'm sure we'll have a good time tonight. Girls, there are some snacks in the fridge. You will be good for Mrs. Dorsey, won't you?"

∽∾∽

The dance hall was located on a farm about fifteen miles outside the city. At the door sat an elderly man with a cash box selling tickets.

"Hello, folks, I haven't seen you before."

"No, this is our first time here," said Karl.

"Welcome. I'm Uncle Willy. I'm the owner. And what are your names?"

Karl made introductions all around.

"I probably won't remember the names, but welcome. Admission is twenty-five cents a person. Now you hang on to your tickets, you might win the door prize."

They sat at a small table surrounded by four chairs. Newspapers served as a table cloth. A waitress asked them what they would like to drink. Soon she brought a pitcher of beer and four glasses.

"That'll be seventy-five cents."

Walter pulled out a dollar and gave it to her. "Keep the change."

Soon the three-piece band began playing. They started out with a lively polka and half the people in the hall got up to dance. Next they played a waltz and more people ventured onto the wooden dance floor. All the dancers moved on the floor counterclockwise in unison. Sometimes Walter danced with his mother while Erika danced with Karl. Then the whistle blew and everyone hit the dance floor for a Paul Jones. After the last exchange of partners, the gentlemen walked the ladies back to their table.

While dancing a slow waltz, Erika gave Walter a big hug and kissed him on the cheek.

"You do know that I really love you. I want to tell you that I'm really happy."

"Yes, and I'm happy you're my wife."

"There is something else I want to tell you."

"Oh, what is it?"

"I'm quite certain we are going to have another baby."

Walter said nothing.

"Walter, what's the matter? Don't you want another child?"

"It just comes as a total surprise. I have to get used to the idea. What makes you sure?"

"I've missed my second period, and they have always been so regular. I'll see a doctor next week. Shall we tell your parents tonight or wait?"

"Let's wait until after you see the doctor. Okay?"

Walter kissed her gently on the lips while the dance ended.

Back at the table Kate commented, "You two look so good on the dance floor. It sure would be nice if Herbert and Betty could come here, too. The waitress said that on Sundays people bring their children out here. In three weeks they will have a children's Christmas party with Santa Claus and presents for all the kids. Karl, we just have to buy a car, too. Don't you want to learn to drive?"

"I thought we were saving to buy a house. A car would cut into the house money."

"Just think how much fun we could have with a car. If you don't want to learn to drive, I will."

"Okay, first a house then maybe a car," Karl said in an assertive manner.

Kate knew not to mention cars for the time being. She could only hope that Herbert might consider buying a car. Eventually owning a car was something Kate determined was going to be in their future.

CHAPTER 23

Wednesday evening the following week, Erika and Walter took the two children to a playground near their house. While Sigrit was pushing Conrad in a swing, Walter asked Erika what the doctor said.

"I am starting my third month of pregnancy."

"I was afraid of that. Here we were, doing so good. With your little job at the restaurant, you made enough money to get us into a position of being able to save for some of the better things of life. Now with a baby coming along…" Seeing her jaw drop and the sadness in her eyes silenced him. "Oh, honey, I'm sorry. We'll make the best of it."

They walked home in silence. Sigrit wondered if the heavy atmosphere was because of her. Had she done something to displease her guardians? That was the last thing in the world she wanted.

At home, Erika complained of a headache, went into the bedroom, and closed the door. While Sigrit got her cousin ready for bed, Walter read him a bedtime story. Then both of them kissed the little boy good-night and closed the door. Sigrit said she had some homework to do and went into her room. Walter sat in the living room in silence. After a while he got up and reached for a bottle of wine. When the bottle was empty, he went upstairs and to bed. If Erika was still awake, she gave no indication of it.

The next morning Walter and Karl were walking to work together. The small factory was only about a twenty minute walk from their houses, and both men enjoyed the exercise and camaraderie. Walter told Karl about expecting another child.

"Wonderful. I was wondering when that would happen. This is perfect timing. Conrad is not too old to be a big brother and companion for the little one. I'm sure Kate will be happy. You and Erika must be delighted."

"I did not take the news with pleasure, even though I had warning that it would be coming."

"*What*? What did you say?"

"I'm worried about the money a baby costs and the loss of her income and I told her so."

"You fool, how do you think that made her feel?"

"She said nothing and went to bed."

"You better go home with a big bouquet of flowers and a huge apology. I can't believe you can be so insensitive. Remember, you were there too when she conceived this baby."

"I sure was." He chuckled, thinking about the night on the living room floor. "Tell you what. Tonight you tell Mom about it, but when we tell you the news, act like you don't know anything about it. I'll buy some flowers on my way home and eat humble pie. If all goes well, we'll come over tonight and bring you the news."

"Good. I'll be looking for you. We'll open a bottle to celebrate."

"Oh, I have had enough of wine from last night. My head still aches."

While at work Walter had time to think about how much he must have hurt his wife. He wished he could take her in his arms right then and apologize profusely. Suddenly, he felt a sharp pain in his left hand. He looked down and saw red. Quickly he lifted the drill press and saw the he had run it through his hand between the bones of his thumb and index finger. The colleague working next to him took him to the office where they called an ambulance. Walter sat there on a hard chair with a white towel wrapped around his hand. While he watched the red spot increase in size he became nauseous. Just as the ambulance arrived, Karl came to the office too and went with him to the hospital.

At Johns Hopkins Hospital they took him right into the emergency room where he was treated. The doctor told him he was really lucky that he had not drilled through any bones. After he was bandaged up with a bulky wrapping, a receptionist called a cab to take Walter home. Karl walked him into the house then took the same cab back to work.

The house was empty when Walter entered. Erika was at work, Conrad was with Kate, and Sigrit was in school. After all that excitement, Walter felt exhausted. He went upstairs and went to bed. Soon he fell asleep.

Erika came home with Conrad and their talking woke Walter. He figured that she did not know he was in the house. He did not want to startle her, so he kept quiet.

After a while, he got up and started down the steps calling, "Erika, it's me. I'm home."

"What are you doing home?" Then she saw the bandage. "What happened?"

"I ran a drill press through my hand. But before you say anything, I want to apologize for the terrible way I acted yesterday. Erika, thinking about it, I am happy we are going to have another baby." He reached for her with his good hand. "Can you ever forgive me for being such a jerk?"

She looked him in the eyes and saw genuine regret. He looked so small and vulnerable. At the moment she had the power to crush him or uplift him. No one was perfect, and they had to accept each other with all their imperfections. She embraced him and kissed him. Words did not need to be spoken. Conrad came up to them and they both stooped down for a family hug.

"It will be good for Conrad to be a big brother," Walter said, embracing and kissing his wife. "I'm looking forward to adding to the family. Just think. We'll have a genuine American baby."

When Sigrit came home from school she was happy to see Walter and Erika looking happy again. Whatever the problem was the day before seemed to be over. Then she saw the bandage.

"Dad, what is wrong with your hand?"

"I did something real stupid and as a result ran a drill press through my hand. But I'll be all right. Don't worry about it, Siggy. I'll just have to take a few days off from work."

"Will you get paid?" Erika asked.

"There is such a thing as workman's compensation, but that will take a while to get."

"I could work another shift at the restaurant. They were shorthanded the last few days."

"You should not work that hard in your condition," Walter said.

Sigrit gave him a puzzled look.

"Sigrit, my dear," Walter said. "Erika and I are expecting another baby."

"That is wonderful," she said and hugged Erika. "If you excuse me, I have some homework to do." She took her schoolbooks and went upstairs to her room.

A baby! Will there be room for me when they have another baby? Will I be just a built-in babysitter? If it's a girl, they'll want my room. Where will I go? I'm too young to get a job and live on my own. Why can't things ever just stay the way they are? Homework, gotta do homework. Hey, I'm thinking in English. Wasn't long ago I could not imagine thinking in English. Get the homework done and worry about other things when you have time.

Sigrit was studying her spelling words when Erika knocked on the door. On entering she asked, "Siggy, do you need any help with homework?"

"Yes, could you dictate my spelling words?"

Erika read the words, which Sigrit all spelled correctly.

"You are doing so well, I'm proud of you. You certainly learned English quickly and are doing well in school."

"I hope to make the honor roll next semester. Now that I don't have to go to English class anymore, I can concentrate on my schoolwork."

"Sigrit, I just want to tell you that both Walter and I love you very much and nothing will change that, not even another baby. You are an important part of our family and always will be." Saying that, Erika opened her arms and Sigrit accepted her embrace eagerly.

That evening the family walked to the parents' house. Walter said, "Mom, Pop, Erika and I have something to tell you." After putting his arm around Erika's waist, he announced, "We are going to have a baby."

Kate hollered with delight. "A new baby. Just think, Karl, we'll have a *new* American baby."

At that moment Herbert walked in the door. "What does that make me, your *old* American baby?"

Everybody laughed.

"Yes, little brother, you're the old American baby," Walter teased.

"Thursday is Thanksgiving," Kate said. "That means we have to dine together. You are invited to come over here for dinner."

"That would be nice, but I'm afraid that I have to work," Erika said. "The restaurant will be very busy that day. They tell me the whole day is booked. Walter, Siggy and Conrad are certainly available for dinner."

"I would like to invite Betty to join us for dinner," Herbert said.

"Wonderful," said Kate. "We'll certainly miss you, Erika. When do you expect to get off?"

"I don't know. It will probably be a long day."

"Now don't overdo it with all that working," Kate said.

"Don't worry, Mom. I feel fine."

સ્જાજ

Thanksgiving Day was rainy and dreary, but the atmosphere in the Huber house was festive. Kate was up early preparing the traditional American dinner. Sigrit and Caroline helped by peeling potatoes, cutting up fresh string beans, and releasing the peas from their pods. The music playing on the radio was drowned out by the singing and laughter of the women in the kitchen. Karl and Walter were in the living room with Conrad, watching him play with his cars, and discussing the state of affairs in the world.

"I figured the Soviet blockade of West Berlin would be over by now," said Karl.

"Those Russians are tenacious," Walter commented. "It's the West that has the hard job, keeping all those planes in the air. I hope they will resolve the issue diplomatically soon. It will probably cost us something to get the Russians to back down."

"When you say 'us,' who do you mean?"

"The Americans, coming to America was like coming home. I can't wait to get my citizenship back."

"You have to wait," Karl said. "In four more years, I'm going to make my citizenship. There are problems here, but after what we have been through, this country is wonderful,"

"Amen and I'll drink to that," said Walter.

The two men raised their beer glasses. The scent of the roasting turkey spread through the whole house out into the street as if to invite any passersby to come in. The door opened and Herbert walked in with Betty. Shortly thereafter, every one took their place at the table. It was set with china that had been brought over from Germany—white porcelain with a wide blue rim accented with gold.

Karl said the prayer then finished with, "I thank thee Lord that we are in America."

"I thank thee to have a nice house to live in," said Kate.

"I thank thee, oh Lord for my wife and job," added Walter.

"I thank thee for my dear family," said Caroline.

"I am grateful for my home and family," said Sigrit.

"I have so much to be thankful for," Betty added, "and that includes Herbert."

"And I thank thee Lord that Betty has consented to be my wife, Amen."

"You two are really engaged?" Kate asked.

Betty showed her left hand that had a gold band with a small diamond. "Yes, we got engaged on the bus coming over here."

"A wedding, we're going to have a wedding. Wonderful. Isn't that exciting?" Kate inquired. "What are your plans?"

"I'm just planning something low-key and simple. My parents don't have the money to give us a wedding. My father drives a cab, and my mother is her mother's caregiver, so she has no salary."

"I'm sure they are fine people," Karl said. "Kate, we have to invite them over for dinner."

"Yes. Betty, how do I get in touch with them?"

"They have a phone. I'll give you their number. Let me tell you that everything is just delicious. You'll have to teach me a few of Herbert's favorite dishes."

"Thank you, I'll be happy to teach you some cooking."

After dinner Betty took a stack of dirty dishes and carried them into the kitchen.

"No Betty, you don't work," Kate told her. "This is your engagement day. The girls and I will take care of the dishes."

Karl and Herbert walked into the kitchen. "You girls have been cooking all day," Karl said. "We boys are going to take care of the dishes."

Kate gave her husband a loving and grateful look. "Thank you, that is very sweet of you." After giving him a big kiss she went into the living room and gratefully flopped onto the couch.

Karl started washing and said to Herbert, "Now if I really wanted to have my wife rush into the kitchen and tell me to leave, I would drop a good plate on the floor right now. But after the appreciation she showed me, I would feel like a real jerk."

Walter joined them in the kitchen. "I can help, too. I still have one good hand."

While the three men were doing the dishes the women discussed the upcoming wedding.

"We want to get married as soon as possible. Maybe even before Christmas."

"Why so quick?" Kate asked. "Are you pregnant?"

"No." Betty jumped up with eyes wide and nostrils flared. "I am not pregnant, and I am insulted that you should even think that."

She went into the kitchen and told Herbert that she was ready to go home right now.

"Why? What is wrong?"

"Your mother thinks I'm pregnant."

Herbert stormed out of the kitchen and confronted his mother who sat there looking quite startled.

"Mother, how dare you accuse Betty? As far as I know, she is still a virgin."

"Gosh, I'm sorry. It just seems strange that you want to get married so quickly."

"What's strange about that? We love each other and we want to be together."

"Oh, Betty, can you ever forgive me for shooting off. Sometimes I speak before thinking."

"You do have that problem," Karl said on entering the room. "She is a good woman after all. Betty, I hope you can forgive her."

Betty looked at Kate who sat quietly, looking doleful and studying her hands in her lap.

"Kate, I forgive you, but I do want to let all of you know that Herbert is a true gentleman and I am a lady."

Kate rose and hugged her future daughter-in-law.

"I still want to go home as soon as the guys finish with the dishes."

"If you want, I can drive you home," Walter said.

"That would be nice, brother."

"Conrad's ears perked up when he heard the word drive. "Car, Daddy, we go car?"

Walter could not resist the pleading look in his son's face. "Yes, Conrad can go with us in the car."

"Betty," Kate said. "I'll call your parents and we set a date for dinner. I hope you and Herbert can join us then, too."

"That would be nice. See you then. Goodnight."

The sun had dipped below the clouds illuminating the horizon in shades of orange and red, promising a beautiful day tomorrow.

CHAPTER 24

Erika was still at work when Sigrit came home from school. She emptied the mailbox attached to the house and found a letter from Bavaria. Since her name was on the envelope, she eagerly opened it. Both Greta and Ludwig had written letters. She read the letter written in Greta's neat handwriting first.

> *Dearest Siggy,*
> *All of us are well and we had a good harvest. Now we are getting ready for Christmas with lots of baking and smoking of pork. I'm sure you remember Christmas four years ago and the big event in the stable. The other day we got a letter from Sarah, the first one ever. You can't imagine how happy Mama and Papa were to get that letter. She and Ruben along with little Samuel went to Israel. She opened a ballet school and has lots of students. Ruben is active in getting a ballet company started in Ashdot where they live. They managed to re-*

main in Switzerland until the war was over. Papa's friend kept them hidden in a cabin in the mountains. He was afraid that the authorities would turn them over to the Nazis.

I can imagine that you miss your dear brother, but he is quite happy here. He is a big help to Papa. We have five cows now and sell milk to the cheese factory. I'll close now, to leave something for Ludwig to write. Give greetings to Erika and Walter too from everyone.

With Love, Your "sister" Greta

Sigrit looked at the enclosed picture. Ludwig was standing next to Sepp, dressed in Bavarian folk dress—short leather pants elaborately embroidered with green silk, a white shirt, and a green vest. On his head was a green velour hat decorated with a *gamsbart,* made from the chin hairs of a mountain goat. Martha and Greta were both dressed in their full green skirts and white silk aprons and shawls. Everyone had a big smile on their faces.

Sigrit stared at the picture for a long time. Tears came to her eyes. She wondered when she would ever see them again. Suddenly she felt so far away and alone.

She had not yet read Ludwig's letter when Erika came home. Erika steps were heavy and the first thing she did was flop into the upholstered easy chair.

"Siggy dear, I'm exhausted. Would you be so kind and get Conrad?"

"Yes, *Tante,* oops, I mean, Mom. I got a letter from Bavaria, you can read it," she said, handing the papers to Erika.

"I'll read it in a little while. Right now I need to just close my eyes for a few minutes."

Now it's starting. The baby is not even born yet and I'm the built in babysitter. Oh, Greta, I wish I was with you in Bavaria. When I was living there I did not realize how lucky and happy I was.

When she arrived at Kate's house, Sigrit could smell the sweet inviting odor of baking.

"Oh, Sigrit," Kate said. "You are just in time to help with baking Christmas cookies."

"Yes, Siggy," shouted Caroline. "I get to paint the Springerle. You can help,"

"Paint Springerle? What is that?"

Kate explained that those were traditional cookies of the Swabian region. Their history went back to ancient times when horses were sacrificed to the gods. Poor people made cookies with bass relief carvings of horses pressed onto the dough. With Christianity other pictures were used too. In the really artistic households not only were highly detailed wooden carvings made, but the figures were painted using egg yolks or whites mixed with food coloring.

Sigrit picked up a small paintbrush and concentrated on painting the dough that had already set for a day to harden before baking. Even little Conrad got in on the fun by decorating sugar cookies with colored candies. Christmas music was playing on the radio adding to the festive atmosphere.

"This is fun," Sigrit said. "What are you going to do with all the cookies?"

"Some we hang on the tree, others we give away, of course we eat most of them," answered Kate.

"It smells good. Is that our supper?" asked Karl, coming home from work.

"Oh, is it that late already? We are having so much fun," Kate said, picking up a plate of sugar cookies and passing them around. "We still have some turkey."

"I better get home. I'm surprised Erika has not come looking for me and Conrad."

When Sigrit got back, Walter and Erika were in the kitchen both making supper. "Sorry, I'm late, Mom, but I was helping bake cookies. Conrad helped, too."

"That is fine. I fell asleep and feel a lot better now. We're almost ready to eat. Good thing you all like Spam."

※

It was a Saturday in the middle of December when Walter drove Herbert, Caroline, and Sigrit to the Cathedral of the Assumption. Both men wore dark suits and the girls had on matching green velvet dresses recently made by Kate.

"You nervous, little brother?"

"No. What's to be nervous about?" Herbert asked, looking at the small bouquet of red roses in his lap.

"It's a big step getting married."

"It's part of growing up. I love Betty and I know she loves me. That's the only way we can be together all the time. Look, there's her father's taxi."

"You better close your eyes. It's supposed to be bad luck to see the bride before the wedding."

"I've got my eyes closed," replied Herbert. "You girls will have to give Betty this bouquet. I hope Betty is wearing something old, something new, something borrowed, something blue, and a penny in her shoe. Sigrit, will you make sure she has all that?"

"Yes."

"There's a taxi with Mama and Papa and Erika," observed Caroline.

Church bells were ringing as Walter escorted his brother in the side door of the cathedral. Betty desired to have a very small wedding, and her wish was granted. The only guests from her side were her sister, Anne, and her sister's husband, Russel. Betty's mother wore a dark brown suit that was straining to contain her body. Anne wore an attractive light blue jersey dress and was carrying a small bouquet of yellow mums. Sigrit and Caroline approached Betty, whose face was beaming with happiness. She had on a royal blue satin dress, a gray little hat with feathers, and a veil over half of her face.

"You look absolutely lovely," Sigrit said, giving Betty a little hug. "Now I have to go over the checklist. Something old?"

"My necklace."

"Something new?"

"My dress."

"Something borrowed?"

"Earrings from my sister."

"Blue is obvious. How about a penny in your shoe?"

"Dad, do you have a penny you can give me?"

He laughed and reached into his pants' pocket, pulling out a shiny copper penny. "This wedding is getting to be expensive."

Betty slipped it into her gray suede shoe. "Okay, I'm ready to get married."

Caroline handed her the roses, then her father took her by the arm and they walked down the aisle of the large, mostly empty, oldest Catholic cathedral in America.

After the service, taxis were waiting to take the wedding party to a famous Baltimore restaurant for lunch. The two sets of parents picked up the tab and split it evenly. Since the taxi drivers were friends of Mr. Burger, they donated their services. After lunch, which included wine, Herbert and Betty were taken by cab to their apartment.

Kate's eyes started to water. "They are moving all the way out to Hamilton. We'll probably never see them anymore."

"Of course we'll see them," Karl said. "The streetcar goes to Hamilton. Maybe we can buy a house there."

"A house?" said Kate, perking up. "You think we can afford to buy a house in Hamilton?"

"In America all things are possible," Karl answered firmly.

എൟ

Just a little over a week later the newlyweds were seen again. The occasion was Christmas Eve. It was celebrated at the parents' house like it had always been. They could not bring themselves to condense Christmas into one short day where the children got up Christmas morning, found presents under the tree, and the next day was a work day again. Try as they might to be American, there was always at least one leg on the other side of the fence. In Europe, Christmas had two days, not counting the evening before. Betty would experience a Christmas the German way for the first time.

The little living room was crowded, especially with a fresh spruce tree in one corner. The tree reached almost to the ceiling and was decorated with glass bulbs, cookies, and handmade ornaments. Betty had never seen a tree decorated with real candles before. The clip-on holders had been brought over from Germany but the small candles were bought locally.

"First we eat," Kate announced. "And then we light the tree and do our celebration."

After a supper of hot dogs from a German butcher shop on rolls from a German bakery and homemade potato salad, the ritual could begin. First the candles on the tree were lit, in addition to some others around the room. Sigrit and Caroline, both dressed in their green velvet dresses, sang *Away in a Manger* together. Everyone clapped and cheered. Then Karl read the Christmas story according to Luke from *The Bible*. After that everyone sang "Silent Night" in German and English. Then slowly the brightly wrapped packages were handed out by Kate.

Walter and Herbert expressed joy over the hand-knitted sweaters made by their mother. Conrad eagerly started playing with his fire engine, rolling it on the floor and making siren noises. Erika received a maternity top, also made by Kate, and Betty got a pretty pair of earrings and matching pendant on a silver chain. Caroline received a large baby doll whose vinyl skin felt almost real.

"I think that is everybody's present," Kate said.

Sigrit's mouth assumed a downward curve. *No present for me. What have I done to be treated this way? I thought they all loved me.* Tears came to her eyes.

"Wait," Karl said. "I hear something. There is a noise out back." He went out the back door and came in with a new bicycle. "That was Santa Claus leaving it. Siggy, it looks like it fits you exactly."

She shrieked with delight. "A bicycle, how did you know that is what I wanted more than anything? How wonderful! Thank you, thank you."

"It is a gift from everybody to you," Kate said.

"That is more than I could hope for. Thank you." She went from person to person hugging and kissing everyone.

After a few more Christmas Carols, Herbert asked, "Does anyone want to know what Betty and I are giving each other?"

"Yes, what is it?" Walter asked.

"You have to come outside to see it."

"It must be a car," Kate said to no one in particular. "Herbert and Betty got a car."

After extinguishing the candles, everyone walked a few houses away to a dark green car parked at the curb.

"There it is," Herbert said with a wave of his arm. "It's a 'thirty-eight Ford."

"Congratulations, I didn't know you could drive," Karl commented.

"I got my driver's license without you knowing, in order to surprise you."

"The things you kids do," Kate said. "It's good, it's all good. We are proud of you, all of you. But we better get back into the house before we catch cold."

CHAPTER 25

It was March and Erika was working a busy lunchtime shift. Up to this point, she was able to hide her pregnancy pretty well under a full red skirt, white peasant blouse, and green apron with big pockets, in which she carried her tips. When she was about to go home, Tony asked to see her in his office.

Upon entering his office, Tony said, "Erika, I just want to tell you that you are a really good waitress. Many customers ask to sit at your tables. Let me just ask you this—are you pregnant?"

"Yes," she answered in a proud voice.

"I'm afraid that I can't have you wait on tables in your condition."

"Why not?"

"Carrying all those heavy trays, I'm afraid you might miscarry."

"I'm beyond the miscarriage stage"

"How far along are you?"

"Six months."

"Really, and you did not say anything."

"I was afraid that if I did you would fire me, which I know you are about to do."

"No, not fire you, but give you a leave of absence. You are welcome to come back after the baby is born."

"Does that mean you don't want me to come in anymore?" she said with a lump in her throat.

"Tell you what I'll do. I'll let you work another week, but you have to promise me that you will tell your regulars why you will not be in the restaurant for a while."

"I can do that, thank you."

"No hard feelings?"

"No Tony, no hard feelings."

For the next week when Erika told her regular customers why she would not be waiting on them anymore, they gave her an especially big tip. She made enough that week to almost pay for her part of the medical expenses. Walter's insurance covered the rest.

Erika missed the camaraderie of the employees at the restaurant, but she was also glad not to have to rush off to work every day. She also saved by not paying Kate anymore. Kate did not want to take any money at first, but Walter and Erika insisted. She also enjoyed having her own mad money as she called it.

Once she was no longer obligated to go to work, Erika looked around the house for projects. The bare backyard screamed for attention. There were all these little backyards that might contain clotheslines, but otherwise went uncared for. Children played in the street or the nearby playground, but no one used the backyard.

"Walter, don't you think it would be nice to do something with the backyard?" Erika asked over supper one evening.

"What do you have in mind?"

"Make a place to sit, and maybe put in a fruit tree or two, plant some tomatoes, and who knows what else? Maybe even a patch of grass and flowers. Yes, flowers, that would be lovely."

"And who will pay for all this?"

"We can do a little at a time. It wouldn't cost that much. Just think how much pleasure that could be. Really, sitting on the steps to socialize is not the most comfortable way to go. We could invite the neighbors to enjoy our backyard, and maybe they would do it, too. Next thing everybody will have a nice little garden with trees and birds and butterflies. Just think what a happy neighborhood that could be."

"Before we do anything, we better ask Mr. Petucci if it would be agreeable with him. He might have other plans for the house."

Erika looked at her husband and smiled. She knew that she would get her garden.

"I can help, too," said Sigrit. "I did some gardening in Bavaria. Maybe we can get some chickens and have fresh eggs."

"No chickens," Walter said.

෴

Mr. Petucci was delighted that Erika wanted to improve the property. That meant they had the intention of staying a long time. They were the kind of tenants a landlord wanted to keep, always paid their rent on time, were gentle on the house, and now willing to put in a garden.

"Tell you what I'll do," said Mr. Petucci, "I have some flagstones I don't know what to do with. I can bring them on down and you can make a patio out of them."

"That would be wonderful," Erika said.

"You know, that fence is old and ready to collapse. I'll have a new wooden fence installed. How would six feet high be? That way you can run grape vines up on the fence."

"Grapes? I hadn't thought of grapes. That's a great idea. I can see it now. It will be a beautiful garden."

"Do you have any garden tools?" asked Mr. Petucci.

"No, not a thing."

"I have more than enough of that stuff. Sometimes I bought a house and the people would leave a lot of the tools and things. Before you buy anything, let me scrounge around and see what I can come up with."

The next day Mr. Petucci drove up with a trailer hitched to his Cadillac. He also had Tony along and another young fellow who was a dishwasher in the restaurant. After the car drove into the alley, the two young men unloaded the flagstones and made a neat pile in the yard. Meanwhile Mr. Petucci took a gas tiller and tilled the soil.

"There, it's an easy job with the tiller," Mr. Petucci said. "Otherwise, you'll break your back."

"Thank you. I was concerned about having Walter dig up that hard soil. He will be happy to see that done."

"Tomorrow the fence people will be here to install a new fence. I'm sure you will like it. I'll be here to check it out and pay them. I'll have them put a big gate opening to the alley. That way you can bring in plants and things from the back. You might even decide that you want to park your car back there."

"Oh, Mr. Petucci, you are a wonderful man," Erika said, giving him a hug.

"It's easy to be nice, dealing with nice people," he said, blushing.

It was dark by the time Walter came home from work, since he was asked to work overtime. Erika heated up supper for him and did not say a word about the garden. She figured that would be a pleasant surprise.

Sigrit could really enjoy riding her bicycle when the weather got warmer and there was no more danger of snow or ice. Sometimes she would ride through neighborhoods where all the occupants were Black. There the houses were unkempt and the people wore really old-looking clothes. The next day in school she spoke with her teacher.

"Miss Smith, why don't Negro children go to our school?"

"It is called segregation. They have their own school to go to, just like they have their own neighborhoods and beaches. They want to be with their own kind, just like you want to be with your white friends. Does that answer your question?"

"For now," she said, but right then she decided that no one would pick whom she associated with.

On her way home from school she saw a boy delivering newspapers. He wore a large canvas bag across his chest filled with the evening papers.

That would be a nice job for me, she decided. *I could deliver papers and earn some money.*

She asked the boy about his job.

"I'm just substituting here," he replied. "They are looking for a paperboy in this neighborhood. Know anybody who would be interested?"

"Yes, me."

"Too bad, they only hire boys."

"Why is that?"

"You couldn't carry a bag this heavy."

"Want to bet?"

"Sure, I'll bet you a paper," he said, taking off the bag and handing it to her.

"See? I can handle it. You owe me a paper. How much does one earn?"

"A good paperboy can earn up to five dollars a week," he said, handing her a paper.

"Five dollars." That seemed a fortune to her. "Who do I see about getting a job?"

"They won't hire you, but you can try. Go to the paper building on Conglin Street."

That night in bed she thought about all the things she could do with five dollars a week. The next day as soon as she got home from school she hopped on her bicycle and headed to the newspaper. She found the circulation department and went in. The receptionist told her that the manager left early for the day, but he should be there tomorrow.

"Please tell him that Sigrit Lachmann would like to see him tomorrow afternoon."

"May I ask what about?"

"Yes, I would like to have a paper route."

"Oh, for that you have to be at least twelve and a boy."

"I qualify on age. The other requirement takes some debating. See you tomorrow."

The next day at the same time Sigrit appeared in the office. She read the name *Harold McCoy* on the glass office door.

"Hello, I believe I have an appointment with Mr. McCoy," Sigrit said in a low, business-like tone.

"Yes, he is expecting you. Go right in."

The man behind the desk was middle-aged and appeared to lack exercise. He gave Sigrit an amused look. Yet the determination in the girl's face prompted him to listen to her. She looked at the large map of Baltimore on the wall at the right side of the desk.

"Mr. McCoy, I understand that you are in need of a paper delivery person in that area," she said, circling her neighborhood with her finger. "I am the person for that job."

"What makes you say that?"

"I know the area and the people. I am conscientious and a good worker."

"You have an accent. Where are you from?"

Darn accent, people hear that and right away I get questioned on where I'm from. Is it really their business? Since I'm asking the man for a job, I better tell him. I have to get rid of the accent, but how?

"I'm from Germany. Do you have a problem with that?"

The man was surprised at the outspoken demeanor of the girl. He figured that not much intimidated this child. He liked her aggressive manner and decided to go against his unwritten rule about hiring only boys.

He picked up a canvas bag full of papers and asked her to put it on. Even though the bag was heavy, Sigrit lifted it without showing any strain and put it over her shoulder.

"See? I can handle it easily."

"Okay, young lady, you've got the job. Can you start tomorrow?"

"I can start today," she said with a big grin. "Thank you, Mr. McCoy. You won't be sorry."

༺༻

A few weeks later the newspaper had a contest for the carriers. The one who got the most new subscriptions won a prize. Sigrit went knocking on her neighbors' doors, those who were not subscribers or took the other Baltimore newspaper. She introduced herself, handed them a paper, and inquired if they would like to get the best newspaper in town from the best paperboy. Looking at her fine-featured and very feminine face, people chuckled. Many became new subscribers. Her route skimmed the edge of the Black section. She knew it was out of her delivery territory, but she had a supply of extra papers to give away. She knocked on the door of the first row house in the block. The paint was peeling, but the windows were clean with white lace curtains. An attractive full-buxomed woman answered the door.

"Hello, my name is Sigrit and I deliver papers. Here is a free sample for you," she said, handing the woman a paper. "If you wish to subscribe, I would be happy to bring you a paper every afternoon."

"Well, bless you, my child. No one has ever offered to deliver on this block. I'm glad to see they're hiring girls now."

"As far as I know I'm still the only girl."

"And you would bring a paper every day, including Sunday?"

"Yes, Ma'am, every afternoon and Sunday morning."

"How much is it?"

"Two dollars a month." She saw the woman hesitate over the two dollars and quickly added, "But you can save over two dollars by clipping the coupons in the paper."

"Yes, I like coupons. Okay, I'll give it a try. Sign me up."

"Now you're sure that no one else is delivering papers here? I don't want to invade anybody's territory."

"No, child, no one delivers papers here."

By the end of the day, Sigrit wondered how she would ever carry all the papers she had promised to deliver. *I suppose, I will just have to divide my route into two sections. I'll go out, get half done, then go back, fold the other papers, and go out again. I can do it. I am strong.*

A few days later Mr. McCoy personally brought a big pile of papers to the Huber house.

"I want to meet the parents of my wonderful paperboy personally," he said, observing Erika's swollen belly. "I want to say that you must be very proud of your daughter."

"Yes, we are. She is a wonderful child."

Looking at the girl who was sitting on the floor folding papers and putting them in the pouch, he asked, "Where did you find all the new subscribers?"

"In the Colored Section."

"You mean you went into the Colored neighborhood and knocked on people's doors?"

"Yes, of course."

"Did you go alone?"

"Why not? All the people are very nice. You, as the manager of a newspaper, should put the colored population into a more positive light."

"What do you mean?"

SIGRIT

Sigrit continued folding papers. "When you report on a crime, when the criminal caught is a Negro, it always says Negro. Never does it say when the burglar was white. How many feature articles do you have about a colored person? Not many."

Erika could not believe her ears. Here sat her little niece on the floor, chastising a system to her boss. He just looked at her, showing no expression. Then rising to his full six feet, he offered to take Sigrit to deliver the papers in the Black Section in his car.

"Now this is just a one-time event. Don't get used to it, but I do want to see about adding a new route."

After those papers were delivered, he dropped Sigrit off at her house for her to get the rest of the papers. Driving back to the office, he smiled. Now he knew what the big prize would be for the winning paperboy.

CHAPTER 26

Two weeks later the newspaper had a party for all its carriers. It was on a Sunday afternoon and held in a park. Most of the carriers and their parents attended along with brothers and sisters. A tent was put up in case of rain and the paper treated everyone to hot dogs, soda, and ice cream. Several hundred boys and three girls were all in a festive mood, playing games and getting acquainted. Finally the highlight of the day was about to commence. Mr. McCoy shouted through a megaphone for everyone to pay attention.

"Now I want all of you to give a big hand to the following carriers who have added the most subscriptions."

He read the names of ten carriers who went to stand next to him. All of them got a fifty-dollar savings bond. "And for the grand prize winner who not only showed me that girls can do the job, but added sixty-eight new readers, please give a big hand to Sigrit Lachmann. Come on up, Siggy."

Sigrit blushed as she walked up in front of several hundred people while they clapped and cheered. The loudest among them was Walter and Conrad. Big tears rolled down Erika's cheeks.

Oh, dear sister and brother-in-law, Erika thought. *If you were here now, what would you say? How proud you would be of your Sigrit. To think of all we have done in five years, how much our lives have changed. Wherever you are, I hope you are happy.*

"Not only will she get a fifty-dollar savings bond," announced Mr. McCoy, "but she and her family will get to go by limo to Washington to spend the day with our congressman."

"Thank you, sir. Thank you, Mr. McCoy," was all she could say, shaking the man's hand as he handed her the bond, a big envelope, and also a certificate naming her the carrier of the month. Softly he said to her, "You will have to be on our staff longer to be carrier of the year."

Quietly she asked him, "Don't you have any colored kids as carriers?"

"We're getting ready to add some, thanks to you. We'll talk about it later."

After the presentation of awards everyone prepared to go home. While Walter was sitting in a line waiting to get out of the parking lot, Erika said, "Walter, you better drop me off at the hospital."

"You mean it's coming?"

"Yes, and I don't think it will be long. I did not want to spoil Siggy's day, but I have been in labor all afternoon. It hasn't been painful, but I could feel it."

"How close are the pains?"

"Three minutes, and it's starting to hurt."

Sigrit saw the long lines of cars and a police officer slowly letting out one car at a time. She jumped out of the car, ran up to the front of the line, and told the officer in a loud voice that her mom was having a baby—now.

"Just have them pull around the other cars."

When Walter pulled around, he got some dirty looks from other drivers, but he just shouted, "My wife is having a baby—now!"

The angry looks turned into smiles and cheers. Erika waved thank-yous. After Sigrit jumped back into the car, Walter sped off to Johns Hopkins Hospital. At the maternity entrance, Erika extracted herself from the car with Walter's help. She asked that if anyone gave her flowers to make sure they had roots on them. She wanted to plant them in her garden.

The children stayed in the car while Walter took his wife in. Soon he returned and took both children to Karl's house where everyone was eager to hear about all the excitement of the afternoon. Walter went back to the hospital where he waited in the father's waiting room with two other fathers-to-be.

Three days later about a dozen women from the neighborhood gathered in front of the Walter Huber house. When Walter drove up they all cheered. He hopped out of the car and opened the passenger door. Erika emerged with a pink bundle in her arms. The neighbors cheered, including Kate. Each woman had a small flowerpot with brightly colored flowers in her hand.

Kate grinned. "We have come to congratulate you and bring you flowers. Let us see the baby."

Erika pulled the blanket away from the baby's face and let everyone see the little pink face. A pink bonnet did not hide the thick, dark hair completely.

"What did you name her?" asked one of the neighbors.

"Rosalie."

"Oh, that's a pretty name for a beautiful little girl," commented one woman with sounds of agreement from the others.

After many ohs and ahs from the women, Erika went into the house and sat on the rocking chair. Kate followed her in with a trowel in her hand.

"Erika, would you mind if the ladies come in and plant their flowers?"

"No. Walter can supervise. He knows how I want the garden."

Walter went to the door and waved the women in. They had to walk through the house to get to the garden. Everyone inspected the flagstone patio on which there was a table with an umbrella. A flagstone path went by a small apple tree and a fig tree. Grape vines were making progress along the redwood fence, promising a harvest in a few months. There were flowering bushes and ground-cover flowers. The women could not get over how beautiful it all was. There was even a fountain Mr. Petucci had added to the garden. It had three tiers and water flowed out the top, cascading from one bowl into a larger bowl. The electric cord needed for circulating the water was hidden under some plants.

"What a beautiful outdoor living room you have here," commented Mrs. Dorsey. "We too have an unused garden."

"We own our house," said another. "And we could do something like this, too. Would you mind if my husband comes to see this?"

"Not at all," answered Walter. "When Erika recovers, we would like to have a garden party for the neighbors."

"That sounds like fun. I hope to be invited."

"We wouldn't think of having a party without you, Stefanie. Now all of you with petunias can put them there," Walter said, pointing. "Impatiens can go over there. Sweet William would look really nice near the apple tree."

One after another the flowers were planted, and the women went home.

After a brief nap Erika went into the garden. She looked at all the colorful flowers, the butterflies hovering over her bushes, and the birds getting a drink at the fountain and taking a bath. Tears came to her eyes. Walter rushed to her side and asked what was wrong.

"Nothing is wrong, Walter. I was just thinking how beautiful it is. I'll be able to sit out here with the baby in the carriage and Conrad playing. We'll have to invite the neighbors over for a get-together soon. I want to share our blessings."

"Yes, dear, we'll do that."

A few weeks later on a Saturday evening, the neighbors came to the party, carrying snacks and drinks, plus folding chairs. Some brought instruments. Karl and Kate, with Caroline and Herbert and Betty, came, carrying folding chairs, too. It was not long until the little garden was bulging with adults and children. Soon guitars were released from their cases and people began to sing. Some did solos, but most of the songs everyone knew and sang along. The evening passed with people bonding into a tight neighborhood.

Farewells were accompanied by hugs and kisses on the cheeks. Everyone seemed to be happy as they headed for their own homes. Karl and Kate kissed Walter and Erika good night.

"Mom, Pop, is there something bothering you?" Walter asked.

"Why do you ask?" Karl inquired.

"You seem a little quiet tonight."

"Well, there is something we want to tell you. We were going to wait 'til tomorrow—" Karl hesitated. "But since you ask, I'll tell you now."

"What is it?" Erika asked anxiously.

"We are going to buy a house."

"That's great. Congratulations," Walter said. "Where at?"

"In Hamilton."

CHAPTER 27

It was a hot day in August. Sigrit was out delivering papers. Conrad was hanging onto his mother's skirt and kept following her everywhere. The baby was colicky and continued crying even when held and rocked. Erika had a load of wash in the old washing machine in the basement. She put the baby into the baby carriage that served as a crib. She had bought it at Goodwill. Every day she walked to that store, hoping to find a crib before Rosalie outgrew the baby carriage.

When the baby finally fell asleep and Conrad was content playing with cars on the cool wooden floor, Erika went down the steps into the musty dark basement. Reaching into the washing machine, she found only sopping wet clothes. Seeing an oil puddle on the floor, she realized that the old machine, left by a previous tenant, was beyond fixing. At the moment they could not afford to replace it. The thought of having to walk with two little children and a load of wash to the local laundromat in this heat and humidity was discouraging. In her mind, she knew that this was only a small problem, but her emotions felt otherwise. She started to cry, as she took each item out of the wash machine and wrung it out. She carried the heavy load upstairs and out into the garden where she had a clothesline beyond the fruit trees. She was still crying, while hanging up the wash, when a butterfly landed on the line. Just seeing the beautiful creature with its bright orange wings, beautiful black patterns, and white spots made her smile.

"Garden," she said out loud, "you have done it again, making me happy."

That evening over supper the dying of the washing machine was a topic of conversation.

"Can you wait a few weeks?" Walter asked. "The rent is due now and after that we can take a look and see about getting a machine."

"How much is a washing machine?" inquired Sigrit.

"In the used appliance store I have seen them for as little as forty dollars," answered Erika.

"I have fifty dollars," said Sigrit. "I can cash in the savings bond I won. I'll be glad to let you have it."

"That's very sweet of you, Siggy," Walter said. "But your fifty-dollar savings bond is only worth twenty-five dollars."

"Really? But why do they call it a fifty-dollar bond?"

"It'll be worth that much in seven years or so."

"I have more than fifty dollars in my savings account," Sigrit said. "I'll be glad to give it to you to buy a washing machine. After all, I like wearing clean clothes, too."

"We don't expect you to give it to us," Erika said. "But as a loan we would appreciate it." Sigrit's face broke out in a big grin. She liked the feeling of being rich enough to make a loan.

"Mom, Dad, we still have not used my other prize yet, the trip to Washington. We'll have to go in the middle of the week and I will have to coordinate everything through my boss. He'll have to have a substitute for me and, Dad, I really would like for you to go, too. Wouldn't that be fun? Maybe Oma can watch both of the little kids and we could take Caroline. We'll get to eat lunch in the capital where all the congressmen and senators eat. Mom, what are we going to wear?"

"I'll have to see about getting off," Walter said. "We have been pretty busy at work."

"Tomorrow I'll call Mr. McCoy and get the ball rolling. It sure is nice to have a phone in the house. Don't you think so?"

"Yes," Erika said. "Especially with the baby. I still consider it a luxury I have not quite gotten used to."

Two days later Walter went to see his boss in the office. "Mr. Henshaw, I really need to take a day off next week on Thursday,"

"What do you have to do that's so important?" asked the man of about sixty, stroking his gray mustache.

"My daughter won the newspaper contest and that includes a limo ride to Washington to meet with our congressman and to spend a day with him. She can take her family along."

"We really need you here, but to meet our congressman as a VIP, well, for that I have to give you the day off. It never hurts to have a foot in the door with a politician. Give the man my greetings, whatever his name is."

"His name is Edward Garmatz."

⁕⁕⁕

"Mom, does this dress look good on me?" Sigrit asked at seven in the morning. "I thought it looked great in the store, but now I'm not sure."

"It is beautiful. That blue really brings out the color of your eyes," said Erika, noticing that her niece was beginning to develop. *I'll have to have a talk with her soon about what it means to become a woman.*

Walter was still getting dressed when Caroline and Kate knocked on the door.

"I brought over one child in exchange for two children," Kate said with a big smile.

"Wonderful exchange," Erika answered. "Shall we keep it for a few years?"

"No, I think one day will be enough." Kate laughed. "Now, Caroline, you be real good and have a wonderful time."

"I will, Mama."

"That is a lovely dress you're wearing," Erika said. "I love the flowered print."

"Thank you. Mama bought it new. It's not from Goodwill this time. I like your blue dress too, Erika, and you look nice, Siggy."

Just then Walter came down the steps. "What a beautiful bunch of women I get to go out with. Am I ever the luckiest man—oh, good morning, Mom," he said, giving his mother a peck on the cheek. "What are your plans for the day?"

"I get to play grandmother today. Maybe I'll get a little packing done. We should settle on the house in a few weeks."

"We're happy for you that you can buy a house," Walter said. "But we will certainly miss being this close to you. Pop will have quite a commute to work, won't he?"

"He might be changing jobs. But there is nothing definite yet. Has Conrad had breakfast?"

"Yes, we all had a bowl of cereal," Erika said. "But in another hour he'll be ready for more."

"No problem, I'm not going to let the kids starve."

Erika loaded the baby carriage with clean diapers and baby bottles, kissed Rosalie and Conrad and, with Walter's help, carried the carriage with the baby in it down the steps. Kate got underway toward her home before Conrad could see the limousine and make a fuss because he could not go.

Soon a black Cadillac limousine with whitewall tires pulled up in front of the house. A large black man dressed in a gray chauffeur's uniform got out, wished everyone good morning, showing a smooth set of white teeth, and opened the door of the vehicle.

"What is your name, sir?" Walter asked, getting in first.

"I'm James."

"Pleased to meet you, James," said Erika stooping down to get in.

Caroline got in next and sat behind them.

"Mr. James," Sigrit said. "I would like to sit in the front next to you."

"Your wish is my command," said James, opening the front passenger door.

A limousine was not a sight seen often in that neighborhood. Soon the neighbors gathered and watched. They had been told what this was all about and clapped and cheered as the long car pulled away. Erika felt like the Queen of England as she waved to the cheering people. Sigrit just sat there, staring out of the windshield with a big smile on her face.

The drive through the city was slow. Every time a streetcar was stopped, all the cars had to stop, too, to let the passengers get from the sidewalks to the middle of the street so they could get on the streetcar. The streetcars stopped at every other block. Only a few cars could get by while the streetcar was rolling.

After a long time they made it to Route One, the road that had connected the two cities since George Washington's time. There the going was faster because there was no streetcars.

Sigrit expected that the pleasant-looking driver would start talking with her, but he remained silent. There was a glass pane between the driver and the passengers in the back, so she could hear none of the conversation going on back there. Finally, she had enough of the silence and told the driver, "Mr. James, you are doing a good job. I admired the way you got this big car through all the traffic."

"Thank you, young lady."

"Oh, you can call me Sigrit or Siggy."

"That's a pretty name."

"Thank you. We have been in America for a whole year now."

Seeing that the girl was eager to talk, he asked the question he did not like asking too soon in the conversation. "Where did you come from?"

"Germany."

"Oh, really, I've been to Germany."

"I suppose it was during the war."

"No, it was right after the war was over. I was with the occupation forces. I really like the German people. They treated us real nice."

"I'm happy to hear that. I know the American soldiers treated the children real good, too, by giving us candy and chocolate. I'm glad that horrible war is over and we are in America. We are going to meet our congressman. I won the trip by selling the most subscriptions to the paper."

"Yeah, I heard you were quite the go-getter. When you see President Truman say hello from me, too, and thank him for integrating the military."

"President Truman is not on our schedule, but who knows who I might see today? I'm real excited. Is it much farther?"

"We're going through Beltsville now. It won't be long before you see the Capitol. One can see that and the Washington Monument a long way off."

Soon they were driving through the streets of Washington. Sigrit was surprised that many streets looked run down and the houses were ill kept.

"This is the Colored Section," said James. "Many landlords do not take good care of the houses here."

"Can't the people just move into nicer houses?"

"There are only certain areas where the Coloreds can go. It's called segregation."

"You mean a colored person cannot buy a nice house anywhere?"

"Few Coloreds can afford to buy a house. We just don't make that much money. There are only certain jobs we can get. You don't see Coloreds working as sales people in fine department stores. In the army I was a supply officer. I can't get an executive position on the outside."

"That is terribly unfair. If I see the president, I'll tell him about that."

"Oh, Mr. Truman knows very well what is going on. Now Congress is another matter, that's where we have to look for change."

"Well, when I see Congressman Garmatz I'll talk to him about that. Your people have been in this country for generations. We just got here, and we can buy a house anywhere we can afford."

"Young lady, I can see that you are very fair minded and I have hope in the future after meeting you. When we round the next corner, you'll see a beautiful sight."

What she saw through the windshield brought tears to her eyes. There in front of her was the white marble dome of the Capitol Building. The size and beauty so overwhelmed her that she could hardly catch her breath.

She opened the glass pane and called back that there was the Capitol Building. Everyone leaned forward and admired the view with ohs and ahs.

When the limo stopped in front of the Capitol Building's steps, an attractive young lady greeted them.

"Hello, I'm Linda, Congressman Garmatz's personal secretary." She shook hands with everyone as they were introduced by Sigrit.

"The congressman is on the floor right now, getting ready to vote on a bill. We can go to the gallery and watch if you like. Or would you rather have a quick tour of the Capitol, see his office, and then watch the vote?"

Sigrit looked at Walter who suggested that a tour would be good.

"Smart choice," said Linda. "They are still discussing the bill."

She turned to James and arranged for him to be at the same place by one in the afternoon. Then Linda led them up the steps into the domed building.

CHAPTER 28

They entered the rotunda and looked up. One-hundred-eighty feet above them was the top of the dome. None of the Hubers had ever been inside such a magnificent building. The pure size left them speechless. They all stood there with their necks craned, absorbing the sheer beauty of their surroundings.

Linda finally spoke. "The statues around the rotunda are former presidents and other great statesmen. If you like, we can go up to the congressman's office and meet some of his staff."

They took the elevator to the third floor and walked down a long corridor. The length of the hallway and all the closed doors on both sides was almost nightmarish. Sigrit expected the office to be totally opulent, but they were led into a modestly furnished room occupied by two young men and one middle-aged woman. After brief introductions, Linda took them to the galley overlooking the House of Representatives.

"All those men," Sigrit said. "So many bald heads. Aren't there any women in Congress?"

"There are about five or six women members," answered Linda. "See? Over there is a woman and there are two."

"We need more women lawmakers," was Sigrit's definite opinion.

"Where is our congressman?" Walter asked.

"Third row back and fifth seat over," said Linda, pointing.

"Another bald head," Caroline commented. After getting a strange look from Erika, she quickly added, "I like bald heads. Papa has one."

Congress was discussing mortgage insurance. Finally, the voting began and everyone was mesmerized, watching the Yea and Nay lights illuminating next to the names. After a while Linda said, "We can go to the House Member's dining room now. Mr. Garmatz will meet us there."

They went to a large dining room containing mostly round tables with white table cloths. They took a table near the window and sat down. A Black waiter handed them a menu and took their drink order. Soon he returned with iced tea and Seven-Up for the girls. Congressmen and senators entered in small groups. Some sat together. Others met someone at a table. A tall, slim man in his mid-forties briskly approached their table.

"Here he is," Linda said, standing up.

His small mustache emphasized his genuine-looking smile. The frameless glasses added a decorative sparkle to his hazel eyes. Everyone stood up and shook hands with the man as Linda introduced them.

Sigrit felt that she was the hostess for this outing and spoke first. "Mr. Garmatz, your honor, thank you very much for taking time out of your busy schedule to meet with us."

"It always is a pleasure to meet my constituents. My friend Mr. McCoy told me about you, young lady. Please, all of you, order anything you like off the menu. Now, is there anything going on that you have concerns about?"

"We are doing well," Sigrit said. "Wouldn't you say so, Mom and Dad?" They both nodded in agreement. "But I am concerned about the colored people," she continued. "So many live in substandard housing, and they are not allowed to move into nicer neighborhoods. What can you do about that?"

"Let me tell you that we are doing something about that. We passed a bill called the Urban Renewal Act. A lot of these old houses will be torn down and we will build nice apartment houses for all the people to live in."

"Will there be gardens?" Erika asked.

"No, there are no plans for gardens, but they'll have room for flowerpots."

"Then you should add to the bill that there must be room for gardens or park areas," Erika insisted. "I know how much my garden means to me, and now my neighbors are putting in gardens, too."

Then Walter added, "Yes, I have a happy wife with her garden. Then there is another matter I would like to discuss with you."

Sigrit was curious what that might be.

"I work in a small factory. I'm an A-1 machinist and my father is just a machinist in the same plant. The man working next to my father is a Negro and does the same job yet he gets paid less. Why is that?"

"Has your father worked there longer?"

"No, the Negro has."

"I'll have to look into that," the congressman said with concern. "The same is true with women. They can work next to a man doing the same job and get paid less. There has been a buzz about introducing a fair wage bill. Unfortunately, these things take a long time. We really are working hard and appreciate getting input from people like you."

When the waiter came with lunch, conversation diminished. The food was fresh and delicious. Erika and Walter enjoyed their juicy steaks. The girls had ordered chicken and the congressman was content with soup and a sandwich. When everyone had finished eating, the congressman needed to get back to work.

"I was so pleased to meet all of you," he said. "Now if you have any problem I can help you with, don't hesitate to call on me."

"Thank you," said Walter. "We are certainly happy to have met you."

Looking at Erika, the congressman said, "I'll see what I can do about getting the people gardens. Linda is going to show you around Washington a bit. She'll use the limo for that."

"Thank you again. Goodbye," they all said, shaking hands before the congressman walked away with an energetic stride.

When they emerged from the Capitol Building, James and the limo were waiting for them at the bottom of the stairs. The afternoon was spent driving along the mall. They stopped at the Washington Monument. They would have liked to take the elevator to the top, but a long line of people were waiting to do that. It would have taken hours to get in.

"One can walk up," Linda said. "But there is more to see on the ground."

"We'll pass on walking up today," Walter commented. "We'll just have to come some Sunday and plan on walking up to the top. I'm sure the view is fantastic."

"That would be fun, Dad."

"Can I come too, Walter?"

"Yes, Caroline, you can come too," promised her brother. "Are you sure you can do five-hundred-fifty-five feet of steps?"

"I'll practice at home running up and down the staircase."

"Conrad and I will take the elevator," Erika said.

The next stop was the castle, as the red brick Smithsonian Institution Museum was called.

"There are plans to build new buildings for all the displays," Linda told them. "There are warehouses full of artifacts that just have no room here. It will be beautiful when the mall is surrounded by white marble buildings."

"Linda, we really would like to see the White House," Erika requested.

"We can drive by," Linda said. "It is not open for visitors right now."

James drove them past most of the famous landmarks while Linda commented about each one. They managed to make a quick stop at many of them to take pictures.

"Siggy, my dear," said Erika, "this is your special day and we just have to immortalize it."

"Yes, I need pictures to send to Ludwig and the Wagners. And make sure you get a good picture of Mr. James and me with the limo."

On the drive back to Baltimore, Sigrit relayed every word spoken with the congressman to James. Suddenly he became very quiet. She felt the darkness of his mood and asked him what was bothering him.

"Miss Siggy," he said. "I don't want to live in no high-rise."

CHAPTER 29

Baltimore 1951:

"Mom, do I look okay?" asked Sigrit, now fourteen years old. She slowly turned around. "Please make sure everything is in place and I have no loose threads hanging out."

"Yes, the dress is beautiful. You did a really good job of sewing it." Erika inspected the white nylon dress with edged embroidery. On top of a white taffeta slip, the dress had full, round sleeves, going to the elbow, and a full skirt, pleated at the waist. A white taffeta sash with a large bow in the back completed the look.

Her legs were clad in her first pair of nylons and she wore white pumps with a two inch heel. Gone were the long brown braids. Her hair was coiffed in a sophisticated page boy. Her full lips had the slightest trace of lipstick.

"I hope my dress is prettier than Sonja's. She's always bragging how much her clothes cost."

Erika smiled. "I'm sure yours is just as pretty, if not more so."

Walter, dressed in his suit, came down the steps with Rosalie in his arms. He set her down on the floor. The little two-year-old looked like a doll. She wore a miniature version of Sigrit's dress, made by Kate out of leftover fabric.

Conrad came down the steps wearing light blue slacks and a white cotton shirt. "Dad, can I take my car to church?" he said, holding up a small truck.

"You can, just don't forget to bring it back home," Walter said. "Now the service will be pretty long today, so after Sunday school, you'll go to the nursery where your sister is."

"I know, Daddy. Siggy is having her comformation."

"That's close, but the word is confirmation," Walter corrected. "We better get going. We don't want to be late. After church we go to Oma and Opa for dinner and a party."

"Oh goody, a party," Conrad said, all excited. "I like playing with the dog."

The car was parked in front of the house. Sigrit started to get into the back as usual.

"You can sit in the front," said Erika. "This is your special day."

Before getting into the car, Sigrit turned her sash to put the bow in the front. Erika, dressed in her best red dress, took the backseat with the two little ones. Soon they arrived at Zion Church near city hall.

The elder Hubers were already there with Caroline and Betty, who had driven Herbert's car. Normally Betty went to a Catholic church, but for this occasion she joined the family. Herbert was in Seoul, South Korea, courtesy of Uncle Sam. After warm greetings, Sigrit and Erika, with the two children, went around the church to the Sunday school rooms. The "confirmants," six boys and five girls, assembled there, getting ready for their grand entrance into the church. The boys were dressed in suits and the girls wore white dresses. All the girls inspected each other with a critical eye. When Sonja looked at her, Sigrit knew by Sonja's expression that Sigrit's homemade dress was the prettier.

After church, the two cars drove to Hamilton. The two-story, craftsman house was located on a quiet street surrounded by a garden with lawn and trees. The upstairs was a separate apartment occupied by Betty. Herbert had moved in with his wife and shortly thereafter was drafted into the army.

Betty's parents were invited for dinner, and her sister and brother-in-law came later. All of them brought Sigrit a card with some money.

"Thank you very much, everybody. I'll put the money into my bank account. I'm saving for college."

"Do you have any idea what you want to study?" asked Mr. Burger.

"Not yet, but to college I will go. I have been saving my newspaper money, too."

"I like that, a determined young woman," Mrs. Burger said.

That is the first time I have been called a young woman. I like it.

On the drive home, Walter said, "My parents did a smart thing buying a house. I wish we could afford to get into our own house. Real estate is always a good investment."

"We will, dear," said Erika. "I can manage to save a little bit each month."

"The only way we really can save is when I get overtime, and that isn't that often. Maybe I can find a part-time job on weekends."

"Walter, our family time together is so important. As soon as Conrad goes to school in the fall, I could find a babysitter for Rosalie and go back to the restaurant. Yes, that's what we can do. We'll get a house, too, you'll see."

A few weeks later Mr. Petucci called. "Erika, I would like to talk with you and your husband. Could I come over and see you this evening?"

"Yes, we'll be home. Would seven o'clock be good for you?"

"Seven it is. See you then."

All day long Erika wondered what the landlord wanted to see them about. When Sigrit came home from school, she noticed her aunt had a sad demeanor.

"Mom, you look down at the mouth. Is anything wrong?"

"The landlord is coming over after supper. He wants to talk to us. I'm afraid he wants us to move. I don't want to leave my garden or this neighborhood." The thought brought tears to her eyes.

As soon as Walter got home that night Erika told him about the upcoming visit. Walter gently took her into his arms and told her not to worry.

"Sometimes life takes a turn for the better through an action that is forced on us," said Walter. "Let's see what the man has to say before we can determine what we will do."

At seven sharp there was a knock on the door. Mr. Petucci came with a bottle of red Italian wine in his hand.

"It is such a lovely evening," Erika said. "Let us sit out in the garden."

"I was hoping you would say that," said Mr. Petucci.

Walter got three wine glasses out of the cupboard while Erika carried out some crackers and cheese. They sat around the metal table on cushioned metal chairs. Sigrit was upstairs putting Rosalie to bed. She was curious what the landlord wanted to discuss. To her delight, Mr. Petucci spoke loud enough for her to hear through the open bedroom window.

Walter pulled the cork and filled the glasses. "*Salut* to the world's best landlord," he said and everyone drank a little.

"I suppose you're wondering what I want to see you about," said the landlord.

"Yes," Erika said. "I hope everything is well with you and yours."

"Fine, just fine. What I really want to discuss with you is this," he said, taking a pregnant pause. "My intention is to sell some of my property."

Oh no, thought Sigrit, *Here it comes. He'll ask us to move.*

"What I want to do is offer to sell you this house."

Before anyone could say that they couldn't afford to buy it, he raised his hand. "Before you say anything, here is the good part. I would have my lawyer write up the contract that I sell you this house for five thousand dollars. You pay me fifty dollars a month until the house is paid for. I will charge you no interest."

"No interest?" said Walter "Then it would be just like paying rent."

"Precisely. You would have to pay the taxes and insurance. But other than that, it's just like paying rent."

"Mr. Petucci," Erika said, "that sounds wonderful, but why would you want to do that?"

"'Cause I like you people and I like to help young people. I had help when I was young and just came off the boat. If I hadn't gotten some breaks who knows where I would be today?"

Erika and Walter looked at each other across the table. Then they watched the compassionate, old Italian man raise his glass and enjoy the sip of wine. They exchanged glances again.

"I have a few questions," said Walter. "How much are the taxes and insurance?"

"I pay about two-hundred a year, might be less if the homeowner lives in the place."

"We can afford that," said Erika. "Especially if I go back to the restaurant when school starts. I hope Tony still wants me."

"Tony will be happy to have you back," the old man assured her.

"This calls for a celebration," said Walter, refilling the glasses.

Everyone raised their glass and said, "*Salut.*"

Then Erika got up and gave Mr. Petucci a hug and a peck on the cheek. "Thank you, Mr. Petucci,"

Walter shook the man's hand. "We can't thank you enough. Thank you, thank you."

"I'll contact my lawyer in the morning and tell him to get busy on the paperwork. As far as I'm concerned, you folks are now homeowners. Congratulations."

Upstairs in the bedrooms, the little children were asleep. Sigrit had heard everything that was said. She clasped her hands together and waved them in the air like a fighter having won the match.

"Thank you Lord," she whispered. "Thank you for keeping my world constant for a while longer."

CHAPTER 30

Walter and Erika took home ownership seriously. Their first project was to clean up the musty basement. In one corner they found some old furniture left by a previous tenant along with old buckets and other things not worth moving, but too good to throw away. Everything was hauled through the house into a far corner of the backyard to possibly be fixed up and utilized at a later time.

"I sure wish we had a basement door," Erika said to her husband one Saturday morning.

"You know that is something we could do," responded Walter. "Dig out here, put in some steps and a door. We could even put in a little window over here," he said, pointing to an empty space above ground. "It will be a hard job. Maybe some of the guys in the neighborhood will help."

The basement job went like many projects. Once started, it began steamrolling. After a door was installed with glass panes and a window, the dark basement looked a lot more cheerful. Walter continued patching the concrete floor and painting it. The brick walls got a coat of white paint.

The beams on the ceiling were scrubbed and left exposed. Since Walter was always available to help the neighbors, the men volunteered to come to his aid. Work times turned into party time. Talking and laughter could be heard throughout the house while the men worked.

"Okay fellows, lunch time," Erika shouted down to the basement.

Four men stomped up the steps, washed their hands, and sat around the dining room table.

"Something smells good," said one of the men. "What is it?"

"Pizza," Erika said.

"Pizza? What is that?"

Erika produced a large flat pan, filled with dough and covered with tomato sauce, pepperoni, and onions, topped with shredded mozzarella cheese, out of the oven.

"It's new. I hope you guys like it. It goes good with beer. Who wants one?"

"Me…I'll have one…Me, too…I'll drink mine out of the bottle."

Everyone liked the never-before-seen dish. Erika showed how to just pick up a piece and eat it out of the hand. She could see that one pizza was not enough. She went into the living room and called Tony at the restaurant.

The men looked disappointed looking at the empty pan.

"Don't worry. There will be more pretty quick."

Soon there was a knock on the door. It was Tony with two more pizzas. He came in and joined everyone at the table.

"How do you guys like this new item on my menu?"

"It's great…I like it…Do you think it'll catch on?"

"I hope so. Well, you know where to come to get more."

"I hate going out to eat with five kids," said Joe, the neighbor who was a plumber. "If I call you, would you bring it to my house, too?"

"You know, Joe, you might have something there. Delivering pizzas to the house, hmm, it might catch on."

After lunch the men went back into the basement to work.

"You know, Walter, you just have to make this basement into a party room. We need a gathering place on this block."

"You all can come here any time, you know that, but why don't you do something with your basement? Don't all of you own your houses?"

For the next few months the women in the neighborhood always knew where to find their husbands—in the house where the noise was and where the big pizza box went.

ಲಾಲಾ

Sigrit was a good student and carried a heavy schedule in high school. Going to an all-girl high school helped by not having any boys distracting her from her studies. Between her morning and afternoon paper route, studying, and helping Erika around the house and with the little ones, she had no time or inclination to date. Her goal was to go to college, and she saved just about every penny she earned for it. She even made good use of the long summer vacation by going to summer school to get ahead on her credits toward graduation. She was looking forward to graduating from high school shortly after she turned seventeen, a year ahead of her contemporaries.

As Conrad and Rosalie got bigger, the house got smaller. One evening at the supper table Sigrit said, "Mom, Dad, you really could use my bedroom for either Conrad or Rosalie. How would it be if I moved into the basement?"

"Are you sure you would like that?" Erika asked.

"In less than a year I'll be away at college and then you would take over my room anyway."

"You know," Walter said. "That might not be a bad idea. There is plumbing down there, I could put in a toilet and sink."

"Then it would be like a private apartment," Sigrit said. "How about a shower? Would that be possible?"

"Everything is possible," Walter promised. "I'll speak with Joe about it."

"If money is a problem, I could even pay for some of it," Sigrit volunteered.

"Thank you," said Erika. "But we have enough put aside for house projects."

"Talking about money," Walter said. "Just how much have you saved?"

"I have almost three thousand dollars," she said proudly.

"That is wonderful," said Erika. "We are proud of you."

"Yes, we are," Walter agreed. "That should be enough for two or three years of college."

"Siggy is going to college," seven-year-old Conrad explained to four-year-old Rosalie. He took his job of big brother seriously. Whenever he learned anything new, he explained it to his sister.

A few weeks later Sigrit moved her belongings into the basement near the window and the door with the glass pane. To have her own bathroom was, in her mind, beyond luxury. She felt that for the first time in her life she had her own space. The Bavarian doll she received for her eighth birthday had a prominent place on her dresser. It was a constant reminder of Greta and Ludwig and the happy days in Bavaria. Occasionally the last moments of Opa entered her head. When that happened, she concentrated on happy times like the sleigh ride into Switzerland, going on picnics with Greta and Ludwig, or just helping Frau Martha with cooking. Slowly the horrible scenes of her young childhood were replaced by good memories.

Shortly before Christmas of 1953, she received a letter from Greta. Sigrit did not open it until all the day's chores were done and she went into her private space. Reading the letter was her way of rewarding herself. She was lying in bed when she read:

> *Dearest Siggy,*
>
> *It has been several weeks now since I have been trying to get Ludwig to write to you. He always says he will, but nothing happens. It is not that he doesn't love you, it just is that he is lazy when it comes to writing. Mother just says, "typical man." Other than that, he is a really hard worker. Father could not run the farm without his help.*
>
> *Mother and Father are well and send you and yours their love. Oma too sends special*

> *greetings to you and your dear family in America. I want to remind you that years ago I made you a promise. Remember, it was New Year's Day 1945 and you made me promise that I would invite you to my wedding. Well, my dear "sister," that time has come. When I get married in July, we will become sisters under the law. You guessed it. Ludwig and I are getting married. I really love him and I believe his feelings toward me are the same. He treats me really nice and lovingly. We plan on having a typical Bavarian country wedding. Whether we will hold it in the church in town or Opa's chapel has not yet been decided. It is our biggest wish that you, my dear Siggy, come to the wedding. I know it is a very long way and terribly expensive, but it would mean so much to us to see you here. Of course, anyone else or all of the family are welcome, too. I send you and yours lots of love,*
>   *Your "sister" Greta and Ludwig.*

Sigrit carefully folded the letter and put it back into the envelope. She did not wish to get out of the warm bed and run upstairs to show it to Erika and Walter. She figured in the morning would be soon enough.

Bavaria? How can I possibly afford to go to Bavaria? It would be wonderful to see them all again, but to squander my college money on a trip? What is more important, college or a trip? As much as I would like to go, I will just have to tell them that I can't be at their wedding.

She looked at the doll and happy memories of Bavaria entered her mind. *I have never named the doll. I'll call her Siggy. Maybe I can just mail them Siggy as a wedding present. Stupid thought. Greta has a doll like it already.* Thinking about her life in Bavaria as she fell asleep took her into dreamland and she was there with her brother and Greta.

೧೨೧

It was shortly after Christmas when Sigrit received a phone call from her boss, Mr. McCoy. When she hung up the phone, Erika saw the puzzled look on her face and asked,

"Is anything wrong, Sigrit?"

"I don't know. Mr. McCoy wants to come to the house tomorrow afternoon and see me. He hasn't done that in years. I wonder what he wants." She shrugged her shoulders. "I suppose we'll know tomorrow at this time."

All the next day the thought of what Mr. McCoy wanted to see her about kept popping into Sigrit's head. *I don't think he'll want to fire me, at least I hope not. Maybe he thinks I'm getting too old for the job, or maybe he has a relative who wants my route. I hope I can keep the job until I get out of high school. The money sure is nice. I'm too young for many other jobs.*

When she returned home from her afternoon paper route, she saw Mr. McCoy's car parked in front of the house. He and Erika sat in the living room, drinking hot tea, with Conrad and Rosalie playing on the floor.

"Good afternoon," Sigrit said upon entering the house. "All the papers are delivered. How are you, Mr. McCoy?"

"Thank you, I am well," he said, reaching for a home-baked cookie on the cocktail table. "I'm sure you're wondering what brings me here today."

"Yes, I hope you are still satisfied with my work."

"More than satisfied. You did not get to be carrier of the year twice for nothing. I have come here to ask you what your future plans are."

"I plan to go to college when I graduate from high school this coming June."

"Do you have any idea what you will major in?"

"No, not yet. I figure a liberal arts program would be best to begin with, maybe find a major later. I don't know, but I might want to eventually get into politics."

"Are you a U. S. citizen yet?" asked Mr. McCoy.

Erika quickly answered, "Yes. Walter and I made our citizenship just a few months ago. Sigrit insisted on taking the test herself, too. She could have gotten it from us getting our citizenship, but she said that she did not want to take any chances that there might be a technicality and she would not be a citizen. You, see, she is my niece and we are her legal guardians."

"Congratulations on becoming Americans."

"Thank you. We are proud and happy to be here."

"Now what I really want to discuss with you," continued Mr. McCoy, "is college. Sigrit, if you want to major in journalism, the newspaper can offer you a full, four-year scholarship to the University of Maryland in College Park."

Sigrit looked at Erika who burst into a big smile. "What exactly does a full scholarship mean?" Erika asked.

"They would pay for tuition, books, room, and board, and any other fees associated with college."

"Wow," Sigrit said, amazed. "They would do that? What do I have to do to get it?"

"Apply for the scholarship, get good grades, and promise to work for the paper for at least two years after you graduate."

"Wow, to be a reporter. I think I would like that. How do I apply?"

"I just happen to have the application form in my car." He rose and went outside to get it.

"A full scholarship. Oh, Mom."

Mr. McCoy came back with a handful of white papers. "You can take your time filling these out. There are also papers for your teachers to fill out. There should be no problems with your record as a paper carrier and your grades in school."

Gratefully, Sigrit took the bundle of papers. "Thank you Mr. McCoy," she said. "That is the best news I've ever had." She looked at Erika. "Well, one of the best news."

Then Erika spoke up. "Mr. McCoy, Sigrit has really been working too hard for a girl her age. She has no time for anything social. Between the morning route and afternoon route and keeping up with her studies, she has no time to participate in any after school activities. I would like to see her drop the afternoon route."

"That is doable. There are several kids around here who would be happy to have the job. If you want, you could even quit the morning route."

"I'm afraid then I would not know what to do with myself. I'll keep the morning route and do the morning collections, if that is agreeable with you, Mr. McCoy."

"It certainly is. When I think of it, Erika, four years ago she came to my office and convinced me that girls can do the job. Since then I have hired many girls and they, in general, do a better job than the boys. Sometimes it takes someone like her to show people the nose in front of their faces. You are going to go far, young lady," he said, rising and shaking her hand.

Sigrit looked him straight in the eyes. "Thank you, Mr. McCoy, thank you for giving me the opportunity and now thank you for the scholarship." She let go of his hand and gave the man a hug, the first one ever.

He responded by saying, "Erika, you have every reason to be proud of Sigrit."

"Thank you, we are, very much so."

After Mr. McCoy left, Sigrit, Erika, and the two children held hands and danced around the living room.

"Mom, do you know what that means?"

"Yes, you don't have to worry about college money anymore."

"That, and now I can afford to go to Bavaria for the wedding. I could even afford to take you."

"I could not go," Erika said. "We can't afford for all of us to go, and what would I do with the family for that long? But I think it would be an excellent idea for you to go."

"You would do that? Let me go by myself? How would I get there?"

Erika laughed. "Well, you can either fly, take a ship, or swim."

"Hmm, between the three choices, I think I'll take a ship. I'll call a travel agent right now and see about it." Sigrit spent the rest of the afternoon on the phone getting facts and requirements about such a trip. When Walter came home from work, supper had not been started.

"I smell excitement in the air, but no supper," he said after he kissed his family.

"I ordered pizza," Erika told him. "Tony will bring it over and join us. We have a celebration tonight."

CHAPTER 31

Baltimore 1954:

"Mom, I have a problem," Sigrit lamented in early April while she and Erika were working in the garden. Conrad and Rosalie were playing on the swing set.

"What is it, dear? Anything I can help you with?"

"The tickets to the senior prom go on sale now. I really would like to go. It's being held at a big hotel downtown, but I have no idea who I can ask to go with me."

"Surely there must be a dozen boys who would be more than happy to take you. You are pretty, you are intelligent, and you are talented. Do any of your girlfriends have older brothers?"

"The ones that do, I would not want to be with. So many of the boys my age are so stupid."

"Surely not all of them. Is there anyone in church who might be a candidate?"

"There might be one or two. That's the problem with going to an all-girl school, I just haven't met many boys at all. But on the other hand, I've had no distractions from my studies."

"When we go to church on Sunday, maybe some young men will be there and you can ask one of them."

"I'll do that. Thanks, Mom, for your suggestion."

಄಄಄

Sunday after church Sigrit did get a chance to speak with a fellow named Gunter, who was a relatively new immigrant from Germany. After she assured him that the suit he was wearing to church would be nice to wear to the dance, and he was not expected to go to the expense of renting a tuxedo, he consented to taking her to the prom.

"Are you doing anything special this afternoon?" Gunter asked.

"No, not really,"

"How about I take you to a movie?"

She gave him a happy smile. "I would like that."

"How about I pick you up at your house at two? What would you like to see, House of Wax in 3D or Roman Holiday?"

"I hear House of Wax is really scary. I think Roman Holiday would be nice."

The movie house was near Sigrit's residence. It was a nice day and they enjoyed the walk to the theater. After the show, they stopped at an ice cream parlor and each had a milkshake. Then Gunter walked her back home. He shook her hand, told her he enjoyed her company, then left after she was in the house.

"How was your first date?" Erika asked as Sigrit came into the dining room where they were eating a cold supper.

"The movie was good, then we had a milk shake. He said he'll see me at church and for the prom."

"He didn't ask you for another date?" Walter asked. Sigrit shook her head. "Well, that's his loss."

"He's nice, but really very uninteresting. Talking with him is like pulling teeth. But at least I have a date for prom night and he's fairly nice looking. There, we don't need to talk. We'll just dance. He says he likes to dance."

"Sigrit, when do you want to go and buy your graduation-slash-prom dress?" Erika asked.

"How about this week, one day after school? I would like you come along, Mom."

"I'd like that, we'll have fun. Walter, you won't mind me going with Siggy one evening this week, or will you?"

"You know I'll enjoy being alone with the kids. Why don't you go and eat supper out, and I'll take the kids for some fifteen-cent hamburgers?"

"Oh boy, hamburgers," eight-year-old Conrad said, clapping his hands.

"Hamburgers," echoed Rosalie now five, clapping her hands, too.

☙❧☙

The night of the prom, Erika and Sigrit were in the master bedroom upstairs and Erika was pinning small white roses into Sigrit's curled and partially put up hair.

"Now when Gunter comes, Walter will talk with him for a little while, then I'll go downstairs and tell him that you are almost ready. Then after a minute or so, you will walk slowly down the steps and make a grand entrance. When he sees you in that lovely white dress he will surely fall head over heels in love with you."

"Well, not too much in love. I'm going to college and he is being drafted. But a little in love for just tonight would be fun."

"What time are you expecting him?"

"Seven thirty."

"He's already five minutes late," Erika said anxiously.

"He said he's coming by cab. Maybe the cab was late."

At ten to eight, Sigrit said, "I'm getting tired of sitting up here, I might as well ditch the grand entrance and go downstairs and read a magazine."

By eight o'clock Walter was losing his patience. "I hope there was no accident. Give me his number and I'll call his house."

Gunter's mother answered the phone. "Gunter is not here. He left for the army over a week ago. He never mentioned having a date with your daughter. Gosh, I'm sorry. He must have forgotten all about it. To not even call and tell you, that was rude of him."

When Walter told everyone what Gunter's mother said, Sigrit's mouth curved downward and her eyes suddenly lost the sparkle.

"What a jerk," she said. "What a number one jerk. I paid twenty dollars for the tickets, got all dressed up, and here I sit."

Erika looked anxiously at her husband, nodded her head, and signaled with her eyes.

"Sigrit dear," Walter said. "Would you give me the honor of allowing *me to* accompany you to the ball?"

"You would want to do that? Oh, Dad, I love you." She ran to his chair and hugged him. "Yes, yes."

"It will only take me a few minutes to get dressed," he said, going up the steps.

Erika went out into the garden and cut a red rose for his lapel. A half an hour later they entered the large elegant ballroom while the band was playing the number one hit, "Oh, my Papa." Most of the girls wore white gowns, the same ones they would wear for the graduation ceremony. The young men wore mostly white sports coats and black slacks. Walter in his dark suit and Sigrit in her white taffeta gown made a handsome couple and got the attention of her classmates.

"Who is that handsome guy with you tonight?" asked one of her classmates sitting at the same round table.

"Well I must confess," Sigrit whispered in a conspiratory tone, "he is a married man." Seeing the shocked look on the girl's face made her laugh. "It's okay. His wife knows. She's my Mom."

After the dance number others returned to the table. Sigrit stood up and announced, "I want all of you to meet my Dad."

"You all can call me Walter," he said after they all introduced themselves and their dates.

The rest of the evening, Walter and Sigrit showed the teenagers how to dance. He had lost none of the skills that so impressed Erika nine years earlier, and Sigrit could easily follow him.

On the way home in Walter's car, she said, "Now I'm glad Gunter did not show up. You, Dad, are a lot more fun than he would have been."

"I enjoyed it too, and talking with that English girl, she has a good brain between her ears."

"Yes, she is one of my favorite classmates."

"They all are nice kids, I wish them all well."

༺༻

A few days later, Sigrit came home from school with her face glowing. "Mom," she said, when entering the house, "I made it, I made it. I'm valedictorian. It was close with two others, but I made it."

"Congratulations," said Erika, giving her a big hug. "Is there anything special you need to do?"

"I get to address the graduation ceremony. I have to write a speech. I never spoke in front of that many people."

"You'll do just fine. Sometimes it is easier to speak to many people than just a few."

"I have two days to write my speech. I might need your help."

"Anytime."

༺༻

The auditorium was filled to capacity. The school orchestra played "Pomp and Circumstances" while all the girls, dressed in long white gowns, marched in single file and took their seats on the stage.

A minister opened the ceremony with a prayer then, after some welcoming speeches by the school principal and the class president, the principal introduced the valedictorian.

"And it is my pleasure to introduce Sigrit Elisabeth Lachmann, our class valedictorian."

Sigrit took a deep breath, walked to the podium, and looked at the sea of faces. She only exhaled when she saw her family sitting in the second row.

There was Betty with Herbert who recently returned from Korea, Karl and Kate with Caroline, and Erika and Walter. She had begged and bought extra tickets from her classmates since the graduates only got a limited number of tickets each.

The audience was silent and expectant.

"Mayor D'Alesandro, school faculty and staff, family and friends of all the graduates, and fellow classmates, I thank all of you for being here tonight to help celebrate this happy occasion.

"As we leave high school we also leave our childhood behind. Now we go forward, armed with knowledge and the beginning of wisdom. In Geometry we learned to think logically, in History we learned to be careful, there are parts we don't want to repeat. We can all be thankful to have gone to this school with such a fine faculty, to live in 'Monument City' in our lovely state, but most of all, we can all be thankful that we live in the United States.

"I thank my teachers and classmates who helped me shed a foreign accent. And I certainly thank my Mom and Dad. Without them I would not be here."

There was a chuckle for that last sentence. Most people had no idea what she really meant.

"Now, as we venture into the future, free to choose the paths we tread, a Dickens book comes to my mind and, to quote Tiny Tim, I close with 'God bless us, every one.'"

Big tears rolled down Erika's cheeks while she added to the resounding applause. "Short and powerful," she said turning to Walter.

"The best speeches are always short," he replied.

After a few more people said what they had to say, the winners of the scholarships were announced. Sigrit again got a big ovation when she received a certificate that she had won a total four-year scholarship to the University of Maryland.

After the mayor of the city handed each graduate their diploma, the orchestra played "Land of Hope and Glory" as the graduates marched out of the auditorium. Several hundred girls, all dressed in long, white evening gowns, reunited with their loved ones and left the school in small clusters. The Huber family drove to Walter's house for a family party.

All the Hubers, plus a few neighbors they were close friends with, crowded into Walter's small house. It was almost dark in early June when the get-together started. Rosalie was already asleep, but Conrad was excited about a party.

He told all the guests, "When I graduate from high school I too will be valedictorian, maybe even salutatorian," he said proudly, having recently added those two words to his vocabulary.

While people were sitting in the living room and dining room and spilling into the kitchen, Sigrit addressed everyone in a loud voice. "I want to thank you all for coming to my party and for all the cards and gifts. I want to tell you that I appreciate your love and friendships. All of you are a happy part of my life."

They all clapped and affirmed that the love went both ways.

"Now I want to show you all something about which I am very excited." Sigrit brought out her left hand that had been behind her back and held a document above her head. "This is my ship's ticket. I am going to Germany for my brother's wedding."

"All by yourself?…When is that?…You must be thrilled…How exciting," Everyone tried to get close to her to hear all about it.

"Here is what the plans are," said Sigrit in a loud voice that carried all the way to the kitchen,

"I take the ship from New York on July seventh to Rotterdam arriving on the seventeenth. Uncle Ernst and Aunt Lydia will pick me up there by car. We'll drive to Stuttgart and I will stay with them for a few days. Then I will take a train to Bavaria and stay with the Wagner family.

"Uncle Ernst and his family will drive to Bavaria for the wedding. On the twenty-first of August the ship will dock in New York again and I plan to be on it. Any more questions?"

The rest of the evening Sigrit answered what seemed to be hundreds of questions concerning her upcoming trip and about her time in Bavaria when she was a child.

"We want to invite you to our house on Sunday," Kate said to the family members, "for dinner and another little graduation celebration. Karl and I hope you don't have other plans."

"We'll be free," Erika assured her. "Thank you, that will be nice. We're looking forward to it."

After everyone had gone home and Walter, Rosalie, and Conrad were in bed, Sigrit was still too stimulated to go to sleep. It was a clear and warm evening and she and Erika sat in the garden, enjoying the full moon and talking. Graduation was yesterday when they finally went to bed.

CHAPTER 32

A few days after graduation Erika received a letter from Jutta in Goerlitz.

Dearest Erika,

It has been a long time since you received a letter from me because nothing is really new in my life, which is probably a good thing. I am quite content living here. Your apartment is in good shape should you ever wish to return to it. With my job in the department store I earn enough to pay the rent and put food on the table.

There is not much else to spend money on. Occasionally there is a sale on china which has been rejected for export. When those go on sale there is a big rush to buy it. The clothes they sell nowadays do not match the style and quality of the clothes you left in the closet. Fortunately, I can wear those dresses with little al-

teration. The day I met you was a very blessed day for me.

Occasionally I go to the Lutheran church. The door is still open and the pastor is a very nice man. The other day I learned that if the boys make confirmation, they will not be accepted as apprentices to learn a trade or be allowed to get higher education.

My boys are ten and twelve now, and I have to do what is best for them. I just teach them The Bible *at home.*

A few months ago I got a new neighbor upstairs. When she saw me come out of your apartment she asked me if I knew you. I figured since you are in America, it would be safe to talk about you.

The lady told me her name is Frau Kempf. She has a big birthmark on her face. She also has an eight year old daughter. Over coffee in the living room, she told me about herself and how she met you. She told me that she was ordered to take your niece and nephew to a family in Bavaria.

On the way, the Volksturm came on the train and drafted the boy—I did not tell her that he returned and told me a different story. Then she confided in me that the daughter she has was the result of a rape by some Russian soldiers. The girl is a pretty child and very polite, and Frau Kempf seems to be a good mother.

She also mentioned your niece and what a pretty and courteous child she was. Now she wishes she would have shown some affection to her while they were traveling together.

I told her that Sigrit is in America and she was happy to hear that.

I hope you continue to be happy with your dear family. I am always pleased to receive a letter from you and treasure the photos you send me.

Your grateful friend, Jutta

Erika gave the letter to Sigrit to read. The only comment she had was, "Mom, I think it would be really nice if we send her a box of nice stationery. That paper she writes on only belongs in the toilet."

"I suppose that is the best she can buy."

౪౩౪౩

The next few days Sigrit spend her time packing, unpacking, and repacking. She would be on the ship ten days then go to a wedding. At first she planned to take her graduation gown, but realized that needed ironing every time before wearing it. She tried on her confirmation dress and decided that with different colored sashes, it gave the appearance of another dress. Since ballerina length gowns were becoming a fashion statement, she felt well dressed with that outfit. A few more wrinkle-resistant summer dresses, along with some slacks, shorts, skirts, and blouses should serve for almost four weeks in Germany and also the two ocean passages. A wool cardigan and light top coat rounded out her wardrobe. She was pleased that all she would need was one moderate sized suitcase.

"Now remember, Sigrit, don't accept any invitations to a man's cabin," Walter said. "If you go into a man's cabin, he thinks you only come for one thing."

"Yes, Dad, I remember."

Walter, with Erika and Sigrit, were driving to New York. At first they planned to leave Baltimore early in the morning and drive to New York with the whole family. Sigrit was afraid that if anything bad happened on the road, like a flat tire or a traffic jam, they might miss the noon sailing of the ship. She said that she would feel a lot more secure to go up the day before, stay in a hotel in New York, then have plenty of time to get to the ship.

Erika and Walter decided to take her, do a little sightseeing, and have some long-needed couple time. Since Walter had lived in New York, he was eager to see some of the old haunts. The little children were on a several day visit with their grandparents.

When they arrived in New York they found a modest priced hotel and checked in. The next morning after breakfast, they drove to the ship. At the pier all the activity of loading the gray-hulled ship electrified the air. Sigrit's cheeks turned red as if she had put on a heavy dose of rouge.

"Oh, Mom, Dad, don't you wish you were going with me?"

"No, I'm not ready to go to Germany yet," Walter said. "I was there much too long. When my parents went in 'thirty-nine it was only supposed to be for six weeks, that turned into nine years. I suppose they did not want to miss the war." He chuckled. "You, my dear, have a good reason to go there, to see your brother and your good friend Greta again—to go to where you have happy childhood memories…"

Sigrit winced. *Opa. I remember Opa and the last time I saw him. Oh how horrible. Think happy thoughts, think about the sleigh ride, the flowers in the field, the picnics with Greta. Oh, it will be good to see all of them again. I wonder what my roommate will be like. I hope it is someone young I can pal around with.*

Walter and Erika were able to go aboard with Sigrit. They located her cabin, which was a tiny space with a bunk bed, a sink, and a little hanging locker. The toilets and baths were down the hall. A girl of about twenty came in while they were inspecting the cabin.

"Oh I'm sorry, I must be in the wrong room," she said checking the number on the door.

"No, this is my Dad and Mom. They just brought my suitcase aboard. They'll be leaving."

"Well, nice to meet you, roomie. My name is Natalie."

"Pleased to meet you. I'm Sigrit. You want the top or bottom?"

"I like top," she said while throwing her coat on the bed.

"We better get ready to get off the ship," Walter said. "Otherwise they'll sail with us aboard."

"Yes, Dad, you don't want to be a stowaway," said Sigrit as they walked down the passageway.

Erika paused at the gangplank. "You have a wonderful time. It looks like there are lots of young people aboard. You'll have all kinds of friends by the time you get to Holland. Now don't forget to write as soon as you get there."

"I will, Mom. I'll mail a postcard as soon as I can. Thank you for coming with me. I really appreciate it."

"That's the least we can do for our daughter," Walter said, giving her a lingering embrace. "Now remember, when you get back, Herbert and Betty will pick you up."

"I hope they remember. Goodbye."

Erika hugged her, kissing her on the cheeks. "Goodbye, sweetheart, bon voyage,"

Walter and Erika were among the crowd of people waving farewell as the ship, with the help of tug boats, slowly pulled away from the dock. Sigrit waved until the ship went to full steam ahead. Then she walked to the other side so she could see the Statue of Liberty as they sailed by. After that she went to the dining room to find her assigned table for lunch.

It was a large round table, seating ten people. Two were lady school teachers going to Europe for the summer, there was a mother and her middle-aged daughter. Two young men had just finished an apprenticeship in organ making and they were going to Europe to see old organs. Another couple was from Holland who had visited relatives in America, and Natalie was an Irish girl who lived in New York, going to visit her parents. Conversation flowed easily and the good looking Dutch steward was friendly and efficient.

This is going to be a fun passage, Sigrit decided.

The next week was a relaxing and also a busy time. Delicious meals were served in the dining room, and soon the table mates became friends. In the evening there was a movie in the lounge and, afterward, the band played dance music. During the day Sigrit would lounge on the deck and use the pool. She enjoyed the company of Natalie and the two organ makers, especially the taller one from Boston. They liked to dance together and, by the time they reached Ireland, he had even given her a shy kiss when they parted to return to their cabins.

The ship anchored off Cobh, Ireland, and several passengers, including Natalie, disembarked. The girls promised to keep in touch with each other through letters. Two days later the ship motored up the Nieuwe Waterweg and docked. Before Sigrit disembarked, she stood on the deck and spotted her aunt and uncle waving from the terminal. Soon she was ashore and in the warm embrace of her relatives.

"My, my, what a beautiful young lady you have become," said Aunt Lydia who was the epitome of a well-groomed, attractive woman, but now shorter than Sigrit.

"It is wonderful to see you again," added Uncle Ernst. "We have heard so much about you. Your mother and father would be very proud of you."

Sigrit frowned. *Mother and father? Oh yes, he is talking about my real parents. I think of Erika and Walter as my mother and father. Just the thought of the real ones brings that horrible scene to my mind. Come on, girl, try to get over it. I hope they won't mention my parents anymore. Happy thoughts, think happy thoughts. Here I am in Holland, enjoy.*

"Siggy!"

She turned around and there were the two organ makers.

"We just want to say goodbye and wish you a good time," said the tall one. "I enjoyed dancing with you."

"Thank you, this is my aunt and uncle, and these two fellows were my table mates. They are off to study the great organs of Europe for a few months."

Everyone shook hands and the two young men left.

"Is that all your luggage?" asked Uncle Ernst, pointing to the fairly small suitcase.

"Yes, it is."

"Good for you, traveling light," he said.

"I could never have all my things in one little suitcase like that," Lydia commented.

"Yes, you could," Ernst assured her.

Lydia gave him a hard look then continued. "The car is close by. We have a nice guest room in our new house. You'll like it, and the boys are eager to meet you. They are nine, six, and three now. I hope this next one is a girl," she said while patting her belly.

"Oh, Auntie, congratulations. When will that be?"

"Not until January, I hope."

Sigrit thought, *Four children? That is more than I would ever want. From what Mom tells me about her, I hope she has some household help.*

"The children are at home with their nanny. Your uncle has his own practice now and is doing well."

The streets of Rotterdam were chockfull of bicycles. There were very few cars, but thousands of bicycles. The new Mercedes did not take long to reach the flat countryside of Holland.

Once in Germany they traveled on the Autobahn at what Sigrit thought was a frightening speed. Never had she been in a car going at hundred and twenty miles an hour or more. She was glad when they got near Stuttgart and left the Autobahn.

"Welcome to our home," said Ernst as he led his niece in the door of the house. Three boys rushed to greet their parents, followed by the nanny, a girl of around eighteen. The boys greeted their cousin in a formal manner.

First, the nine-year-old shook her hand, said, "Good day," and bowed from the waist.

The six- and three-year-olds followed suit, except the three-year-old gave his cousin a warm hug on the legs. She stooped down and hugged the little blond boy.

The nanny took Sigrit upstairs and showed her the guest room.

"And here is the bathroom," the nanny said.

Sigrit inspected the light green tiled bathroom with tub and shower. "That is wonderful."

"Yes, this house has two bathrooms, one on each floor and a toilet downstairs off the entrance hall. I have never seen a house with this many bathrooms. The Zellers sure are clean people."

"Where is your room?"

"Upstairs," the nanny said, pointing up. "I like living here. The family is much nicer than the last one I was with. I better get downstairs and help put supper on the table. We'll eat in about ten minutes," she said, leaving the room.

Sigrit decided ten minutes would give her enough time to take a shower and put on another dress. While she was combing the large waves and curls in her shoulder-length, blonde-streaked, brown hair, she stood at the window.

Across the street, Sigrit saw a young woman, looking out of the window of the room she used to occupy a few months before they left for America.

That could be me, looking out of the window to see who is walking by. I am so glad I live in America, that I can speak English, and for all the experiences I've had.

"Sigrit, supper is ready!" called Lydia.

"Coming," she replied. She went downstairs to join the family.

CHAPTER 33

Ludwig and Greta were sitting at the train station, holding hands and speaking in low tones to each other while they waited for the local 3:15 to arrive from Munich. Both of them were trying to control their excitement by concentrating on their love. The last few weeks had been very hectic, and waiting for the train gave them time to relax and appreciate each other. Suddenly the repose ended when the steam engine pulling the train entered the station. Several people disembarked and both sifted through them. They both spotted a very attractive lady in a light blue cotton dress, with a full A-line skirt, wearing a little white hat, shoes, and gloves.

"Siggy!" Greta jumped up and waved, then both of them started running toward the passenger. Greta was the first to embrace her dear friend. When she let go, Ludwig stared.

"Is this really my little sister? No, it must be a movie star from America." Then he gently embraced her. "I remember nine years ago when I met my little sister again in maybe this very same spot."

"Yes, you picked me up and swung me around, and then I introduced you to Greta."

"Who would have believed it then—" Ludwig almost choked with emotion. "I am so happy you could come for the wedding."

"Yes," added Greta. "You should have seen the joy in the house when we got your letter that you would be coming. Mama and Papa are home awaiting your arrival and so is Oma."

"Good, I am eager to see all of them."

"How was your sea voyage?" inquired Ludwig.

"Wonderful. I really had a good time. Uncle Ernst and Auntie send you greetings, and they'll make it for the wedding."

"It will be good to see them again," said Ludwig, picking up her suitcase to carry it home.

As they walked along the street they saw several people of the village.

"Hallo, Hans, this is my American sister," Ludwig said to his neighbor.

"We have an American in town. Welcome, miss," he said, tipping his hat.

Sigrit grinned. *An American. That is the first time I have been referred to as an American. In America I'm always the German girl. I just hope I don't get my German accent back.*

Everyone was waiting for her in the Wagner's kitchen. There stood Sepp, Martha, and Oma. Sigrit could not contain the tears of joy when greeting them. Then she noticed three more people. "No. Can it really be? Sarah and Ruben, is that really you?"

"Yes," Ruben said. "We came from Israel for the wedding."

Ruben and Sarah gave Sigrit hugs as a nine-year-old boy stepped forward.

"And here is Samuel," Sarah said. "The little doll you smuggled out of Germany.

The boy extended his hand to Sigrit. "Shalom, Miss Sigrit."

"Shalom, Samuel. My, what a handsome fellow you are."

After dinner, eaten in the large kitchen, they sat outside as friends and neighbors came, bringing fresh baked goods, bottles of wine, and homemade spirits. If one did not try their culinary creations, it was an insult. In order to keep peace, Sigrit had to sample everything. Soon accordions came out of their cases and provided dance music. One very handsome, young, blond man dominated that art with his lively music. He used his accordion like it was a yo-yo, letting one side drop almost to the floor and never missing a note.

"Is he a music star?" Sigrit asked Greta.

"He could be, but he refuses to sign contracts. He'd rather go up into the mountains. We are fortunate that he is here tonight and hope he makes it to the wedding."

When a certain march was played, the men, all wearing short leather pants, got up, reached for a partner, and made a circle. Then the men swung their partners out of the circle, and the girls twirled around the men with their skirts belled. The men then faced each other and beat a precise tattoo with their hands on their legs and shoes. After some athletic jumps, they pursued their partners and waltzed with them. This was repeated two more times until, at the end, the men knelt next to the girls. Everyone clapped and cheered.

"Ludwig, Greta, that was wonderful," Sigrit said after they returned to their seats. "I had no idea you, Ludwig, could dance so well or that you, Greta, could keep up the twirling on the grass."

"That dance is called a *Schuhplattler*. It's the Bavarian national dance," explained Ludwig. "Every village has a slightly different version of it with the music a little different. I learned dozens of them."

"I can see that you really have found a home here. I am happy for you."

"Thank you," said Ludwig. "And have you found a new home too, little sister?"

"I love America, but at times I still feel like a foreigner there. The people are very friendly and easy going. On the other hand, there is a *Gemuetlichkeit* about the Germans, which is hard to put one's finger on. There is not even a word in English for it. Now if you can mix the casualness and the *Gemuetlichkeit* you have a good mixture. The German community in Baltimore is about the best at doing that. Did I tell you that Walter and Karl got together and started a soccer club there? They also hold dances and other social events where the children are welcome."

"I must confess, dear sister, that sometimes I am reminded that I am a foreigner, too. Then they call me a *Preis,* which means Prussian. To them any German not a Bavarian is a Prussian. For example, I treat women as equals, something that is not the Bavarian way."

"Yes, I noticed that. When the men handed out their drinks, they always served the other men first."

"The saying is, that in Bavaria when one greets the family, one starts with the man, then the dog, and then the wife. Children might or might not be greeted."

Sigrit laughed, "I hope you, my dear brother, will never become *that* Bavarian."

"I don't intend to."

Sigrit lodged with Greta in the same room where she had slept years before. On a hook on the wall hung a long, blue brocade, dirndle dress with a white linen blouse and a white silk apron.

"Is that your wedding dress?" asked Sigrit.

"Yes. Mama and I made it. I like looking at it."

"It is beautiful. I see you are not doing the total traditional Bavarian wedding where everybody wears black."

"We considered it, but to me that seems too stuffy. I want something a little more casual. I'm sure some of the old ladies will show up in their black wedding gowns, but they are so expensive with all the ruffles and smocking and so many yards of silk. What are you going to wear?"

"I have a white dress," said Sigrit lifting it out of her suitcase, "and I could wear a blue sash with it or another color."

"Blue will be lovely. Oh, Siggy, I'm just more than excited, not only to be marrying Ludwig, but that you could come and now we'll really be sisters." Greta flopped down on the bed and kicked her legs in the air. "We'll just have to do something together before the wedding."

"Where will you live after you're married?"

"There is a large bed in Ludwig's room which will be ours, and I'll make this room here into a sitting room. Oh, Siggy, I hope you will find someone to love too, soon."

"I am going to college, first of all, then after I get my degree, and only then, will I have time for love."

"You never know, love sometimes sneaks up on you," Greta said with a happy smile.

ぴがひ

The wedding was held in the baroque church in town. Everybody in the village, and a few relatives from afar, were there. Uncle Ernst and Aunt Lydia, looking almost out of place in their sophisticated clothes, drove down in their Mercedes with the three boys and the nanny. They lodged in a guest house in the village. Everyone wore their best clothes, but most of it was old and a bit shabby. What they lacked in glamor was made up for by the music and general atmosphere of celebration. When the new pair came out of church, their path was blocked by a big log resting on two sawhorses. While the local musicians played a lively march, Ludwig and Greta sawed the log in half with a two-man saw. The first obstacle of their married life was overcome to applause and cheers by everyone.

The entire wedding party marched to a field on which a big tent had been set up. In the tent were tables and chairs for all the guests. Everyone had contributed to the buffet set up on long tables.

Flower, the old cow, added beef to the bounty. People brought their own plates and flatware for eating and drinking. Beer in kegs, other drinks in glass bottles lubricated the party way into the night. Greta and Ludwig sat with relatives at an elevated table overlooking the dance floor.

Occasionally groups danced a *Schuhplattler* in their honor. At midnight Greta took off her small veil with its Myrtle wreath, and all the single girls made a circle around her. Blindfolded, she put the veil on the head of one of the girls. That was to determine who the next bride would be. There were groans of disappointment when it turned out to be the Zeller's nanny. Everyone was hoping to have another wedding in town soon.

With music and shouting, along with much laughter and teasing, the bride and groom were accompanied not only to their house, but into the bedroom. Ludwig pushed them out and closed the door, but he knew they were outside listening. To tease them, he and Greta had a loud dialogue going. After a while, Greta alone kept asking for more, to the amusement of the listeners. While everyone was listening, Ludwig snuck up behind the fellows at the door and asked them who was in there. They were so surprised to see Ludwig, and when they realized that the prank had been played on them, they all went home, laughing.

"Peace and quiet at last," Ludwig said as he came back into the bedroom then crawled into bed and gave his bride a very loving embrace.

જીન્જી

After the wedding celebration, which went on for two days, Sigrit still had more than a week before she had to be back on the ship. She decided that it would be a good time to do some sight-seeing, something she had not been able to do when she was little. She had no desire to go to Goerlitz. There was no one there she wanted to see. Besides, that part of the country was behind the Iron Curtain, and travel there was restricted. She just bought a train ticket good for multiple rides.

"Aren't you afraid to prance around the country by yourself?" asked Ludwig while he and the whole Wagner family walked her to the train station.

"What is to be afraid of?" Sigrit answered with a shrug of her shoulders.

"Don't you think you'll get lonely?" Martha asked, then without waiting for an answer, she added, "But I do admire your courage."

"There is always someone traveling alone that I can talk with, don't you think?"

"If you get too lonesome, you can always come back here to Hollstein," Sepp assured her. "There will always be room for you in our house for as long as you want."

"Thank you. I will never forget the time you were like a mother and father to me. And you, Oma, I will always remember you and your love for me."

"That, my dear, is still with you. God bless you, dear child."

When the train stood in the station, Sigrit only had time for quick hugs before the whistle blew and she had to jump on board for departure. She had a compartment for herself, of which she was glad.

She did not want anyone to see her crying. She left the window shut while the train pulled out of the station. The last thing she saw of Hollstein was Greta running beside the train, waving and blowing her a kiss.

൞൞൞

In the ten days before Sigrit got aboard the ship in Rotterdam, she visited mostly small cities, numerous castles, and many old churches, some still undergoing repairs from war damage.

I wonder how the organ makers are doing. Wouldn't it be funny if somewhere I would run into them? That would be too much of a coincidence to hope for.

When she arrived at a town, usually early in the day, she found a small guest house and rented a room, which often was not ready to occupy at that time. The host was always happy to store her suitcase until her return. Some days she rode a cable car up a mountain, ate lunch on the top, and either hiked down or rode the cable car back to town.

She enjoyed her freedom, doing what she wanted to do without asking or waiting for someone else. When she was hungry, she went into a busy restaurant. There she would be seated at a table that was already occupied. Some people were interesting and talkative while others did not want to bother speaking. Then Sigrit pulled out a small note book and wrote in her journal until her food was served.

She did buy a few souvenirs, not only for herself, but also her relatives in Baltimore. The American dollar went far in those days. She had the shops mail the wood carvings and porcelain she bought directly home.

൞

She silently said goodbye to Germany when the train crossed the border to Holland. As the ship completed its transit of the Nieuwe Waterweg and entered the ocean, she waved farewell to Europe.

Goodbye, Europe, goodbye, Germany, goodbye, Ludwig and Greta. It was so good to see you again. Have a long and very happy life together. Goodbye, Sepp and Martha, thank you for offering me a place to live. But no, thank you, I'm going back to America. Yes, America, I'm coming home.

The End

About the Author

When Ellynore Seybold-Smith was just a kid, she knew she wanted to be a writer. Her first book, *The Wooden Mistress*, was published in 1994. Then in 2012, Smith was diagnosed with cancer. She thought if it was time to die, okay. After all, her husband was waiting on the other side. Then a miracle happened, and the tumor turned benign. Smith saw this as a message from God that she had better do something creative with the rest of her life, and she began to write in earnest.

Made in the USA
San Bernardino, CA
07 November 2013